PLAY MAKER: ALTERNATE COVER

MM COLLEGE HOCKEY ROMANCE

BAR DOWN 2

AVA OLSEN

Play Maker (Alternate Cover)

MM College Hockey Romance (Bar Down 2)

Copyright © 2025 by Ava Olsen

http://avaolsenauthor.com/

Beta-reader: Jennifer Sharon

Proofreader: Melissa DaSilva

Cover Design: Covers by Jo Clement

Warning: Mentions of mental health issues, eating disorders, past bullying, abuse (not SA), death of a loved one, homophobia, drug use, smoking.

Copyright and Trademark Acknowledgments

The author acknowledges the copyrights, trademarked status, and trademark owners of the trademarks and copyrights mentioned in this work of fiction.

FOREWORD

For my readers. Thank you

CHAPTER 1
AXEL

TWO YEARS AGO (AGE 18)

"You can't tell anyone."

How many times had I heard that phrase?

Too many to count. I was raised in a household of secrets. Secrets and lies. Navigating my family dynamic was like walking barefoot in a room full of broken glass; you couldn't move without getting cut. I couldn't escape the suffocating tension at home, but I had hockey. At least on the ice, I had my skates to protect me.

But secrets were tiring; the more I had, the heavier the burden, and the more I wanted to hide.

"I won't," I replied as I stared at Preston Pearson, my best friend. After class, we'd snuck off to the local park to smoke and shoot the shit. "You know I won't."

Unlike my parents, I was true to my word. And to my friends like Preston. We met two years ago when I got roped into volunteering for our high school musical. I had no idea what I was doing—I was an athlete, not an actor—except what the teacher told me. Thank fuck I was tasked with something simple; coordinating the props. Preston was new to the school, but he'd secured the lead role in said musical within a week of his arrival. It wasn't surprising to me because he was outgoing and persuasive. The guy could charm anyone into doing anything. That first day in the theatre, he teased me about my shaggy hockey hair, and despite the razzing, we became fast friends.

"Promise me," he implored. "I almost got caught in a lie last week and I freaked out."

"I get it."

"No, you don't," he snapped. "Because you're straight. You don't need to hide. I'm only telling you about Friday night because I trust you. And I need you to give me an alibi."

"Alibi? Are you committing a crime?" I quipped.

"It'll feel that way if my parents find out I'm fucking a guy."

I didn't care if Preston was gay, and I didn't understand why other people did. What did it matter to them?

It mattered to Preston's parents. They were always pushing him to date one wealthy debutante girl or another. We both came from wealthy Connecticut families where the bottom line was the only line. Keeping up with the neighbors and being seen with the 'right' people was everything. Appearances were important and they wanted Preston to have the whole 'wife and two kids' scenario, just like them. Their idea of the perfect family. Hah. Like that existed.

"Ax? Did you hear me?"

"Yeah, sorry," I muttered. "You know I've got your back. I've got practice tomorrow, but I'm done by seven. So, what's our story after that?"

"We're going to your place to watch movies and binge on pizza, then studying first thing Saturday morning at the library."

I rolled my eyes.

"No one's gonna believe that. Me, studying early in the morning? Please, I can barely get through class as it is."

"My parents will believe anything as long as I'm with you," he replied. "You're a Lund. That means you're trusted without question."

"Barf. If only they knew."

Preston ignored my comment. I'd told him a few things about my dysfunctional family, but not everything. Secrets, remember? I was good at keeping them. Even from my best friend. Not that he didn't try to get me to talk, but I tended to keep myself to myself.

"Just two more weeks until graduation, and then I can kiss this lame fucking town goodbye," he admitted.

Getting away from Redgewick was my dream. Not that the small town near Rochester, New York was a bad place to live, but everywhere I went people knew me. I wanted a fresh start, a place where I could do my own thing without everyone stuck in my business. Unlike Preston, who got accepted to college in California, I was headed to Langston, my father and grandfather's alma mater. With the top-ranked hockey team in the country, I should be thrilled. But I wasn't. Why? Because the campus was in my hometown and that meant I was still within my parents' controlling reach.

"Not me," I griped, taking a long drag of my cigarette.

"Why don't you just tell them you want to go to another school?"

Preston didn't get it. His parents were first-generation wealthy so there was no 'tradition' to uphold. Tradition was a pain in my ass. But my parents were paying the bill, and I wanted to play nice until I had access to my trust fund. Only three more years. Then I could tell Bradford and Venetia, AKA my parents, to take their Lund expectations and screw off.

"You don't understand how it is with them," I explained. "I *have* to go there. It's a done deal. I probably didn't even need to send in an application. I'm sure my admission was taken care of when I was born."

I know, I know. *Poor little rich boy.* But while it was true that money opened a shit ton of doors, what was behind some of them was scary as fuck. The things I knew about people in my family, no one would believe. And that had my brain working overtime. Maybe there was still a chance for me to escape? I'd do my first year at Langston to keep my family off my back, and then apply elsewhere. But I'd need an excuse. A damn good one. Or, something I could use as leverage.

"Unless I come up with a way out," I admitted. "Do my freshman year and then transfer to another state. I've got time to think up a reason. One they can't argue with."

As my mind whirled, searching for a solution, Preston sighed and stood up.

"Okay, so, back to *my* problem, which really *is* a problem," Preston insisted. "I'm meeting Jace in Hillington tomorrow. Can you give me a lift after practice?"

I'd never met Preston's boyfriend, Jace Rowland. Well, not in any social context. The guy was one of the best hockey forwards in the state, so yes, I'd played against him. But that was it. Preston insisted I steer clear of Jace given their secret relationship, so I did. Jace wasn't out either and that was no surprise. I didn't know anyone on my hockey team, or any sports team, who was queer. I was sure there was rep some-where, but things were slow to change in the world of sports.

I still had a hard time picturing Preston and Jace together. They'd met, funnily enough, at one of my hockey games. But Jace lived a half hour and a whole world away. While Redgewick was host to the Langston campus and affluent families, Hillington was a former factory town turned ghost walk. I'd only been there once, driving through, and I had no desire to return. Bleak didn't even begin to describe it.

"Sure," I replied and took another drag of my cigarette.

"Wait, his place? Do I finally get to meet him? I mean, like outside of the usual 'hey' at hockey games?"

Preston snorted. "Maybe. But I'm warning you, his place is a dump."

"That bad?"

"He lives with his aunt in a ratty two-bedroom apartment over a garage. It smells like gasoline and despair." Preston shook his head, a lock of black hair falling into his eyes. "Whatever. It's been a long week, his aunt's out of town, and I need to get laid. Jace is hot as fuck, and more importantly, he knows *how* to fuck. Shit, what he can do with his tongue and cock is just…I can't even begin to describe it."

Not for the first time, I was jealous. Not of Preston, since I wasn't into guys, but of the way he talked about sex. I'd had my first time with Olivia, a classmate, a month ago. But it wasn't exactly the life- changing experience I expected, or the kind of sex that everyone at school bragged about. Fucking was fine; I got off, she got off. But I expected…more? I don't know. Like the way Preston talked about it. Every time he got laid it was the best time in the history of ever. What the fuck was I missing out on?

"What about college?" I asked, desperate to change the subject. "Where's he going? Or, *is* he going?"

"He got a full scholarship to some college in Vermont. I can't remember the name."

Typical Preston, too busy for the details.

"You still gonna see each other?"

"From across the country?" Preston scoffed. "Jace lives for hockey and I've got my acting career to launch."

"So, that's a no? What happened to being boyfriends?"

Preston shrugged. "It is what it is for now. Who knows about tomorrow? I'm a realist."

"Does he know this?"

"Of course he does. We have an understanding," Preston replied and stood up. "It's all good."

I nodded and threw my cigarette on the ground. What did I care about his boyfriend anyway? It was Preston's business, not mine. And relationships came and went. Nothing lasted forever.

He was right, it was all good.

Until the weekend hit.

I dropped off my bestie near Jace's on Friday as planned, but I still didn't get to meet the guy. Preston insisted there was no point. The next day, when I picked him up, Preston was in tears. I'd never seen him cry and it shocked me. Preston confided that he'd called things off with Jace, and Jace, in turn, had flown into a rage. Preston insisted he wasn't physically hurt, but he was trembling. I was about to tear up the steps of that crumbling apartment and show Jace exactly what I thought of his shitty treatment of my friend, but Preston held me off. My friend was shaken up and just wanted to go home.

"This isn't the first time he's lost his temper, but thank fuck it's the last," Preston admitted. "I'm so glad that's over."

What the hell? I was seething, but my bestie warned me to let it go. And now wasn't the time for me to get into a fight and into trouble. I needed to get away from my family, not give them a reason to hold on even tighter.

Not that I forgot about Jace or how he treated my friend. I knew that somehow, someway, Jace was going to get what was coming to him.

Two weeks later, Preston left for California, and I headed with my family to France for our annual summer vacation. Vacation. Right. My father worked every day and night, my mom was off with her latest fuck friend, and my younger brother was either getting high or ignoring me as usual.

My best friend was gone, and I was alone with only my secrets for company.

That fall, I headed to Langston College as planned. And because of hockey, I couldn't avoid facing off against Jace

Rowland on the ice–he was, after all, Sutton University's star forward.

But I let my anger simmer, biding my time. Revenge would come.

It wasn't a matter of if, but when.

CHAPTER 2

AXEL

A YEAR AGO (AGE 19)

My freshman year at Langston could only be described as claustrophobic. My parents always popped up, attending one college event after another. Not to see me and not to watch my games, nope. They showed up when there was a public event with press around. I was brought in to smile and prop up their image. It was all about public relations.

Like today, when I got called in to the Dean of Students' office. The college was opening a new international business school, and the campus was crawling with anticipation. And media. I knew exactly what that meant and why I was called away from class.

Inevitably, my parents would be here. Fuck.

As I passed the hallway that led to the dean's office, I noticed several pictures of my father and grandfather. Their photographs were all over the damn school. Given that they'd attended Langston and more importantly, were one of the college's biggest donors, it wasn't surprising. There was the Lund Scholarship Fund, the Lund Football Field, and the

Lund Library, to name a few. They'd probably rename the whole college in a few years. Everywhere I looked, they were there. It creeped me out because it was like being watched twenty-four seven. Not only that, but my teammates and fellow students acted weird around me. I was always invited to parties and stuff, but no one wanted to have any real conversations with me, like they were wary of saying a bad word. They were probably worried that if I didn't like them, I'd have them thrown out of the school, or something. Not that I would ever do anything like that.

My parents, on the other hand…

Fuck, I needed to get out of here. Like, yesterday.

Instead, I swallowed down my frustration and gave my name to the dean's receptionist, who quickly guided me to his office, a room with dark wood walls, shelves of books, and the heavy scent of leather and old money.

Dean Jacobs sat at his desk with my parents opposite him.

Like I did when I was ready to hit the ice, I pushed aside my fear and faced my opponent head-on.

I got my size from the Lund side of the family, and thankfully, I was now taller than my father. Finally I had one advantage. His formerly auburn hair was now gray, and his brown eyes showed no expression. He stared at me like he was looking at a stranger, rather than his own son. My mother matched him perfectly, her icy blond bob accentuating the bluest, but coldest, eyes I'd ever seen.

My parents stood up to greet me with a nod and an awkward hello. No hugs in this family.

"Axel, good to see you," Dean Jacobs announced with a polite, but entirely fake, smile. "We need you for photographs at the opening this afternoon."

"I'm sorry, but I can't do that," I replied. "I've got hockey practice."

Dean Jacobs waved his hand. "I've already spoken to Coach Williams about your absence."

"But—"

"You heard the dean," my father snapped. "This is far more important. Every major donor to this college will be there. It's time for you to forget about this stupid fixation with hockey and focus on your future. Your real future. Making connections. That's why you're here."

"Hockey's my future," I bit out. "And I don't care about making connections. I don't want or need that kind of education."

"It's what's expected," my father insisted with a clipped voice. "You're a representative of this family and this school, and you will do well to remember that."

There was no point in arguing in front of the dean, it would only make life harder for me.

Instead, I nodded and crossed my arms.

"Good." Dean Jacobs smiled at me, but it was like looking at a shark, all blank eyes and razor-sharp teeth.

Jacobs creeped me out. Then I noticed the way he glanced at my mother, the once-over, and the way she looked back at him. I barely held back an eye roll.

Get me the fuck out of here.

"You'll be joining us for lunch with the donors," my mother commanded. "Go change into a suit and meet us at the new pavilion in half an hour."

"Do you have a script for me too?" I snarked.

"Don't question us, just do it!" my father barked.

With my father's booming voice still ringing in my ears I left the room, feeling worse than when I first entered. No surprises there. Being around my parents always left me feeling like total shit, and I desperately wanted to run away.

I stumbled out of the building and headed across campus like a zombie. Was this really going to be *my* life? Always taking their orders? Never getting out from under their grasp?

I couldn't do it. I needed a breakaway.

By the time I got back to the dorm, changed, and headed to the pavilion, it was raining heavily, and the gloomy weather suited my mood entirely. I arrived early, but it was fine. I needed a moment to myself. That dreaded spiral of panic set in, and I just knew that no matter what I did or said, I was going to screw this up. And I also knew that tomorrow, I'd replay every word and action in my head. Only, I'd still be lost. I'd hardly want to leave my bed, never mind attending class or hitting the rink.

I sighed as I glanced up at the newest building on campus.

The inaugural international business pavilion was all glass and sharp angles, modern compared to most of the facilities on campus. It didn't really fit in.

Kinda like you.

I entered the lobby, which was already filling up with attendees, many of them college representatives, donors, and press.

There was a sign near the elevators indicating that the private luncheon was being held on the second floor, but I decided to take the stairs. I needed the walk. Hell, I'd need to walk more than one set of stairs to settle my nerves but it would do for now.

Up here, there was hardly anyone around. It was so eerily quiet that the only sound I heard was the echo of my lonely footsteps.

Until I heard a voice somewhere down the hall.

I followed it but as I drew closer, I realized it wasn't a stranger, but my father talking. Instead of entering the room right away, I waited outside and listened.

"I've had it. I don't want Axel being brought in for any more of these events," my father stated. "He's more of a hindrance at this point. I don't care about the photo ops, as soon as he opens his mouth it's clear he won't or can't sell the Lund story. He's fucking useless."

His words didn't shock me. Did they hurt? Yes, but I'd

learned a long time ago to push that down. Feeling bad for myself didn't get me anywhere.

I leaned in closer, but stayed behind the door, not wanting him to see me.

"He takes a great picture, and it looks good for the school and therefore for us," my mother replied. "And we need that publicity now more than ever."

"If you'd stop fucking every married man you meet, maybe we wouldn't be in this position," he snarled. "I'm done paying out hush money. There's hardly any left to pay out."

"Make more," she snapped. "And like you're one to talk when it comes to spending."

"I spend money to make money."

"There's hardly any of that happening lately."

Interesting.

"It's a slow quarter. Property values in some markets are tumbling, and we're all being hit hard," he grumbled. "And here's a novel idea, Venetia, why don't you find a way to bring in some cash instead of sitting on your ass, or rather, lying on your back?" my father hissed.

"Fuck you, Brad. I did my part. You wanted a son to carry on the family legacy, and I gave you two."

"Maybe if both of them were mine, I'd agree with you."

Wait, what?

"Lower your voice," she whispered. "He's still a Lund, so what does it matter?"

"Really? Fucking my brother and then passing off his kid as mine doesn't matter? You're unreal," he scoffed. "If Axel was a genius, I'd overlook it. But he's not. Not even close. All he wants to do is act like a goon with that stupid hockey he's obsessed with. Fucking idiot."

I knew there were a lot of family secrets, but I'd never guessed one would be about me. I was suddenly nauseous, feeling like I was going to throw up, until it hit me.

They don't want this news to get out.

This wasn't the worst day of my life, but the best.

Instead of hiding outside, and fueled by shock and adrenaline, I stalked into the room.

"Gotta love these family reunions," I stated.

My comment was met with silence. Silence and frigid glares.

"I think it's time we talk about my future," I added. "The one that doesn't include Langston."

Maybe I wasn't as smart as the rest of the Lunds, but I knew one thing. In life, sometimes you had to play dirty to win.

———

Two months later

Unfortunately, transferring colleges wasn't as easy as all that. My grades weren't great, and I relied on my hockey stats to get an acceptance letter.

Only, I didn't have a choice. I had one offer and that was it. Take it or leave it.

I couldn't wait to get out of this place. I felt suffocated and at the same time, isolated, and I hated it.

Preston was the first, and only person, I confided in.

> Axel: Hey, I've got good news and bad news. I'm leaving Langston.

> Preston: You finally made it happen. How? Are your parents freaking out?

> Axel: They are. I don't care. And the how isn't important.

The fuck it wasn't. Still, I didn't tell Preston about what I'd done, using a secret to gain favor. Maybe I was more like my family than I wanted to admit? That idea was even scarier than staying here at Langston.

> Preston: Don't push them too far. You still need their money. And their name carries weight.

> Axel: I'm not worried.

> Preston: And the bad news?

I paused for a moment. I didn't want to hurt my friend, but he needed to know.

> Axel: I only had one offer. From Sutton University.

The college where his ex, Jace Rowland, played.

> Preston: Are you shitting me?

> Axel: Nope.

> Preston: He was such an asshole to me, and now you're on the same team? WTF?

> Axel: I know. But don't worry. I can handle it. And he'll get what's coming to him.

Confronting my family was one thing.

Confronting Jace? Well, that didn't quite work out the way I imagined.

CHAPTER 3
JACE

There was nothing like the smell of a hockey locker room; a combination of musky jocks, funky pits, and ripe feet, along with the hit of ammonia that lingered from the cleaning crew. To some people, it's intense, even gag-inducing. To me, it was a reminder that no matter how shitty things got, this was home.

Hockey wasn't just a game to me; it was my destiny. That might sound dramatic, but it was true. I was eight years old when my aunt gifted me a hockey jersey with the number to match, along with a pair of secondhand skates. There was trepidation but mostly elation when I stepped out onto the ice for the first time, like a wobbly newborn deer discovering how to walk. But it didn't take me long to get my footing. Soon, I was outskating every kid in my town and on my team, and I didn't look back.

For a guy like me, whose professional league dream was just within reach, it wasn't a matter of doing what I love, but needing it, like a drug. Everything in my life up to this point was a fight to get here.

And I always played to win.

According to my aunt Josie, I'd been born scrappy, a preemie with a tiny body but a huge set of lungs. And nothing had changed in twenty years. I was still loud and determined to beat the odds.

My first year at Sutton U had felt like a dream and after every game I pinched myself. This was my life. And now, more than halfway through my second year, my goal was to secure the coveted center spot. Coach Banning hadn't decided yet and it was chafing my balls. I was the highest scorer on the team and ranked fourth in the national college standings. That spot was fucking mine. I knew it as sure as I knew every inch of ice that we played on.

But there was a problem with my plan. A problem named Axel Lund.

He was a new forward, but an old reminder of the life I'd left behind. Axel wasn't just a teammate; he was also my ex-boyfriend's best friend. My stomach roiled at the thought of my last semester of high school and everything that had happened with Preston. I thought I'd put it all behind me but having Axel here brought back shit I didn't want to face.

But I'd survived tougher enemies than Axel. I could handle it.

I *was* handling it. Sort of.

This past fall was nothing but me and Axel circling each other with wary glances and sharp comments. The tension was undeniable, but given that we barely spoke to each other, we kept it contained. But we couldn't maintain this distance forever. I was dying to ask him questions. Like, what the fuck was he doing here at Sutton anyway? Why would Axel transfer from the top-ranked team in the country? Did he miss his mark as Langston's play maker? The guy didn't score as much as me last season, but he sure as shit had more assists, so the nickname suited. And I knew that he was also vying for the same spot.

He was close, too close, and now my competition for everything I'd been busting ass for.

And here we were, in late January, ready to ramp up again. And it wasn't just hockey that had my gut churning and my nerves riding high. I'd recently come out to the team. I'd known I was bisexual since high school but living in a small town stuck in the nineties didn't exactly encourage me to tell people. Axel already knew, of course he did, and I was surprised he didn't tell everyone the moment he landed here, since he hated my guts. But he didn't. As to why, I still didn't know.

More questions whizzed around in my brain like a puck bouncing off the boards, and my pregame anxiety turned to full-on panic. I fought hard against the urge to run to the bathroom.

"Jace!" a familiar voice shouted, snapping me out of my doomsday headspace.

I looked up to find my friend, and the captain of the Cougars, Dane St. Pierre, standing at the doorway to the locker room.

"You coming or what? We need our best forward if we want to smash this fucking game," Dane teased with a big grin on his face.

I could always count on Dane to cheer me on, and I couldn't lie; I was a total praise slut. Hey, I was a hockey player, we all have big egos that need stroking on the regular.

"Yeah, I'm coming already," I fired back and popped to my feet.

Grabbing my stick from the stall, I followed my friend as we made our way out of the locker room and down the chute to the rink. The closer we got to the ice, the faster my pulse thrummed. My stomach flipped over again but it was more about excitement.

As long as I kept moving, my intrusive thoughts wouldn't win.

"Everything okay?" Dane asked.

I glanced at my friend and nodded. Now wasn't the time to unload all the shit I'd been working on in my head since high school.

"Just school stuff."

Dane's eyes surveyed my face, and he shook his head. "Not buying it."

I rolled my eyes and playfully smacked his padded chest with my gloved hand.

"Later, okay. We've got the game to worry about first."

Dane smiled. "Jackson's got the whole crew here today to make noise."

I wasn't the only one who came out recently. Dane told the team about his boyfriend—and dormmate—Jackson. They'd dated secretly in high school and reconnected here at Sutton. Since Jackson was a member of the rowing crew, he always had a group of friends with him to help cheer on our home games. Their antics were loud and sometimes crazy, and I wouldn't have had it any other way.

"There's nothing like the buzz of playing for a home crowd," I replied as we shuffled down the chute, the noise around us getting louder and louder. "I swear, I could live off of this feeling for weeks."

"I know, right?"

We joined the rest of our teammates but in the crowded space, I bumped into Ethan Walker, another forward.

"Sorry, man," I muttered.

No one should stand near a hockey player when they're all geared up. On the ice, we had smooth moves. Off the ice, we were all accidents waiting to happen.

"No worries," Ethan replied with a teasing grin. "Just don't knock into me like that when I'm heading for the net, yeah?"

"You? Don't you mean me?"

"Fuck off," Ethan said playfully and nudged me with his arm.

Unfortunately, Ethan pushed a little too hard and I fell back, hitting someone else. Someone who smelled like sweat, grapefruit, and musk. I recognized that unique combination right away and there was no need for me to turn my head.

Axel.

I'd never seen the guy in a good mood. I knew some of his backstory from Preston, and from the fact that the Lund name was well-known in New York state. Axel came from money. A lot of it. Which is probably one of the reasons he looked down his nose at me. He was a snobby asshole times ten, and it pissed me off that he always smelled so damn good. What, did he sit in a bath of cologne before every game or something? I snorted at that idea. Given that his family was loaded, he probably did.

"Do you fucking mind?" Axel growled and shoved me forward.

Thankfully, I had Dane and Ethan around to cushion me.

"Easy, Lund, it was an accident," I explained as I turned around to face him. "Save that aggression for the other team."

"Stop talking and keep walking," Axel muttered, his dark blues full of contempt.

"Bite me."

Axel shook his head, his shaggy blond mullet sticking out from under his helmet. With his six-three height and broad build, number thirteen (I didn't know if that was lucky or unlucky) was a force to be reckoned with. I was shorter and leaner, but faster, and most important of all, I wasn't intimidated. Not by him or anyone else. I'd faced a lot tougher rivals than this spoiled jackass.

"Maybe if you spent more time on your slapshot and less on getting your dick wet, you'd get drafted already," Axel snapped.

"Maybe if you got laid occasionally you wouldn't *be* a dick," I bit back. "Or, do you suck at scoring off the ice, too?"

"Ooh," Ethan cackled as more teammates turned around to stare at us. "The gloves are coming off now, baby."

Axel's face turned ruddy, and I swear I saw smoke coming out from under his helmet. My smart-ass comments often got me into trouble and today was no different.

"Shut your fucking mouth, Rowland," Axel bit out.

Kayden Melnyk, our biggest defenseman, but the sweetest guy ever, grabbed my shoulder and gave me a worried look. "Come on, guys, can't we all just get along?"

"Let them be, Kay."

That gruff comment came from Maddox Rocher, our first-line goalie, and Kayden's boyfriend. Talk about opposites attracting. More like the moon and sun colliding. Mad was one hell of a blocker but snarky and testy as fuck, and not one for the whole 'team spirit' thing. Unlike Kay, who made friends anywhere he went. But thanks to Kay, Mad's initial chilly reception to the team finally started to melt. But the last few weeks hadn't been easy. They'd come out too, and while most of the team were supportive, there was still tension in the air. Or maybe that was just because with every game, we were one step closer to the national championships. Emotions, frustrations, and expectations were riding high.

Kayden gave me another concerned glance but said nothing.

"What the hell are you guys waiting for?" Coach Banning suddenly yelled out. "Get out there and get warmed up! We have a game to play!"

I shoved aside my anger with Axel and followed my teammates. Once my blades hit the ice, I did what I always did, I got in the zone. Out here, I wasn't struggling with my insecurities, or worried about my past, or anything else.

I was exactly where I was meant to be.

The rink was packed with students proudly displaying the Sutton U green and gold, from sweatshirts to jackets and hats, and even banners. And of course, there was our mascot, the roaring cougar, working the fans into a frenzy. I spotted Jackson in the crowd with his friends, waving and clapping. Then Jackson stood up and turned around, showing off his jersey with Dane's name and number on it.

I skated around the net and nudged our captain, pointing to Jackson. Dane glanced up at the crowd and waved to his boyfriend. Their smiles were nearly blinding and for a split second, I envied my friend. Not that I wanted to go down that road. Not with anyone. I'd tried the relationship thing, and it had fucked me up, bad. No way was I doing that again.

And being around Axel was a constant reminder of that fact. I shook my head, needing to cut loose from the past and remain focused on the present.

"Stop poking the bear before every game," a deep voice muttered behind me.

I came to a sharp stop and turned to face another giant on our team, Silas Moss. The guy was a mountain of a hockey player, with long, dirty blond hair, a full beard, and tons of tatts. Silas was a skilled, if somewhat inconsistent, defenseman. But unlike sunny Kayden, this d-man was quietly intense, often sarcastic when spoken to, and had a rebellious air, like he didn't give a shit what anyone thought about him. Defensive, if you will. Maybe it had to do with the fact that Silas was the oldest guy on the team at twenty-two and after taking a year off from school and hockey, he was still trying to find his rhythm and prove his place on this team. As to the reason why he was gone for two semesters, no one knew. There was plenty of speculation but since Silas barely spoke to anyone, he was a mystery. The only other bit of information I gleaned about him, courtesy of Kayden, was that Silas had a younger brother.

"I didn't start it," I replied automatically.

Fuck, even I could admit that I sounded like a petulant brat. With Axel around, that was no surprise.

Silas shook his head. "You don't have to pour gasoline on the freaking fire."

He had a point. I hated to admit it, but he was right. Maybe.

"Maybe my timing wasn't good," I bit out. "I just can't help it. I'm not the type to let insults slide. It's just not me."

Not anymore. In the past, yes, because I wanted everyone to like me. But I learned a hard lesson about being too nice. A lesson that would stay with me forever.

Silas grunted in response and skated off. Okay, then.

"Good talking to you!" I called out and Silas raised his stick in acknowledgment.

At least, I think he was acknowledging me. One of these days I was going to have an actual conversation with that guy. I was a curious person and I made it a point to talk to everyone in my class and on my team. I was a lot like Kayden in that way, except louder and with more sass. The only person I didn't have any urge to get near was Axel; sometimes, a bad apple just needs binning.

The shrill sound of a whistle pierced the air and Coach Banning waved us over to the boards for our pregame scrum.

"Rowland, Lund, St. Pierre, Baran, Melnyk, Rocher, you're up. Like I've said time and again, I want to see you working cohesively. Remember our strategy. Mansfield is weaker when it comes to their offensive plays so keep your eyes out for any advantage and press hard. This season's ramping up and there's no time for bullshit," Banning barked. "Get out there and get that win."

Everyone tapped their sticks on the ice and shouted 'cougars!' before we skated off to take our positions.

Dane faced off against Mansfield's captain.

Just before the puck dropped, I glanced to my right. Axel's

glare cut sharper than my blades. I looked down, surprised I wasn't bleeding all over the ice.

Then I remembered Coach's words. Out here, there was no time for bullshit.

The only thing that mattered was winning.

CHAPTER 4

AXEL

The first period was a tug of war, with neither side pulling ahead.

But the game pivoted in the second period. We were ahead by one goal, thanks to Dane scoring in the first five minutes of play. But given the number of shots on goal from Mansfield, there was no telling where this game might end up.

Now Jace was out there, blasting down the ice at full speed like he always did. Just like his smart mouth, his frenetic energy in this game couldn't be contained. He wasn't nearly as big as most of the players on our team, but I envied him his speed. Between that, and his ability to sink the puck, he was often a target for the opposing team, many of whom were ruthless. Not that college hockey is as aggressive as the professional league but still, players played to win, and hard hits happened. The potential to be drafted meant everything was on the line, so it was no wonder that competition was fierce.

It pained me to admit, but Jace Rowland was going to make it and make it big.

Some players had that 'it' factor, a combination of skill,

drive, and kinetic grace. Jace was one of them. Unlike me, he was long and lean, almost too lean. Six feet of pure muscle. But you could count his damn ribs, and it made me edgy. Now wasn't the time for him to drop any weight. If he got smashed into the boards he'd be toast, and so would our chances of making it to the finals. Not that I paid much attention to his body, but in a locker room, you can't help but notice other players. Other than his body weight, Jace was your typical hockey boy; his messy chocolate brown hair was curled at the ends and in bad need of a cut, and he sported a large cougar tattoo on his left pec. A bunch of my teammates got them last year, all on different parts of their bodies. No thanks, I hated needles.

And I hated the mouthy prick that was Jace Rowland.

But I couldn't deny the guy was really fucking talented. Like right now. He snatched the puck away from Danny Daskell, Mansfield's star forward, and deked around so many of their players it was dizzying to witness. Dizzying and frustrating. I hadn't scored nearly as much as Jace in the past four months and this game was proving to be much the same.

Coach Banning expected more of me, and I'd already been warned. Even though my technical skills were strong, my scoring and teamwork wasn't, and that had to change. Professional league scouts didn't give a shit about mediocre; they wanted the best. I was also struggling with school. Honestly, I didn't know what I wanted to do with my life except play hockey. Signing up for a degree in economics was practical, but boring. My GPA wasn't anything to brag about, but the longer I was at school the less I cared about my future outside of hockey. I'd spoken with one advisor when I was at Langston, and he'd suggested that I stick to my program. That didn't sit well because I was bored. The lack of clarity only made me more frustrated with myself.

With every passing week, the pressure I felt on and off the ice kept building.

The worst of it was the recent incident with my team-mates, Kayden and Maddox.

A few weeks ago, I saw them kissing and freaked out. I overreacted and did something that, to this day, had me feeling like shit. My behavior was exactly that. Shitty to the max. My teammates were together, but not out to the rest of the team. All I could think at the time was, if things went ass up between Kayden and Maddox, would it fuck with our ability to win? We were so close to the national championships. Still, I should've kept my mouth shut. Threatening to go to our coach with their relationship was a dick move on my part and one I was still apologizing for. If Preston ever found out what I'd done, he'd never speak to me again and he'd be right. I could blame my reaction on stress, but the truth was, I'd let my fear take over. Kayden accepted my apology, but Maddox didn't talk to me. Then again, our goalie wasn't exactly a people person, and he hardly talked to anyone.

All this to say, mentally I was fucked up, and my game was too.

Which is why, when Jace gave me the stink eye at the first face- off, I gave it right back. Hopefully, none of Mansfield's players noticed. If they so much as caught a whiff of discord between teammates, they'd pounce on me and Jace like the cougars we were named after.

Being witness to Jace's best season ever hadn't helped me either.

No one knew what a dick this guy really was under all that equipment. All they saw was his big smile, outgoing personality, and talent on the ice. I wanted to lay into him about his treatment of Preston, but every time I had the courage to say something, I didn't. And after what I'd done to Kayden and Maddox, I second- guessed every decision and every word before it came out of my mouth. Okay, maybe not every word, and not when it came to arguing with Jace. He had a way of getting under my skin that had me forgetting to play nice. I had no problem insulting the guy, but confronting him about my friend? That was a whole other story.

Caught up in my head, I sat in the box, staring at the ice, surrounded by the roar of students and the flash of players whizzing by. I could've been staring at a blank wall for all I was paying attention.

"Lund! I said you're on!"

I startled at the sound of my name and turned to find Coach Banning frantically motioning for me to get my ass on the ice. Jesus, this wasn't good.

Shaking out of my weird headspace, I launched out of the box as we switched lines. Thankfully, Jace was called off, and I took my place along with Ethan, Dane, Kayden, and Finn Baran, another one of our defensemen. I looked over at our captain, who gave me a warning look, silently telling me to get my shit together.

The crack of the puck hitting the ice snapped me back to the moment and thank God for quick reflexes and muscle memory. Dane took possession of the puck, and Ethan and I took off with him. But Mansfield's players brought their A game tonight, and they were all over us. Dane got an opening and passed to me, but I only got as far as the blue line when I was hit hard.

"Fucking hell!" I yelled out as every bone in my body rattled along with the boards.

Shaking off the pain, I scrummed with Gacey, one of Mansfield's best d-men. I managed to eke out an opening and passed the puck back to Ethan before I got smacked into the boards again. I'd need more than a massage after this game. More like a week of them.

I didn't see Ethan's goal, but I heard the buzzer and the boom of the crowd's reaction.

When I finally recovered from the hit, I turned to find Ethan and Dane hugging and Kayden and Finn joining in.

Hell, even grouchy Maddox skated away from his net and tapped Ethan on the back. I pushed off the boards, slowly, and skated over to celebrate with my teammates. I'd managed to rack up another assist for my records. I should be elated, but instead of feeling like I'd accomplished something, my mind went right back to the idea I wasn't good enough.

"Ethan! Ethan!" Kayden chanted and everyone on our team joined in.

Dane nudged my shoulder and pulled me aside.

"You alright, Lund? You got hit twice and hard," Dane commented.

"I'm good." My body was already aching like a mother-fucker. "Just the usual bumps and bruises, I'm sure."

"Good play," Dane replied. "You're fast and you always see the opening."

"Maybe next time I can take it all the way and sink the puck myself."

I wasn't shitting on Ethan's goal, not at all. Just shitting on myself. I hadn't scored in so long and it was getting to me.

"I'm sure you will."

I wish I had Dane's confidence. Right now, I was running on 'fake it till you make it' but that couldn't last forever. What did I have to be stressed about? Even if I never got drafted, I had money coming, and that meant a shitload of opportunities. But what no one else knew was that I wanted to skate as far and as fast as I could from my past and never look back. Hockey was my only escape, the one thing I was good at on my own, the one thing that was mine, all mine. And I was a possessive motherfucker.

"Hey, Ax, thanks for the awesome pass."

I turned to find Ethan with a big smile on his face, his glove raised. I bumped it with my own.

"No worries. I'm sorry I missed your goal but I'm sure it was a beaut," I replied.

Ethan laughed.

"It happened so fast even *I* couldn't tell you." He pointed to the boards. "Ask our teammates who were watching."

I glanced over at the box and my eyes locked on Jace. Not that I meant to, but the star forward was standing beside Coach Banning, talking a mile a minute and moving his arms around, nearly taking out Silas's head in the process. Our moody defenseman said something in response to Jace and whatever it was, Coach Banning didn't look happy. Jace laughed it off and kept right on yammering.

I wasn't the only one watching the show. A row of students sitting directly behind the box called Jace's name, and he turned to them, waving and chatting. Guys and girls, they all wanted to talk to him. Not just that, they wanted to be near him, to be a part of his inner circle. I'd been to a few of the parties that Ethan's frat hosted, along with the rest of the hockey team, and Jace was never short of company. Then I remembered what Preston told me. How good a fuck Jace was. Ugh, what the hell? I didn't need to be thinking about *that* of all things. Besides, I did okay myself when it came to sex. I'd met and fucked a couple of women from those parties. I scratched an itch but that was it. One wanted a repeat and a date, but I wasn't about to go down that road. My plate was already loaded with problems, and a relationship would only add to it.

But watching Jace charm the crowd fueled my aggravation. If only they knew what a manipulative dick he really was…

Suddenly, Jace turned around, and caught me staring. Damn.

What was worse? I didn't look away.

CHAPTER 5
JACE

What was Axel's problem now? And why did I give a shit?

I didn't, but he and I were going to talk after this game. He could stare at me until his eyeballs mummified, but he better lose that pissy attitude.

Coach Banning suggested we hash things out in his office, and if needed, with the aid of a counselor. I didn't mind the former, but the latter was a hard no. I wasn't in the mood to get analyzed, at least, not with Axel. Besides, there was nothing here that could be fixed. Axel was best friends with Preston, Preston hated me, and it followed that Axel did too. It went both ways. I hated Preston for what he did to me, so...

Not to mention, Axel and I were competing for the same spot. Coach kept saying that he'd have his decision in a few weeks, but weeks turned into months. Every game and every goal told me that I deserved that center spot. I was confident it was mine.

Until the third period happened, and my ego crashed. Hard.

We had the lead at 2-0 but Mansfield wasn't ready to admit defeat. They charged back with an unexpected goal, a stunning corner shot that whizzed past Maddox's blocker. Our goalie was now angrier than a nest of disturbed bees, pacing back and forth and shaking his head so hard I was surprised he didn't hurt his neck. My sixth sense thrummed loudly, and I knew something strange was about to happen. Only, I'd had that feeling since Axel joined our team, so maybe my intuition was jammed up?

Nope, my instinct was right on target.

Axel scored with five minutes remaining in the period. I was elated like the rest of my team that the Cougars were up 3-1 but being witness to the end of Axel's scoring drought? It had me wanting to stomp my feet and slap my stick against the ice until it shattered. Instead, on the next play, I jumped the gun and crossed the blue line before the puck did. The ref called offside, rightly so, and Mansfield had an advantage, a face-off in the neutral zone. Their best forward, Daskell, scored on us again.

The air in the rink was so thick with contention I was nearly choking on it.

But of course, I didn't screw up once, but twice. My temper got the better of me when I battled for the puck with Gacey. Then I was stuck in the sin bin for two minutes for a holding call. It felt like a fucking eternity, and I only had myself to blame. The worst part? I had to spend my time watching Axel score, yet again, and on Mansfield's power play. He managed to score on them with a man down. Unreal.

When my time was up, I shot out of the bin like my ass was literally on fire. Watching Axel score not once, but twice, had that effect. No way was this asshole outplaying me.

I skated past Silas, on my way to take my spot, when he tapped my arm.

"Everyone can hear your teeth grinding," he whispered. "Stay focused."

"I am," I bit out.

"I mean, on the freaking puck. Not on him."

"For someone who hasn't said much in months, you sure do have a shit ton of opinions all of a sudden."

He shrugged. "Maybe I'm finally feeling like a real part of this team. I can see our momentum and I want to go all the way. We all have something to prove. Some of us more than others."

Silas played a great game today; I'll give him that.

And me? This period was a bomb. But it wasn't over yet.

"Stop thinking about yourself," he continued. "Think about what's best for the team."

"Thanks for the advice, old man. And guess what? I'm always thinking about the team. I—"

The ref blew the whistle, thank fuck, and there was no more time for talk.

Axel was on the same line as me, along with Colin Goring, one of our grinders. Silas' advice rattled around in my head, and I begrudgingly admitted that he was right. Putting aside my personal feelings, Axel was just another teammate. And the truth was, I wanted to win this game more than I wanted to show up Axel.

When the puck dropped, Colin took possession, and we mounted our attack. Until Colin got slammed by Gacey, and the puck went wild, bouncing off the boards like a pinball. In the scrum, Daskell got ahold of the puck and took off with it. But Maddox was ready for him and blocked one of the fastest slapshots I'd seen all game. I zoomed around the net, Maddox passed the puck to me, and it was on. The crowd chanted my name and I pushed harder, sprinting down the ice, when I spotted Axel in my line of sight.

When Mansfield's defense closed in on me, I had no choice. With one quick flick of my wrist, I shot it straight to Axel, and he took it the rest of the way home. I deked around Gacey, barely, and saw an opening. This was it. Axel, thank fuck, knew it too and when he shot the puck back to me, I geared up and hit the bullseye, right between their goalie's legs.

The buzzer lit up. 5-2. This game was ours; I fucking knew it.

"Jace, that was amazing!" Colin shouted as he reached me and grabbed my shoulder. The crowd was shouting so loud that I barely heard him. "Great freaking goal!"

"Thanks," I replied and spotted Axel skating towards me. Slowly.

Fuck it. I met him halfway and gave him a pat on the shoulder, whether he wanted it or not. Whether I liked it or not. I ignored the fact that he still smelled incredible and focused on the fact that we'd worked together and succeeded.

"We did it," I announced.

"You're welcome," he growled, his blue eyes as fiery as ever.

"No celebratory kiss?" I goaded him.

"I'd rather suck face with the Zamboni driver."

"He's like, eighty or something," I quipped. "Didn't know you were into dudes and old ones at that, but that's cool. Daddies are hot."

"Shut your mouth, Rowland. The game isn't over yet."

I tapped his stick in response. That was as civil as Axel and I were going to get.

Coach called for a line change, and I gratefully accepted the break.

"Rowland, Lund, Goring, great play," Banning called out as we filed off the ice. "I expect to see more of the same."

"Yes, Coach!" we replied at the same time.

Finally, my roller-coaster emotions settled. Things were only going to get more intense the closer we got to nationals, and I couldn't have a repeat of today. The goals, yes, but the stupid penalty, no. And no way was Axel going to mess with my head. All I had to do was separate the athlete from the person, and I was good. Right?

"Let's go guys! Bring it home!" I yelled out to my teammates.

I glanced up at the clock. There was less than thirty seconds left.

The hometown crowd chanted 'cougars roar' and 'green and gold', the booming echo louder than any concert. I turned my stick upside down and started banging it on the floorboard, making more noise, and the rest of the guys on the sideline did the same, as we cheered on our teammates. No doubt we'd be hoarse and hard of hearing by the time we hit the locker room.

Twenty seconds left and Ethan managed to get another shot on goal, but Mansfield's goalie was faster and blocked it.

Ten seconds remaining and I was vibrating, jumping up and down along with everyone around me, screaming as loud as I could. Gaskell made one last attempt at Maddox, but Kayden and Silas were all over him and blocked the shot.

No goal.

When the final buzzer sounded, everyone in the box jumped onto the ice. A five-goal game was a huge win for any team, and for us, it solidified everything we'd been working on for months.

After the initial celebration on the ice, we did our usual lineup with the opposing team to thank them for a good game and then scuttled back to the box for Coach Banning's postgame scrum. There was always a detailed discussion about the plays at the next practice—what worked, what didn't—but Banning liked to give his initial thoughts while the game was fresh. Coach even offered a rare smile before he started speaking. It only lasted about a tenth of a second and if you blinked, you missed it.

"This is our second highest scoring game this season, and it feels like we're hitting our stride. Things that happened today that I want to see more of; great communication, an aggressive offense, and a defense that's getting more cohesive with every game. What didn't hit right—several unnecessary penalties. Losing our cool now isn't an option. Your head needs to stay in the game and if it's not, come talk to me. Rest up tomorrow and get ready to practice hard this week," Banning paused and scanned our group. "Axel, Jace, Finn, and Silas, I want to see you in my office after you get changed."

Uh oh, Coach used our first names and that meant a long lecture was coming.

No one on the team would dare say anything right now but I knew that as soon as we hit the locker room, the razzing would start. In the meantime, I got nudges and rude gestures (when Coach wasn't looking) and ignored all of them.

With Banning's dismissal, we shuffled off to get showered and dressed. I was already feeling the aches in my lower back and when I sat down in front of my stall to remove my gear, my knees cracked loudly. Thankfully, that was the worst of it. Last year, I'd injured my groin, and I didn't want to go through that hell again. It took me forever to heal and I had to give up sex for two whole months. Sixty days, for god's sake. For me, that was like two freaking years.

Ethan stood up on one of the benches and let out a sharp whistle.

"Party at my place to celebrate the win!" Ethan shouted. "Everyone—and that includes you, Moss—better be there!"

There were claps and hollers and more whistles. Silas grunted so I wasn't sure if that was a yes or a no. He attended the team dinners, which were mandatory, but only rarely the parties on campus. No one knew why and no one felt comfortable asking. If he wanted to tell us, he would. But lately, something had changed. In fact, he'd been at the most recent one, where me, Dane, Kayden and Maddox, came out. Ethan dubbed it the Rainbow Rave. After our teammates got over the initial shock of our news, we partied until sunrise. Even Ethan's frat brothers were impressed by our stamina.

"You gonna feed us?" Kayden asked with a grin.

"Duh," Ethan chuckled. "You think I'm going to invite a group of hungry-ass hockey players to my house without food? I'm crazy, not stupid. We'll order pizza and wings and any other junk food you want."

I grabbed my kit and headed for the shower room. Normally I'd take my time, but I wanted to get washed up and get my lecture over with. While I was heading into the room, Axel was coming out, a white towel wrapped tightly around his hips. An array of colorful bruises near his ribs and on his massive biceps had me looking longer than I should've. I glanced down at my own body and realized I was much the same. Not the body type, the bruises.

Axel knocked into me when I walked past, and I got another whiff of that fucking bodywash.

Ugh, why couldn't he smell rank like most jocks?

"Watch it," I grumbled, pissed off at him, and at myself. "I don't need another hit today."

He either didn't hear me or chose to ignore my comment. Either way, it was a good thing. I was tired and hangry, and I imagined so was he. It wouldn't take much to spark our tempers. I took my shower in record time and headed back to my stall.

After changing into my jeans, black converse, and a sweat-shirt, I threw on my Cougars ballcap—backwards, natch—grabbed my neon green puffer jacket and my backpack.

"Have fun getting lectured!" Dane called out and everyone laughed.

I gave my friend my best finger and headed out the door.

By the time I got to Coach's office, Axel was already there, of course.

"Shut the door, Jace," Banning stated. "I want to speak to you and Axel first."

My stomach clenched hard, but I did as Coach directed, closing the door and taking the empty seat beside Axel. There wasn't much space in this cubbyhole of an office and when my knee brushed Axel's, I jolted hard. Or was that him?

"I've done my best to leave you two to sort out whatever it is you need to sort out," Banning started, and leaned back in his chair, running an aggravated hand though his short, dark hair. "But clearly that hasn't worked, and I've had it. When you work together, like you did in the third period, you're unstoppable. I want to see that happening during every period, every game. So, starting this week, both of you are to report to the rink at six pm on Thursdays. We're going to spend an hour each week working on your offensive plays. Together."

Axel's knee started popping up and down in a nervous rhythm and it was driving me nuts.

"Wait, why—" Axel started.

Wrong move.

"This isn't up for debate, Lund, and I just explained why. It's mandatory," Banning snapped. "You'll also be working with Finn and Silas for another hour, each on your own skills but also, helping each other out. The goal is to learn more about our teammates and to work better, together. Are you getting what I'm saying?"

"Yeah, we're being singled out," Axel huffed.

"And?" Banning bit out, and thankfully, Axel kept his mouth shut. "I'm doing what's best to improve your game and the team's. In a month's time, you're going to thank me."

I wouldn't hold my breath.

CHAPTER 6

AXEL

An extra two hours of practice a week? And one of them I had to spend entirely with Jace?

Fuck. My. Life.

I glanced over at my new 'training buddy' and my blood ran so hot I was either feverish or really fucking pissed. Definitely pissed. Jace didn't look bothered at all, sitting there with his cocky manspread going on. Most of his unruly hair was shoved under his ballcap, and the ends that peeked out were even curlier since his hair was wet.

When he glanced at me, I saw nothing but contempt. No surprise there, he was as annoyed as I was about this fucktastic turn of events.

"And that's not all—" Banning continued.

Please, what else could there be?

I was about to say something when there was a loud knock at the door.

"Enter!" Banning barked.

The door opened and Silas and Finn stepped into the cramped office. You could hardly breathe, never mind move in here. There wasn't enough room for four hockey players, plus our coach, who was a massive guy himself. My chest tightened, like someone had punched my breastbone. Great. Now I could definitely add claustrophobia to my list of problems.

"Perfect timing," Banning added. "Silas, Finn, I need both of you here on Thursdays at seven. You'll be working on drills with Axel and Jace."

"Extra practice?" Silas grumbled. "But Coach—"

"Problem?" Banning replied.

"Kind of," Silas bit out.

"If you want to stay on this team, you need to be there. Am I clear?"

Silas grunted.

"I'm sorry, was that a 'yes'?" Banning snarked.

"Yes," Silas mumbled and crossed his arms, his leather jacket creaking.

"Good. Finn?"

"Yeah, I'm good," Finn nodded with a grin. "Whatever it takes."

"That's what I like to hear. And that's not all—"

"Fuck me," Silas muttered.

"One more word out of you, Moss, and I'll add another hour to your practice time."

Silas shook his head but stayed silent. Banning was at the end of his patience, if the throbbing vein in his forehead was any indication.

Banning leaned forward and steepled his hands. I braced myself for whatever was coming next.

"I've been approached by the mayor of Sutton for a community event they're hosting in April. This is a formal dinner and dance to raise funds for the new firehouse. Axel and Jace, you've been assigned as the school liaison volunteers when it comes to the silent auction and the keynote speaker. Silas and Finn, you're going to assist at the event itself as needed."

Oh my fucking God.

"Uh, Coach, with all due respect," Jace replied. "I've got a shi...I mean, a lot on my plate. It's not just classes, but my kinesiology practicum, plus hockey. My schedule's already packed."

Banning didn't look impressed.

"Make the time, Jace. If it means one less party on the weekend, so be it," Banning replied. "It's a couple of hours a month. You can add it to your résumé and it's for a good cause. One that's important to this town and the school. This isn't just me talking. The mayor contacted our school president personally about this event. This is a priority for the Cougars and the university, whether you like it or not."

"Yes, Coach," Jace replied quickly.

"Does everyone understand?"

Unfortunately, I did. I was about to push back, but I caught the warning glare in Banning's eyes and there was no point in arguing any further. Instead, I kept my mouth shut and nodded.

"The workload won't be as cumbersome as you think. Given my history in the professional league, I've already been in touch with my contacts there and they've agreed to donate signed items for the silent auction. On your end, it's simply follow-up to ensure we receive and track the donations," Coach continued. "I've also confirmed that my friend, defenseman Selwin Kirkland, will be our keynote. His attendance means a lot of press coverage. You need to get in touch with his assistant and keep the event organizers in the loop. And be discreet about it."

I was stunned. Stunned and suddenly stoked. Selwin Kirkland was Chicago's best d-man and a player I greatly admired. Even though I was pissed about having to work with Jace, meeting one of my hockey idols tempered my bad mood.

"I'll email you the details, including the information about the league contacts and you can take it from there. I'm counting on you to get this job done right," Banning added. "This also applies to the game; we only work if we work together. Together or not at all. Got it?"

Everyone nodded.

"Good. Any other questions?" Coach asked.

"Is Kirkland going to visit campus? Maybe give our team some one-on-one guidance while he's here?" Silas asked.

Banning leaned back in his chair.

"I've already asked him, but unfortunately with his schedule, he's flying in and out for the dinner only. But there's always the possibility in the future."

"Next fall?"

"Maybe earlier," Coach replied with an enigmatic expression. "Now, if there's no further questions, you're free to go."

Free, my ass.

The temporary high I had from scoring earlier was gone. Even the possibility of meeting one of the greatest players in the league couldn't quite lift me up. And I certainly didn't want to show up to the party tonight. Why would I? Jace would be there. Then again, now I had even more frustrations to vent.

Food, beer, and a pretty girl to distract me for a few hours sounded just right.

To be honest, I was more excited about the food and beer. Sex? I could take it or leave it. It was yet another secret that I was holding tight to. At least if I got drunk, I wouldn't have any worries.

Not about how shitty I was in class, how shitty I was at sex, and now, how shitty I was at hockey.

Okay, the hockey part was an exaggeration. An assist and two goals wasn't crap by any means. But given the extra practice that had just been handed to me, it felt like I was being punished. All the past nagging from my father about how lousy I was at everything reverberated in my head. No matter the distance, that wily asshole's voice still got to me. But I'd made it this far, and no way was I going to give up. That center line position was mine and if I had to work with my rival to prove I was the bigger and better player, so be it.

As to the rest, and when it came to my classes, I needed to pick a lane. Either stay with my economics major or switch. A decision had to be made and there was no more time for dicking around.

And sex? Dicking around was a given. Maybe I just needed to embrace my inner fuckboy and do it as often as I could. Practice made perfect, right?

"Axel? Is there anything else you need to say?"

Shit, I was still sitting there like an idiot.

"Uh, no. Sorry, Coach."

I finally stood up and filed out of the room, following my teammates. It felt like we lost the game rather than won it. Jace walked ahead with Finn, and Silas with me.

"At least Coach sees our potential," Finn broke the silence. "He's giving us more time because he knows we can do better."

That didn't make me feel better. Not at all.

"I can't believe I'm saying this, but I kind of agree with Finn," Silas replied.

The rest of us stopped short and turned to stare at him.

"What?" he growled and rubbed a hand over his unruly beard. "Okay, so I wasn't expecting the volunteer thing, but having the chance to meet Kirkland? He's the best d-man in the league. Come on, don't tell me you're not excited."

I nodded and so did Finn and Jace.

"And sure, finding time in my schedule for extra practice is going to be a pain in the ass, but I'm starting to find my groove," Silas added. "And if working more closely with you guys is gonna help get me get where I need to be, then I'll do it."

"And where do you need to be?" Jace asked.

"Same as you guys," Silas replied with a frown. When no one responded, he sighed. "On the radar for the scouts."

"You want to go pro?" I asked and received a glare in return. From everyone. "What? He's already twenty-two. That's like, ancient for a hockey draft."

"Not old," Silas snapped. "And I have a hell of a lot more stamina than you."

"Oh really?" I smirked. "I guess we'll see on Thursday."

"Fucking right we will," Silas bit out and stormed down the hallway.

"Don't forget about the party!" Finn called out.

Silas replied with the tried-and-true 'fuck off' hand gesture.

"I'll talk to him," Finn assured us and took off after Silas.

"You don't make a lot of friends, do you?" Jace snarked.

I stepped towards him, but he didn't back up. Not one freaking inch. This close, I noticed that his eyes were more hazel than brown, with specks of green, and surrounded by lashes that were almost too thick to be real. And since when did I give a shit about anyone's eyes? Jesus Christ, I was hallucinating from dehydration or something. I needed carbs, preferably in the form of pizza and beer, and I needed them now.

"I might be blunt, but at least I don't treat people like shit," I bit out.

"What the fuck are you talking about?"

"Don't play innocent with me," I snapped. "You're Mr. Popularity here at Sutton, but students here don't really know you, do they?"

"Are you sure you didn't hit your head in the game today?" Jace bit back, his cheeks flushed. "Because you're not making any goddamn sense."

"I don't have time to stand here and argue with a two-faced narcissist," I hissed.

"Well, you sure as fuck have to play with him and, FYI,

I'm talking about you," Jace sneered. "I'm anything *but* two-faced and look who's talking about narcissism? You're too good for anyone here at Sutton, including the team. You've been here since September, and you've barely made any effort to get to know your teammates. The fuck is that? Maybe if you pulled that elite hockey stick out of your ass, and learned how to use it properly, you'd have a chance at being a decent person *and* player."

"You want to talk about decent? How about—"

"Hey!"

Jace and I turned to find Coach Banning standing outside his door, arms crossed, scowl in full effect.

"What the hell, guys? I can hear you from my office!" he bellowed. "What did we just talk about?"

And I thought we were loud.

"Sorry, Coach," we replied at the same time.

"Sorry is an empty word in this case. Remember what I said. We work together or we don't work at all."

Banning turned on his heel and went back into his office. When he slammed the door, I jumped. Hey, in the narrow hallway, the sound was really fucking loud. I had to get out of here. I needed food and I needed a drink. Several drinks.

"Scared?" Jace quipped. "Going to call Mommy and Daddy so they can yell at the coach for you?"

"You think you're so clever," I sneered. "But you don't know shit."

I stalked off, and didn't look back. If I did, I'd probably either heave my guts out or walk back and punch Jace in the face. Either way, I couldn't afford to go there. And I didn't know how the hell I was going to do this. My parents would be laughing their asses off if they could see me now. The 'I told you so's would never end. Calling them? I'd rather practice with Jace every day than do that. Was transferring schools a mistake? In my gut, I knew the answer was no, but the nagging self-doubt kept creeping up.

Then I thought about my freshman year at Langston. Everyone seemed friendly but that's just because of my family history with the school. I didn't make any real friends there. Just people who invited me to stuff, and who wanted an invite in return. Or an introduction to my parents, and their circle. That's how the one percent operated.

I never fit in there. And I wasn't going back.

CHAPTER 7

JACE

Not even the oblivion of a shitload of beer and vodka shots could erase Axel Lund or today from my head. And, of course, he *had* to show up to the goddamn party. I thought for sure he'd slink back to the dorm and stay there, but nope, he was here, sitting in the corner with Colin and Ethan, surrounded by several beautiful girls all vying for his attention.

Not that I was doing badly myself. I'd already made out with Hailey, one of my classmates. She wanted to go back to my room and fuck, but I wasn't feeling it. We'd had sex a few times and it was fun, but she was always hinting at more. No way did I want to give her the impression that I was looking for a relationship. Then her friend Tyson flirted with me and suggested all three of us go back to his room, together. He was a sexy guy with pouty lips and a confident air, but I wasn't interested in a threesome either.

I know, what the fuck?

Normally I'd be so pumped after a game that I could fuck all night. I guess I drank too much, because my dick wasn't cooperating and there was no way I was going to hook up tonight.

"You look like you need this."

I turned to find Finn standing beside me with several beer bottles in hand.

"Thanks," I replied and gratefully took the offered drink.

Might as well get totally shit-faced if I wasn't going to get laid.

"No worries," Finn took a gulp of his beer and looked around the room like he did when he was on the ice, scanning for opportunities. "I saw you kissing Hailey earlier. She's hot."

"Yeah."

"So, what the hell are you doing standing here by yourself?" he asked.

I shrugged and took another gulp. "She's great, but I'm done with repeats."

Finn nodded.

"Is she looking for a boyfriend?"

"Seems like," I smirked and nudged his arm. "Talk about a boner-killer, am I right?"

Finn bit his lower lip.

"I don't know about that," he replied quietly. "Back in Nebraska, I had a girlfriend, Simone. But when I got accepted here for college, she broke up with me. She didn't want to do long distance."

His voice, tinged with sadness, made me pause and look at him. Finn was scrappy as hell and he was always joking around, always lighthearted. But he was serious right now. Was it the booze in my system or was he confiding in me? We'd talked a lot, but always about hockey and school, with plenty of razzing thrown in. I had no idea he'd ever been in a relationship, never mind that he was obviously upset over it ending.

"I'm sorry," I finally replied. "You miss her?"

"A lot," Finn admitted with a sigh. "But I think it's more that I miss having a partner. I was hoping I'd meet someone here at Sutton, but so far, no dice."

"I've seen plenty of girls come on to you—" I started.

Finn shook his head. "Yeah, that's not it. I'm not into the casual thing."

I stared at him, shocked.

"The way you talk in the locker room, I thought you scored plenty."

Finn rolled his eyes.

"Come on Jace, you know how it is. Everyone mouths off and plays a big game. You think I'm going to admit to the rest of the guys that I'm not interested in random hookups?"

He had a point.

"So, you're demi?" I stated and he nodded in return. "Cool, but why tell me? I mean, I'm glad you did, but why now?"

Finn paused, then nervously peeled the label off his beer bottle.

"You came out, and Dane, plus Kayden and Maddox, and it got me thinking. I've always felt different, but I couldn't really talk about it with my friends back home, you know?"

Did I ever. I didn't want to tell anyone I was bi back in high school.

"My head's been wrapped up in this for months. Man, I'm so relieved to finally tell someone. Maybe now I can focus more on the ice," he admitted. "I can just be myself and it's okay. Shit, that seems way too deep for a buzzed hockey player."

I laughed out loud at his comment.

"This is what college is all about." I tapped his beer bottle with mine and then raised it. "To discovering the best version of ourselves."

Finn let out a wide smile.

"Speaking of best—" Finn motioned to the corner of the

room where Axel was sitting. "He had some phenomenal assists today."

"Ugh, don't even go there. I'm trying to relax, not get worked up again."

At the very moment that I let out those words, Axel turned and scowled at me.

Finn let out a low whistle. "You'd never know you two are on the same team. But Coach is right; save your aggression for the next game."

I didn't know that I could make it that long.

Axel

I should've been paying attention to the conversation around me, to my teammates, and more importantly, to the beautiful girls that were sitting beside me, but I was too caught up in my head.

Ever since that meeting with Coach, and the reality that I'd be spending more time with Jace, I'd been in full-blown panic. A feeling that was all too familiar lately. I thought being far away from my family would ease the pressure inside of me, but instead, I was always on edge. Like I was waiting for them to appear and drag me back. No way could I go back.

Suddenly, the room was both stiflingly hot and freezing cold. I was sweating like I did on the ice, but with none of the exhilaration that followed. My heart pounded louder than the music around me and my chest seized up so tight that I could barely take a breath. When my vision blurred and my ears rang, I stood up on shaky legs.

I *had* to get out of here. Right fucking now.

I don't know what, if anything, I said to the guys sitting next to me, and I didn't care. Plowing through the crowd, I made it outside in record time and when the frigid winter air hit my lungs, I shuddered in relief.

No one was hanging around outside, thank fuck. I could have my meltdown alone.

Deep breath in for four, hold for four, and out for four… Again.

Fuck that holistic shit. I was still spiraling, with anxieties whirling through my mind like a tornado as worst-case scenarios bombarded me. What if I didn't improve? Would I fuck up my chance at a hockey career? What then? And when was I finally going to confront Jace about what he did to Preston? Question after question pinged around in my brain until I wanted to scream. At this point, I was counting down the hours, not days, until I'd have access to my trust fund. Would I be free then? I would. I'd never have to go back to that house. And those people. Even if I didn't have hockey, I wouldn't go back.

Focus on that. It's not much longer. Just play hard, keep your head down, and do the work.

Finally, I was able to suck in some air, but the sweet relief was short-lived. I reached into my coat pocket for my cigarette pack, but there was nothing there and then I remembered that I quit a month ago. Still, this was an emergency, and fuck knows I needed something to calm me down. There were pills I had for immediate relief, but I didn't like relying on them. The antidepressant my doctor had prescribed was fine for my low mood but it was obviously doing jack shit for my increasing anxiety.

"You look like you need this."

I jolted at the sudden deep voice that echoed in the still air.

Turning around, I spotted Maddox standing in the shadows of the porch, a cigarette perched between his lips. He held one hand out, offering me a smoke.

How the hell had I missed him standing there? I really *was* losing it.

"Even though I seem to recall you telling me it was a filthy habit," he added.

"It is. Was." I shook my head. "I've quit, but thanks."

He shrugged, shoved the pack into the pocket of his jeans, and reached into his jacket. When he pulled out a baggie of gummy bears, I stared at him, confused at first.

"Have a couple of these. They'll help you relax better than a cig ever could."

Ah yes, I'd heard about Mad's fondness for edibles.

"Trust me, two of these and you'll be smiling wider than Kay," he added.

I chuckled, relieved to feel, well, relief. Without pause, I took two gummies and popped them in my mouth. They were way too sour for my liking, but the shocking taste distracted me.

"Thanks," I muttered as I quickly chewed. "And no one will ever smile as big as your boyfriend."

Maddox snorted. "True."

He didn't say anything else, and I was grateful. I didn't need twenty questions right now, just quiet. Maddox leaned back against the wall of the house and closed his eyes, taking another long drag of his cig.

Huh. That was a little quieter than I expected.

"Had enough of the party?" I asked, breaking the silence.

Maddox blinked slowly, like a slumberous cat, and nodded.

"Not my thing. I can do ten, maybe fifteen minutes of peopling and then I need a break. Too much noise and shit. But since it's game day, I promised Kay I'd be here."

I leaned against the railing.

"You played great today," I responded awkwardly.

Duh, Axel.

"Could've been better," Maddox offered with a shrug, running one hand through his dark, messy hair. "I've been replaying those goals all night."

"Ruminating?"

He pushed off the wall and walked towards me, shaking his head.

"Nope. I learn from it and then move the fuck on. That's what makes us the players we are. And if you want to get to the next level, you can't let the losses screw with you, right?"

I bit my lower lip and nodded. It sounded right, if only my brain would get on board.

"You did good too," Maddox continued, inhaling sharply then exhaling a long plume of smoke. "There's some weird sixth sense shit you have going on when it comes to the puck."

I rolled my eyes. *Yeah, right.*

"I mean it," he stated and pointed at me. "Your record for assists speaks for itself. And after being on the ice with you these past few months, I finally get the nickname. You've got a knack for making plays happen."

"I want more," I admitted.

"Don't we all?" Maddox snarked.

"Coach does too. He's given me extra practice. With Jace," I scoffed and then leaned against the porch with a sigh. "And Silas and Finn."

Maddox pursed his lips. "Yeah, Silas told me. It's probably a good thing. Especially you and Jace. We can't have our best forwards at each other's throats all the time."

Before I could reply to his comment, the door opened and Kayden stepped out, his six-foot-five frame looming, a beer bottle in one hand.

"Where's my beautiful Bee?" Kayden called out in a teasing voice laced with humor and alcohol, and when he spotted Maddox, he gave a low whistle and motioned with his free hand. "Get your sexy ass over here, Mad."

Maddox's usual scowl deepened as he turned to his boyfriend.

"A bit louder, Kay," he replied with a shake of his head. "I don't think everyone in the entire state heard you."

Kayden's head fell back as he let out a deep laugh, and he pulled Maddox into his side. The goalie's scowl softened to a grin. I didn't fully understand these two as a couple but the look that passed between them was scorching hot, igniting the icy winter air around us. I was curious, and a bit envious, about their intense attraction.

"Oh, hey," Kayden suddenly acknowledged me with a cool smile and a nod.

He'd forgiven me for my shitty behavior, but he obviously hadn't forgotten. Not that I blamed him. I shuffled in place, jittery, hating the feeling.

Just how long were these edibles going to take to kick in?

"You guys have fun," I replied quickly and turned away. "I'm gonna head out."

I was halfway down the stairs when Maddox called out.

"Good luck in those extra sessions," he commented. "And don't have too much fun getting sweaty with Jace."

I stumbled, but thankfully, I didn't fall.

"Asshole," I grumbled.

The echo of Maddox's unexpected laughter followed me all the way home.

CHAPTER 8
JACE

THE FOLLOWING WEEK

I was going to be late for practice. Shit.

Get up and leave.

I'd sat frozen on my bathroom floor for over an hour, staring at the toilet. Fun times. My gut was churning full force, but I fought hard to let the feeling ebb and flow, to let my nerves ease in and out like a long, shuddering breath. That nagging voice in my head told me it would be so much easier to make myself vomit. Then everything would be under control. The uncertainty would be over. That's the way it had been since my senior year in high school. Pressure had been coming at me from everywhere, from hockey, to school, to my boyfriend, Preston. Especially him.

But it was the comments that never got out of my head, stuck there like permanent post-it notes.

You're nothing but trash.

You'll never amount to anything.

You're only good for a fuck.

I fought hard to push back against those thoughts. Like

hockey, sometimes I won, and sometimes I lost. The only thing I could control was my response.

Just throw up, you'll feel better.

Plenty of guys vomited before a game. It wasn't that unusual. Only, it had gotten worse at the end of my senior year, around the time my relationship with Preston came to the breaking point. Never mind puking before the game, I was doing it before class, after every team dinner, and sometimes, in the middle of the night when I couldn't sleep. I kept telling myself that it was fine. I had it under control. I was wiry but strong, and the less weight I had the faster I was on the ice anyway.

Until I fainted during practice. My coach pulled me aside and told me if I didn't stop losing weight, he was going to bench me and call my aunt. She'd already been through enough and had done everything in her power to raise me right after my mom died when I was just a baby. Josie knew something was up with me, but never pushed. That wasn't her way. I couldn't lay my problem on her, not when I was so close to getting out of Hillington.

That day, I searched online and found a therapist and used the tips I earned working at Josie's garage to pay for it. After a month, I confided in her about what really happened. My urges to binge and purge were less frequent. And, feeling stronger, I finally had the courage to put a stop to the toxic relationship that had me questioning every idea in my head and every word that came out of my mouth.

A sudden knock at my bathroom door jolted me back to the present.

"Jace, hurry the fuck up!"

Dane? What was he doing here?

I slowly stood up, washed my hands, and reached for the handle, yanking it open.

"Can't a guy take a shit without being interrupted?" I snarked as I stared at my friend.

Dane sniffed the air. "You shit pretty clean."

"Fuck off," I quipped and stepped out of the bathroom. "What are you doing here?"

"I'm making sure my friend gets his ass to practice so Coach doesn't give us *all* extra workout time this week."

"Gee, thanks." I walked over and grabbed my puffer coat, my backpack, and a beanie. "Now tell me the *real* reason you're here."

"Two reasons. One, Coach made me permanent captain today—" he started.

"Holy fuck! Congrats!"

I reached over and hugged Dane.

"Thanks. Formal announcement coming soon. And second," Dane continued as he pulled back, his smile wide. "I want to make sure my two best forwards aren't gonna get into a fist fight today and get thrown off the team for good."

I shook my head, fidgeting with my keys as we headed out of my room.

"Don't worry," I assured him. "It's all under control."

I think. I was in control, but I had no idea about Axel.

"I trust you," Dane replied as we headed for the stairs. "I still don't know Axel that well, though, so he's kind of a wild card. But I'm pretty sure he won't do anything to fuck this up."

"Does that mean you're not going to stay to watch our practice?"

"Nope, I've got a date with Jackson," Dane offered a dirty grin, and I shoved his shoulder.

"You're so gaga over him."

"Fuck, yeah."

I had a momentary pang of envy, but it passed like one of Axel's assists; fast. I couldn't fathom a relationship. Not now, not ever. Why would I want to go through that shit again? I'd rather wear a funky jock for a year.

"Please think of me while I'm out there sweating my balls

off and you and your boyfriend are—" I paused, smirking at my friend. "Wait, I guess you'll be sweating your balls off too."

I snorted and Dane chuckled as we stepped out of the dorm and into the bitter cold.

"Come on, you know that Coach is doing the right thing. If you and Axel don't click soon, the team's not going to improve."

"We're never going to click," I hissed, my breath releasing like a plume of smoke. "He's besties with my ex. And because of that, I can't even look at him, never mind have a civil conversation."

"You don't need to like the guy to work with him. On the ice, it's not personal," Dane countered. "Remember, he's just another player."

"You don't get it," I sighed. "My ex, Preston, he…fuck, you know what happened. And I can't talk about this now."

I walked faster, needing to move.

"I hate to say it but at some point, you have to open up," Dane insisted. "Not just to your friends but to Axel. Tell him the truth."

"I don't know if I can. And chances are, Axel won't believe me," I admitted quietly, then stopped short. "Preston messed with my head, and I don't want to go back there, to fuck up my concentration. Not now. There's too much at stake."

Dane didn't push any further but instead, patted my back.

"Let me know if I can help, however I can help. I'm here. Jackson too."

"Thanks."

We then walked silently to the rink and surprisingly, Dane followed me inside.

"I'm okay now, Daddy. I swear I'll be fine on my own and I will *not* cause trouble," I announced sarcastically as I rolled my eyes.

Dane messed up my hair and I shoved his shoulder. Everything was back to normal.

"Fine." He walked backwards down the hallway and pointed a finger at me. "Have a great practice. Be good."

"Go on, get out of here!" I teased. "Go have sex with your hot boyfriend."

"Rowland!"

Shit. I turned around to find Coach Banning staring me down.

"Get on the ice, you're already late!"

"Yes, sir," I replied automatically.

I shuffled off to the locker room but before I entered, I glanced over my shoulder to find Dane standing at the end of the hallway, giving me an evil grin and mouthing 'burn'. I gave him my best finger in return and then hauled ass to get changed.

When I snuck out of the locker room all kitted up (in record time, I might add), I ambled down the chute to find Axel practicing with Coach. Great. Ax was already busy kissing ass.

"Add another fifteen minutes to your time tonight," Coach announced, glancing at me and then at Axel. "Both of you."

Axel glanced over at me and his glare was frostier than this rink. Fuck me.

"Do your usual warm-up for fifteen and then we're working on advanced drills," Coach stated.

I did my stretches and then took off down the ice.

We did laps around the rink, Axel skated on one side and me on the other. Around and back the other way, until I felt my muscles loosen up. I glanced over and noticed Coach had set up five sets of pylons and sticks, three in a row near the blue line, and then another two sets leading up to the net.

"Alright," Coach yelled out. "Quick hands, 360 drill. I'm timing. Rowland, you're up first. Lund, notice how he handles the puck, any patterns—good and bad—and how he approaches the net. Rowland, the same goes for you when it's Lund's turn. We're doing ten rounds. After that, you're working on passing drills. Let's go."

For some reason, I was suddenly self-conscious like I never was on the ice. Probably because I'd never practiced one on one with Axel before. Then I looked up and realized Axel's eyes were burning a hole in my jersey. If he thought that was going to make me flub in front of him, he could think again.

With a quick flick of my stick I nabbed the puck and took off, skating between the pylons, flipping the puck back and forth, then around and over to the net, taking my shot. I turned around and faced Axel, giving him my best smirk. He leaned on his stick and stared at me like I was a strange specimen in a lab. Fuck him.

"Was that beautiful or what?" I gloated as I held my arms out.

Coach shook his head, but Axel's hard expression never wavered, his mouth set in a grim line.

He was going to get lockjaw at this rate.

"You're dragging your left foot," Axel stated.

"The fuck you say?" I snapped.

"Hey!" Coach interrupted.

I bit my lower lip. "Sorry, Coach."

"He's got a point," Banning replied with a raised eyebrow. "You tend to lean into your right. Do it again."

Turning around, I headed for the pylons and repeated the drill. This time, instead of being distracted by my dickhead teammate, I focused on my footwork. After I slid the puck into the net, I swiveled around, and spotted Coach's approving stare.

"Better," he said. "Did you notice how much faster you were that time?"

I didn't want to admit it, but Coach—and Axel—was right. I nodded.

"Sometimes we get complacent because skating is second nature to us. Don't make that mistake."

Then it was Axel's turn. The last thing I wanted to do was study him, but then again, if I wanted that center spot, I needed to know everything about him. Keep your enemies close and all that.

When it came to hockey, that is.

Despite his bulkier frame, Axel moved with an agility that was undeniable. But it was his stickhandling that caught my attention (no, not that kind). And this was why he was so great at making assists; his reaction time was lightning quick. If he wasn't such an ass, I'd be tempted to admire him.

He made to take his shot on goal, but there was a moment of hesitation before the blade of his stick connected with the puck. Interesting. Was this just a one-off?

"Take the shot over!" I called out when the puck hit the net. "And don't choke this time."

"Rowland," Coach warned.

I should've watched my words. Instead, I skated over to Axel and got up in his face. If I was going to push my luck, at least Coach was around to referee.

"Why did you hesitate to take the freaking shot?" I asked.

"I didn't," Axel returned, pointing to the net. "Clearly."

"I saw it," I insisted. "You had momentum and then you didn't. The puck barely made it in."

Okay, I was exaggerating but I had to make my point. It was a valid one.

"Fuck you," he muttered low under his breath.

"You wish," I hissed, my adrenaline spiking.

Axel stepped closer, sweat trickling down the sharp angles of his face. His sneer had my temper running so hot I was sure I was going to combust on the spot. Instead of fueling the fire, I skated back to stand beside Coach and Axel started the drill over again.

The same thing happened when he approached the net.

Why was he stalling out? It was weird. And so was my interest in why he was doing it.

"Do it again," Banning demanded.

Axel let out a loud growl of frustration but with each turn, he got better. But not as good as he needed to be. I was about to take my turn when Coach's phone rang. He pulled it out of his pocket and a worried expression crossed his face.

"I've got to take this. Start on your circle passing drills."

Banning glided off the ice. Axel and I were alone for the first time. No coach, teammates, or game to buffer us. He stared at me like I was shit under his shoe and I gave it right back.

"I don't need your fucking advice," Axel spat out.

"Suit yourself," I bit back. "You keep assisting and I'll keep scoring."

Did I push things too far?

I got my answer when Axel dropped his stick and gloves and came at me.

CHAPTER 9

AXEL

Jace skated backwards and laughed. Laughed, that fucker.

"What did you say to me?" I bit out.

I lunged for him, and we slammed into each other and the boards, tussling like the idiots we were. I caught the scent of his musky sweat and something spicy, probably shampoo, and it bothered me that I even noticed. The fuck? I thought I had everything under control. Then again, I'd never been alone like this with Jace.

"Go on, hit me," Jace dared me as I locked eyes with him.

The defiance in his gaze told me he wasn't bluffing, but his sharp, quick breaths made me think he was all for show. He licked his lips nervously and my eyes caught on his mouth. For a split second, I couldn't move or speak. I just stared at him like I didn't know what I was looking at.

"Do it," he goaded again, and I snapped back to attention.

Hit him? And throw away college and my future? I wouldn't give him the satisfaction. Instead, I pushed one finger into his chest, or rather his pads, and shook my head.

"You're not worth it."

Jace paled, his formerly red cheeks turning almost ghostly white.

"Then back off," he warned.

I did just that, pushing away from him, wanting to get as far away as possible.

God, I was stupid. If Coach saw this, he'd kick us both off the team.

"Then shut up about my slapshot," I countered.

There was nothing wrong with it. Nothing. Okay, maybe it was a bit on the slow side, but I was tired, and I was having an off day, and that was it. I'd hardly slept last night, thinking about today. In fact, I'd hardly slept all week knowing I'd be working with Jace. Add to that, an unexpected voicemail from my brother and I was all but ready to pack my bags and leave school for good. Not that I had anywhere to go. I'd have to stick it out here at Sutton until I graduated or got drafted, whatever came first.

"How can you do better if you can't take criticism?" Jace huffed.

"Look who's talking."

"Hey, if there's something I can do to improve my game, I'll do it. I want to be the best."

"And I don't?" I scoffed.

He shrugged, giving me a cocky smirk.

"Doesn't seem like it," he replied. "But then it's not for me to say."

"That's hilarious considering you have opinions on everything."

Jace mimed jerking off. Part of me wanted to laugh at his antics, but then I remembered who I was talking to. *Don't be fooled. Think about how he treated Preston.* Yup, that got my head cleared up quick.

"Grow up," I growled.

"The same advice applies," he bit out. "Your follow-through is weak. Something's holding you back. What the fuck is it? The sooner you figure it out, the better you're going to play. Not that you'll ever be as good as me, but that goes without saying."

"You little shit."

"Not little." His eyes filled with a mischievous light. "And you know I'm right."

Was I holding back? I wanted to argue but something in my gut told me his comment wasn't totally off base. Then I remembered the way Jace took his shot and compared it to mine. Without other players around, I'd tracked every movement of his long body; from his sneaky footwork to the way he geared up to take his shot. How the fuck did he make things look so easy? The guy's slapshot was perfection and it grated on my already frayed nerves. Why couldn't I just let it fly like he did? If I had, I'd be scoring a shit ton more than him. The fact that he'd thought the same and said it out loud made me feel crappier than I already did. And I was itching to wipe that smug-ass expression off Jace's face.

"I don't see my players practicing."

We turned to find Coach standing on the other side of the boards, hands on his hips, staring at us with a disappointed expression. When his gaze veered to the right, I knew that he'd spotted my gloves and stick on the ice. Shit.

Jace didn't say a word and neither did I. Without pause, I skated off and picked up my stuff.

Focus.

Coach stepped back onto the ice, but he didn't lay into us like I expected. Still, I was so damn thankful for the reprieve. If someone else was around, anyone, I'd be okay to manage my reaction to Jace.

We practiced our passing drills over and over, and before I knew it, Silas and Finn joined us.

All four of us worked hard, only stopping to hydrate, until Coach let us go an hour later.

Instead of taking a shower in the locker room like I normally did, I changed quickly and headed out. No way was I staying around Jace any longer than I needed to be. I'd clean up back at the dorm.

With a quick goodbye to Finn and Silas, I hauled ass out of the rink and the tension in my chest finally eased.

Until my phone buzzed. I reluctantly glanced at the message, hoping it wasn't my brother.

It was Preston.

My bestie was texting and calling me less frequently lately and I wondered what was up. Or maybe I was the problem. It didn't seem like we were BFFs anymore. The longer Preston and I were apart, the less we had to say to each other. He was on the west coast, and I was on the east; he was focused on acting and me on hockey. We had no interests in common anymore. Not school or friends or anything really. Oddly enough, the only link we had was Jace.

> Preston: How's things in Sutton? Are you bored out of your freaking mind?

Bored? I wish.

> Axel: No time for that. Just finished practice. Sore and tired as fuck.

> Preston: And Jace? Is he still an asshole? Have you talked to him?

The times when Preston did text me, he always asked about Jace. He was weirded out that I was now on the same team as his ex. Not surprising, but there was nothing I could do about it.

> Axel: Only when needed and when it relates to the game.

> Preston: Really? He doesn't talk about me?

> Axel: I thought you were going to forget about him.

> Preston: I have. I just don't want him spreading rumors about me. If he claims that I hurt him, tell him to fuck off.

That reply made me pause. Preston was in California, why would he care what people here thought about him? And claims about hurting Jace? I thought Jace was the one who hurt him.

> Preston: Don't listen to anything he has to say. Jace is charming when he wants something, but he's such a liar. He lies about everything.

I should've believed my friend, but something about his comments felt off. Everyone at Sutton loved Jace. Dane let it be known several times that there was no one he trusted more as a friend and a teammate, and Dane was, by all accounts, a stand-up guy. Jace, a liar? Given my family history, I had a great radar for bullshit and lies; secrets were our stock-in-trade. But the longer I played with the team and with Jace, the more confused I was about Preston's history with him. My head told me to be wary of falling for Jace's charm, but my instincts were starting to fight.

> Axel: You need to forget about him. He's not worth it.

> Preston: You're right. And not the reason I texted. I have BIG news. I know a guy who knows a guy and...he's getting me a movie audition.

> Axel: Holy shit, congrats!

Preston: If this works out, I'm quitting college.

Axel: What? Your parents will flip.

Preston: I don't care. This is what I want. Nothing's going to stop me.

Axel: I hope you know what you're doing.

Preston: I'm going to be a megastar and fuck everyone else.

Axel: Good luck.

Preston: I don't need it. Later.

Axel: TTYS

I was so busy texting that I wasn't watching where I was walking and bumped into someone.

"Oof."

"Sorry," I replied and glanced up. "Oh, hey."

Ethan grinned at me.

"Hey yourself, glad to see you're in one piece. I thought for sure you and Jace would maul each other tonight."

Mauling made me think of fucking, not fighting, and that train of thought was…disturbing to say the least. I swallowed hard as I remembered the way Jace and I collided on the ice, grappling like angry wrestlers, and of course, the taste of sweat and frustration. My stomach flipped over in the strangest way, and despite the bitter winter air, I was boiling hot again.

"Funny," I sighed and shook off my unease.

Ethan chuckled. "It's the truth."

"Coach was there to play peacemaker. It's all good."

I was a pretty good liar myself.

"If you say so," Ethan nodded. "Where are you off to now?"

"Dorm. I need to shower, eat, and pass out."

"You sound like a rookie."

"You add two more hours of ice time to your week and see how you feel," I snarked.

Ethan wiped his eyes dramatically. "Aw, poor Axel."

Everyone on this freaking team was a comedian…

I was about to reply to his sarcasm when my phone rang.

"See you around." Ethan waved and stalked off.

Looking down at my phone with a cautious glance, I wondered who the hell was calling me. I hated talking on the phone. Not that I had anyone to talk to since arriving at Sutton. Except for Ethan's parties, I didn't have a full social calendar. Not like Jace.

Stop thinking about him.

Only, it wasn't a friend calling. It was my brother, Jonas. *Not now.*

I hadn't replied to his earlier voicemail, and he wasn't one to give up. I tapped *accept* with extreme hesitation, like I was worried about being contaminated.

"What?" I answered.

"Nice to talk to you too, Ax."

The sound of my brother's voice had me shivering in the worst way and I started walking again, desperate to get rid of the feeling.

"You never call me unless you want something. What is it?" I bit out.

That sounded harsh but it was the truth. We had nothing to say to each other. My brother was two years younger than me, but we could've been ten or twenty years apart for all we had in common. He was smarter, got perfect grades without effort, and always knew just what to say to get his way. Especially with my mother. Our parents picked a favorite early on, and Jonas was it. He was popular in school, invited to every party, and the center of attention. I could never measure up to him. And when I found hockey, I didn't need to. It was the one thing that was mine, and that even Jonas couldn't compete with or take away. Still, always being made to feel like I was the screwup of the family messed with my head. You'd think I'd be jealous of Jonas, but I wasn't. The opposite, in fact, because for years I was confused as to why he hated me when I'd done nothing to warrant it.

The reason only became clear last year when I discovered that he was my half brother. The reason I used as leverage to get the fuck out of Redgewick.

"How's college? And hockey?" he asked. "Still coming in second best?"

My footsteps faltered at his dig, but I kept walking.

"You have three seconds before I hang up," I replied, my heart hammering in my chest.

Whatever was about to come out of Jonas's mouth was not going to be good.

"I need money," he hissed.

I bit out a laugh. "Be serious."

"I can't ask Mom or Dad. They've cut me off."

"The fuck you say."

Even if my parents had cash flow problems, they'd find a way to give Jonas what he wanted.

"It's true," he whined.

Jonas blew a lot of money on drugs. If it came in a pill, he was popping it. He also loved to gamble so if there was a bet to be made, he was placing it. My parents looked the other way. If Jonas was happy, they were happy.

"What do you need it for?"

I don't know why I asked, because I already knew the answer. There was a pause on the other end of the line, then a sharp inhale.

"What does it matter? You don't give a shit anyway. Just lend me the money and I'll pay you back in a month."

"Are you using again?"

"It's under control. And don't act pious. You get high too."

"Not every day," I sighed. "How much do you need?"

"Five grand."

Jesus Christ.

"You can't be serious."

"I don't buy cheap shit and I owe some guys for a party last month. Plus, I have a poker debt to pay off. Now, are you going to give me the money or what?"

I sighed.

"Fine. But that's it. I don't have any more to give you."

"Yeah, right."

"I'm serious. I've got enough to cover my expenses until I graduate, but that's it. Mom and Dad have no more cash to pass out."

"You're lying. They have a shitload of money, tons of it."

That's what it looked like on the surface.

"Next time you need a loan, ask one of your friends."

"College hasn't changed you, Ax. You're still the same bastard that you always were."

"Maybe you're the one who's the asshole? You ever think about that?"

Then I hung up. I tapped on my phone again and logged into my bank account, transferring the money to Jonas as requested. For a second, I considered ignoring him, but I knew that wouldn't work. He'd keep calling and texting until he got what he wanted. He was completely relentless and nothing stopped him. Jonas would do anything to get his hands on his next fix. While I knew that his addictions weren't my problem, part of me felt guilty. Maybe if I'd tried harder when I was younger, if I'd found some way to get through to him, things would be different between us. But I never succeeded. Just like I never fit in with the rest of our family, I didn't fit in with Jonas.

I was used to being an outsider—at home, at school, and now, in hockey. Suddenly, desperately, I wanted to fit in somewhere, anywhere, and most of all here.

I just didn't know how.

CHAPTER 10
JACE

THE NEXT DAY

was halfway through my anatomy 201 class when my phone buzzed. A couple of students turned to stare at me and the teacher stopped talking.

"What did I say about phones in the classroom?" Professor Mulligan barked.

"It won't happen again," I called out apologetically.

But I left the phone on my lap and surreptitiously tapped on my email. It was a note from Coach Banning about the spring fundraising event. I needed this added stress like I needed a fucking puck to my head. When I read through the entire email, I realized that this volunteer thing was going to take more than one or two hours a month. It was probably more like one or two hours a week and that meant even more time spent with Axel. Hockey was one thing. At least we had Coach or Silas or Finn to keep us from imploding. This? How the hell were we gonna navigate this? And we could not screw up. Coach would be watching, the school too, and fuck, even the mayor of the town.

I could do this. It would be fine.

Without pause, I texted Axel, since Coach included his contact information to ensure nothing would be left undone. We had to set up a time where we could meet and discuss how we were going to divide up the work for this event. I expected him to reply, but I did not expect him to reply right away.

Jace: We need to meet in person to discuss the fundraiser.

Axel: The only days that work for me are Monday evening or Sunday morning.

Jace: Fuck Sundays, we need one day to sleep in. Monday it is.

Axel: It won't interfere with your hookups?

Jace: We all need a day off. FYI, I don't fuck everyone on campus. And even if I did, don't slut shame me.

Axel: Don't be so touchy.

Jace: Around you? No thanks.

Axel: Monday at seven. The game room at the dorm or the pub in town?

Jace: Pub. The school can at least comp us a meal.

Axel: Are you sure you want to be seen with me in public? Wouldn't want to ruin your reputation.

Jace: According to you it's already shit, so what does it matter?

Axel: Is this what it's going to be like on Monday or are we actually gonna get stuff done?

> Jace: You got the email from Coach. Set up a plan and we can discuss it.

> Axel: Me? Why don't you do it?

> Jace: Aren't you used to attending all these fancy ass socials? This event should be right up your alley.

> Axel: I hate that shit. But since I don't fuck away my responsibilities, fine, I'll do it. You just show up and act pretty.

> Jace: Didn't think you'd noticed.

I didn't get any response after that.

"Mr. Rowland?" Professor Mulligan bellowed.

My head shot up and I stared at my teacher, my face burning hot.

"Yes, sir?"

"If you do not put your phone away, I will confiscate it, and I won't return it for an entire week. Are we clear? Do you understand, or do I need to put it in writing to your advisor?"

"Understood, sir. My apologies."

There was a ripple of laughter in the room from my fellow students, but Mulligan's glare put a stop to it pretty quick.

Like I did when I was playing hockey, I put my conversation with Axel out of my head and focused on what I had to do right here and now, which was *not* pissing off my teacher. Any more than he already was. The last thing I needed was an extra assignment or getting my marks docked.

When class ended, I headed over to the library. I had an hour of free time before my next class and I needed a quiet place to study.

On my way there, I ran into Hailey. This day was just getting better and better…

"Hey, Jace, where are you off to?" She reached for my arm and gripped me tightly. "You want some company?"

"Not today. I've got to get some studying in before I head to my next class."

"What about later?" Hailey smiled knowingly. "I could stop by your room?"

She was a beautiful girl and a lot of fun in the bedroom, but I had no interest in taking things any further. Or spending more time with her. Outside of casual flirting, I didn't see the point. We had nothing in common except sex. Which was great, but strangely enough, *not* enough to make me want her again. In fact, when I thought about any conversation we'd had, it was always about, or leading to, fucking. Otherwise, we'd had nothing to say to each other. And my interactions with her seemed so boring in comparison to…

No. Fuck no. Don't even think about Axel.

I hoped like hell I wasn't coming down with a bug or something because I felt off.

"What about tomorrow?"

I sighed, wanting out of this conversation. Like, now. It was shitty, but I couldn't help it.

"Sorry."

"That's fine," she replied, her grin cooling. "There are plenty of other hot hockey players around. Like that teammate of yours, Axel."

My scowl was immediate. She smirked and tossed her hair over her shoulder.

"He's gorgeous."

He was something alright. I bit my lip, holding back a response.

"He's in your dorm, right?"

"Yup," I replied calmly, despite my heart beating a furious rhythm. "Not sure which room. You can ask around."

"I'll do that," Hailey replied with a firm nod.

"I've got to get going," I repeated and pulled my arm loose.

"Text me later if you change your mind," she added and stepped back.

"Will do," I said politely, lying my ass off.

I turned away, relieved, and scampered off as fast as I could. Given the frozen sidewalks, I nearly slipped and forced myself to slow down. The last thing I needed was an injury.

By the time I got to the library, I was half frozen. Instead of taking the elevator, I decided on the stairs, and sighed in relief when my limbs finally defrosted. Making it up to the second floor, I smiled at the clerk at the front desk and asked if there were any private rooms available, but unfortunately, everything was booked up.

I was about to head up to the next level when I spotted Maddox and Kayden heading my way. They waved and wandered over to meet me.

Up close, I noticed that both guys had swollen lips and red cheeks. Jesus.

"Studying hard?" I chuckled.

"Hardly studying," Kayden replied with a dirty grin.

Maddox groaned and shook his head.

"The library? Seriously?" I asked.

"Don't knock it," Kayden replied and tapped my shoulder. "Those private rooms? No windows, no distractions—"

"No more," Maddox snarked.

Kayden laughed and ruffled Maddox's hair, which only made our goalie scowl harder.

"Plus, this place has special meaning for us," Kayden continued.

Aw. My cynical heart melted. Just a little.

"Kay," Maddox warned, his face bright red.

"What? It's true," Kayden admitted as he stared at his boyfriend. "It was the first time I ever gave you a blo—"

Maddox quickly slammed his hand over Kayden's mouth. "Stop."

"Mrphrm."

Whatever Kayden was *trying* to say was muffled and for once, I was glad that Maddox had silenced him. I didn't need to know any more about my friends' sex life than I already did.

"That's so dirty, and at the same time, oddly sweet," I teased.

"Fuck off," Maddox growled but it had no impact on me.

We were all used to his attitude by now. Instead, I laughed while he rolled his eyes.

Kayden pulled him in tight, but at first Maddox resisted. Until Kay gave him a resounding kiss, and all seemed to be forgiven. These two…

"Well, okay then, some of us really *do* have to study, so—" I stated, pointing to the stairs.

Neither one of them paid me any attention since they were too busy sucking face. I didn't mind though, I was happy for them.

"Talk later," I added and was met with silence.

I wandered up the stairs to the third floor and the place was packed, but I managed to find an empty nook near the window and settled in. Turning my phone off–for real this time—I shoved it in my pocket, grabbed my headphones from my backpack, and started reviewing my biology notes for my upcoming test. I wasn't the smartest student but with dedication and hard work, I was going to graduate at the top of my class and ensure my future. Hockey was the primary goal, but it wouldn't last forever. When I was done playing hockey in the pro league, I'd go back to school for my master's degree. Kinesiologists could work anywhere, with any athlete, but I'd probably stick to hockey or another professional sport.

And I knew there was no fucking way I was going back to

poverty or to Hillington. My aunt Josie had done all she could. She hadn't graduated from high school and though her body shop kept food on the table, it wasn't enough. With my career goals firmly in sight, I was going to ensure that as a family, we never had to worry about money again.

After almost an hour of studying, I turned my phone back on and got ready to head out to my next class when I noticed a missed call from my aunt. *Speak of the angel.* She usually called me on weekends. I hoped everything was alright.

I grabbed my stuff and walked down to the first floor of the building and found a quiet corner, then tapped her number and waited for her to answer.

"Hey sweetie, how are you?" she answered on the first ring.

"I'm good," I announced. "Great in fact. Just on my way to my next class. How's things with you? Everything okay at the shop?"

"Everything's fine. Well, things are a bit slow at the shop, so I figured I'd call early," she replied. "You didn't need to call me back right away. I know you're busy with classes. We can talk later."

"I've got fifteen minutes before my next class. What's up?"

"I just wanted to check in. See how your classes are going and hockey practice. And if you're getting along with all your teammates. Are you still arguing with that Lund boy?"

I told my aunt all about Axel when I returned home for the Christmas break. Come to think of it, I probably talked more about him than I did about anything else. I didn't even want to think about what that meant. Nothing good would come of it.

"He still hates my guts and I'm still better at scoring than he is, so nothing's changed," I replied, cocky as ever. "Only—"

"Only what?" she asked.

"Coach is making Axel and I take extra practice together.

It's torture," I sighed dramatically. "And that's not all. I've been assigned to work with him on a fundraising event here in Sutton. I have no issue volunteering, but I don't know *how* I'm going to work with *him*. We nearly came to blows on the ice yesterday."

"Do you mean he tried to hit you?" Josie asked, her voice filled with concern.

"Well, sort of. I kind of provoked him," I confessed. "And then we just went at each other. It wasn't all him."

My face flushed with heat.

"I mean, it wasn't anything more than grabbing his jersey and trash talking," I added. "Maybe we wrestled a bit."

That didn't sound any better. The image of me and Axel grappling, our bodies so close, all sweaty and frustrated, had my heart beating triple time.

"Jace," Josie warned.

"I can't help it. He insults me all the time and I'm not gonna stand there and take it. You know I'm not made that way. And because he's a Lund, he thinks he's better than everyone else," I snapped. "He hardly talks to anyone on the team, not to mention he threatened to out Maddox and Kayden a while back."

There was a longer pause on the other end of the line.

Josie was calm in situations where I was not. Always level headed. *Think, then act.* Part of it was her personality but a lot of it had to do with everything she'd been through in her life. She'd taken over my care when she was only a twenty-year-old girl herself. My mom died in an accident and my dad wasn't in the picture. I couldn't imagine taking on a child at my age. All that responsibility. Josie grew up fast and sacrificed a lot. Sometimes I forgot that she'd lost everything too when my mom passed.

"He acted like an asshole, that I'll give you," she replied. "But you said he apologized to them and is trying to do right. And you know better than to judge someone based on their name or their shitty behavior. You don't know what he's dealing with."

"Some people are just jerks."

"That's also true," she chuckled, and the raspy sound made me homesick. "But remember what we talked about Jace? A lot of times when people lash out, that's when they're hurting the most. It sounds like Axel has problems in his life and he just doesn't know how to deal with them."

Josie had a point. I didn't want to admit it, but there was something going on with him.

"You're probably right. But I have no idea what it has to do with me. Okay, that's not true," I paused. "He thinks I'm this awful person. I have no idea what Preston said about me, but I have a feeling he's gaslighting Axel like he did me. And if that's the case, how am I going to convince Axel otherwise?"

Josie made a humming sound like she always did when she was pondering something.

"That's tricky," she replied. "You'll probably have to approach this like you're playing offense. What happens when you're faced with an opponent that's out playing you? What do you do?"

"I study them. I watch the tape. Watch them on the ice. Analyze them and figure out the best way to maneuver around them. And then I act. I've got to be bold."

"There you go. You need to watch and listen. Don't just argue with him. Listen to what he's saying, and maybe what he's not. And then you need to be up-front about what happened between you and Preston. If he doesn't believe you, he doesn't believe you, but at least you tried. You've been carrying around that secret for a while now. Maybe it's time you let more people know what really happened."

"I told Dane and that was enough. You know that I don't like talking about it."

"I do know that. And I know that there was stuff that you

shared with your therapist that you didn't want to share with me, and that's fine. If you were talking to someone you trusted, and you were okay, I was okay. I just don't wanna see you hurt yourself like that again," she paused. "Have you been alright lately? Do you need to talk to your therapist?"

"I...I don't know. Maybe," I admitted, lowering my voice. I ran one agitated hand over my head. "Before my practice with Axel last night, I sat in the bathroom for a while and contemplated making myself sick. I didn't do it, but the urge was strong. Just when I think I have everything under control, I don't."

"Says every adult every day," she confessed. "Don't ignore the warning sign. Call your therapist."

"I will," I promised.

"You're doing so well, sweetie, and I'm so proud of you. And I'm just a phone call away. You're not alone. Remember that. You are *never* alone."

Axel's troubled blue eyes came to mind.

No, I never felt alone. But I was starting to think that maybe Axel did. And why that bothered me, I didn't even want to think about.

CHAPTER 11

AXEL

Boots N' Burgers was the busiest place in Sutton, and renowned for their pub food.

Unfortunately, I had no appetite. I was grumpy as fuck knowing that Jace was about to walk through those doors any minute now. The thought of seeing him after our last practice had my stomach clenching painfully.

I'd gone to the gym last night, but even after a long workout, sleep wouldn't come. Instead of lying in bed, staring at the ceiling, I'd opened my laptop and worked on my economics paper. Sure enough, an hour after I started typing, I fell asleep. That should've been a clue right there that I had to change my major ASAP.

"Evening. What can I get you?"

I looked up and gave Phoenix, the owner of the pub, a polite smile. I'd never really talked to him, but I'd witnessed my teammates chatting him up. He seemed like a nice guy, hardworking, and good to his staff, who were also friendly. He must've lived and breathed this place because he was always here.

Phoenix placed a glass of ice water on the table and then tapped on his tablet.

"Just a large Coke with extra ice," I muttered. "Thanks."

Phoenix stared at me with narrowed eyes. "I've seen you in here before with Ethan. You play with the Cougars, right?"

I nodded. "That's right. I'm Axel."

"Phoenix, nice to formally meet you. But you'll need more than a Coke," he quipped. "Come on, we've got the best burgers in Vermont. And you guys have a game coming up soon. You need fuel."

The thought of a juicy burger and a pile of crispy French fries suddenly had my stomach growling. Loudly.

"See?" Phoenix laughed.

I shrugged and conceded. "Alright. A double cheeseburger, the works, but no onion. And fries, extra crispy."

"I'll have the same," a familiar voice added. "Plus, a large Coke."

Jace stepped around Phoenix and smiled at him. My teammate looked casual in worn jeans, a navy cable-knit sweater, and his winter jacket. Only, he didn't have his usual baseball cap on. Instead, he pulled off a black beanie and swiped a hand through his dark curls.

I'd managed to snag a booth, and Jace slid in opposite me, but he didn't meet my gaze. Instead, he kept his eyes on Phoenix, and they began to chat about the upcoming season. I reached for my laptop and tried to distract myself from the complete awkwardness of this scenario.

A few minutes later, Phoenix headed off to the kitchen, and Jace took off his jacket and settled in. He ran his hands through his hair again and gave me a strange look.

"So," Jace finally said, breaking the tension.

I stared right back at him and tried to swallow the lump that was lodged in my throat. My right knee bounced up and down so hard that I hit the wood table with a loud bang. The pain had me swearing and Jace chuckling.

"What?" I snapped. "You're as eager to be here as I am, right?"

Jace licked his lips and nodded. "That about sums it up."

"Okay, so let's get this over with." I showed him my laptop screen. "I put together a spreadsheet with a list of all the tasks for the silent auction follow-up, but we need to divide—"

Jace held a hand up and I paused.

"Can we wait until after we've eaten? I haven't had anything since lunch and if I don't get calories in me soon, I won't concentrate, and if I can't concentrate, I can't—"

"I get it," I snarked and shut my laptop with a snap. "But it's probably going to take at least ten minutes for our food to get here. Are we really going to just sit and stare at each other in the meantime?"

Jace leaned in, giving me a shit-eating grin.

"I know I'm real pretty to look at, but don't stare too long. You'll give me the wrong idea."

Then he winked at me. Fucker.

I gave him the universal sign for 'screw you' and reached for my glass of water, taking a much-needed sip to cool down.

"Don't tempt me with my favorite finger."

I started to choke, but thankfully, I managed *not* to spew water all over the table.

"You just don't quit, do you?" I finally croaked out.

"No fucking way," Jace replied confidently, leaning back and resting one arm over the leather booth.

His hazel eyes were bright under the dim lighting, and for some reason, I struggled to look away.

"Personally, I don't feel like arguing. I mean, if you want to that's fine, but it's Monday. Isn't that bad enough?" I replied with a resigned sigh.

"Long day?" Jace asked, opting for a safer topic of discussion.

I nodded. "Aren't they all?"

"Truth," Jace replied. "I haven't seen you hanging around the lounge in the dorm, and only once or twice at Ethan's parties. What do you do outside of class and hockey?"

"There's life outside of hockey?"

"Funny. Come on, spill."

I didn't know what to say. I hadn't been joking.

"At least tell me what you're studying," Jace continued.

"I'm an economics major. It's boring as fuck, but hey, I'm sure the degree will be useful. For what, I don't know. Unfortunately, school isn't my thing, much to the disappointment of my parents. I'm all about hockey. And I don't really hang out with people here other than the parties."

"Why not?"

I shrugged.

"It's been kind of strange transferring after my freshman year at Langston," I admitted. "Everyone here except me went through first year together, and because of that, they're already friends and I—"

What was I doing? Why was I telling Jace all this? I sounded like a sad loner. Which I was, but Jace didn't need to know that.

"I can't believe I told you that," I hissed and looked away, embarrassed.

"Speaking of friends, we need to talk about Preston," Jace suddenly announced.

Just like that, my hackles went up, and my embarrassment turned to anger.

"Don't even start," I snarled. "I know how you treated him, and I don't need to hear your excuses. I won't hesitate to walk out of here."

"And risk your place on the team if Coach finds out you reneged on this fundraiser?"

I bit my lower lip. Shit. There was no way I could just get up and walk away.

Jace knew it and I knew it.

Phoenix stalked back up to our booth with a cautious smile and set down two plates, along with our drinks. The burgers and fries looked, and smelled, amazing. Too bad I wasn't hungry anymore.

When Phoenix left us alone again, Jace leaned forward, his gaze holding mine. I recognized the look of intense determination on his face, just like he was about to lean into his slapshot.

"I have an eating disorder," he whispered.

What? I wasn't hearing correctly.

"Excuse me?"

He swallowed hard and I watched his Adam's apple bob up and down.

"I said, I have an eating disorder. Bulimia." He glanced down at his plate and back up at me. "It started during high school when I was seeing Preston."

"Look, I don't know what kind of weird head game you're playing with me right now, but—"

"Not a game. Not this. Never this. It's the truth."

He locked eyes with me and my heart kicked up a wild rhythm.

"My last year of high school was a lot," Jace admitted quietly. "I was busting my ass to get the best grades possible because I needed a scholarship to go to college. Then there was hockey of course, and I wanted to make an impression so Sutton would offer me a place on the team. Plus, I wasn't out yet and neither was Preston. We kept our relationship hidden and it was becoming more and more frustrating. I hated lying to my friends and it became a lot. A lot of lies and a lot of pressure. See, my aunt Josie is my only family. My dad left town before I was born and my mom passed when I was three, in an accident at a local factory. It's just been me and Josie since I was a little kid. I told her that I was bi when I was sixteen, but she was the only one who knew."

Jace paused and reached for his drink. It was only then that I noticed his fingers were trembling, the ice in the glass rattling. If Jace was telling me a bullshit story, then he was a damn good actor. Better than Preston.

After taking a long sip, Jace wiped his mouth with the back of his hand.

"Things started to get weird in the months leading up to graduation," he continued, clearing his throat. "Preston was getting angry with me all the time and freaked out when I so much as mentioned that I wanted to stop hiding who I was. He started telling me I was trash and that I was never going to make anything of my life. That I was only good for fucking and that was it. If we'd been a casual, one-night thing, I could have ignored the comment and walked away. But, by that time, we'd been together for months. I had real feelings for him. I thought I loved him, and I thought he loved me. I kept telling myself he's just scared. He's scared and frustrated and taking it out on me."

Jace paused and took another sip of water.

"Two months before graduation, he'd been at my place, and he'd left his phone behind. He started getting all these notifications and I recognized the app. A hookup app. I didn't need to look to know what was going on. I returned his phone and confronted him. Preston denied cheating on me, but my gut told me I was right. My gut and everything else, because I started feeling sick. But it wasn't until I went to my doctor for a physical a few weeks later that I found out the truth. I had an STD. Preston insisted we didn't need condoms and since I thought we were monogamous—"

I sat there in shock, too numb to say or do anything. Even my knee stopped jumping under the table.

"Anyway, Preston denied everything. He gaslighted me, making me second-guess my doctor and everything I thought I knew about our relationship. Between that and the pressure at school and hockey, I felt so out of control. The only thing that comforted me was binge eating. Then I'd feel so guilty, I'd force myself to vomit. At first, I didn't think it was a big deal. I sometimes puked before a big game given my nerves. A lot of guys are the same. But then, I was doing it before every practice, every game, every day. I lost almost twenty pounds. It made me fast as fuck on the ice, but I was getting more anxious, sick, and tired. When I fainted during a practice, my coach intervened."

This couldn't be real, right? Preston lied to me for the past two years? I didn't know what to think or believe. But the longer Jace talked, the more details he gave, the more it made me consider. Had I been played by my best friend? I thought I was good at spotting liars. And if he was a liar, shit, wasn't there one person in my life that I could trust? My stomach cramped and for a moment, I thought *I* was going to throw up. That was irony right there.

"I got into therapy and things got better," Jace added, swiping an agitated hand through messy hair. "At the end of high school, I finally had the courage to break up with Preston. To call him out on his bullshit."

What was I supposed to say to that? Preston was my closest friend. Suddenly, I was just supposed to forget everything and believe Jace? Based on what?

"Preston told me that you'd screamed at him, and that he was scared of you," I bit out. "I picked him up that last morning and he was crying. Shaken up. I almost went into your place to confront you, but he insisted we go home."

Jace shook his head and let out a deep sigh.

"I'm sorry, but the truth is that he was the one with the temper. He refused to leave my apartment after I told him it was over. He was so mad about my decision to end things that he punched a hole in the wall of my bedroom."

"Preston told me it was the other way around."

"He lied."

I didn't know what to say to that. To any of it.

So, I did what I normally did when confronted with shit that I couldn't handle.

"I don't want to talk about Preston or anything to do with him. I can't," I bit out. "Let's just get on with what we came here to do and get it over with."

"We'll play it your way for now. You don't want to hear the truth? You want to go on being an arrogant jerk defending your asshole of a friend? That's fine," Jace snapped and pointed to my laptop. "Let's deal with this fundraising event. At least something good can come out of this shit show we're in."

"Oh, I'm sorry. You dropped a freaking bombshell on me, and what? You think I'm going to change my mind about you?" I snapped my fingers. "Just like that? For real?"

Jace's responding scowl was fierce.

"I said what I needed to say," he hissed. "I really don't care one way or the other if you believe me or not. It's not my problem. And you don't deserve any more explanation."

"Look, Preston and I—"

"I don't give a fuck," Jace snapped. "Just forget everything I said tonight. All of it."

His face was so distraught that it made me sick.

There was no way I could forget. Any of it.

CHAPTER 12
JACE

Facing off with Axel in the pub was harder than facing off with any opponent on the ice.

But I'd done what I came here to do. I'd taken my shot and told him the truth, whether he wanted to believe me or not. Like I told him, it wasn't my problem. It didn't surprise me that Preston had lied to him and was lying still. And if Axel wanted to hold onto those lies, then there was nothing I could do.

Not a goddamn thing.

And, naturally, the rest of the night was awkward as fuck.

Axel kept staring at me as we ate silently. Like he was worried I was going to run off to the bathroom as soon as we were done. And this was the reason why I rarely told people that I had an eating disorder. As soon as they knew, they were watching, waiting, and worrying. That didn't help things at all. Talking about my bulimia was supposed to be good for my mental health but I was starting to wonder. Then again, what did I expect with Axel? It's not like I was talking to Dane or Kayden or someone who was my friend. This guy hated me.

Axel didn't respect me, and honestly, after that conversation with him, I didn't respect him. On the other hand, I knew that if someone had just told me that one of my friends was lying to me, I wouldn't believe them either.

What else could I do? Nothing. Abso-fucking-lutely nothing.

Somehow, someway, we managed to finish eating and then we went through the checklist of tasks for the fundraiser. Distraction was a color-coded spreadsheet and thank God. We agreed on one thing at least; I'd deal with communications with the league contact and Axel would catalog the donations.

For a first-class asshole, he was surprisingly well-organized.

An hour later, I headed out. I didn't want to go back to my room and ruminate about Axel or everything I'd admitted to him, so I texted Dane and hung out with him and Jackson in their room. We played video games, and I won all of them, having so much nervous energy to dispel.

Dane gave me questioning looks but I ignored them.

Like Axel, I just couldn't deal with it in the moment.

I'd almost told Dane everything I'd said to Axel, but I held back. I wasn't sure why. Spilling my guts to my rival? Sure. But my friend? Nope. I guess I was feeling kind of raw. Dane knew, or rather, I'd told him about Preston and that last year of high school, but I didn't go into a lot of detail about the eating disorder. Dane knew about it, but he didn't press me. And I didn't blurt out everything like I did in that pub tonight. God, I wanted to erase that conversation with Axel from my brain forever. Then again, there was a kind of relief with putting it all out there.

The next day was our usual Tuesday practice.

Usual? Not quite.

Knowing that I was going to see Axel again had me so nervous I was all but shaking in my skates. I'd arrived extra early so I wouldn't run into him, and when Dane spotted me pacing the locker room, he pulled me aside.

"What's going on with you? You've been jittery since last night."

"It's nothing."

"Jace."

"You know I had to meet up with Axel, what do you think?" I asked, lowering my voice and leaning in. "I did something stupid. I told Axel about my bulimia. And about Preston."

"Oh shit. What did he say?"

I didn't reply, reliving the conversation in my head.

"Jace?"

"I shocked myself, and him," I finally whispered. "It all came out. All of it. But it didn't change anything."

"He didn't believe you?" Dane asked.

I shook my head and bit my lower lip.

"Nope. He was pissed. He thinks I'm the one who's a liar. That I treated Preston like shit."

Dane's face darkened. It was rare to see him get upset. Not our calm, cool captain.

"Don't get in the middle, D," I warned him. "It's not worth it."

"Now I'm really worried."

I bit my lower lip. "I can separate hockey from Axel. On the ice it's a different thing. I promise."

"You say that, but I know you. And I'm worried for you. As my friend."

"I appreciate that. But there's nothing to be worried about. I said what I had to say to him and that's it. In a way, I feel better. He knows the truth. If he doesn't want to accept it, like I told him last night, that's his problem. Besides, that's the past. I'm focused on the present."

"And that's why you're pacing up and down the locker room like you're about to jump out of your gear?" he said with a raised eyebrow.

"Can you blame me? I have no idea how he's going to act. Or how I'm going to react to *him*."

"Maybe you need to talk to Coach?"

I considered that and nodded. "Let's see how today goes."

I didn't want to go to Banning. At this point, I was old enough to figure my shit out. And I didn't need this drama. Why did everything have to be so fucking complicated? So much for telling the truth. It didn't get me anything in this case. Maybe it would've been better if I had just left things alone and continued to let Axel believe the worst of me. Only, I had a bad feeling that by unleashing all that stuff on him, especially the reality about Preston, worse was just the start.

"Jace?" Dane asked, staring at me with concern.

"Sorry," I replied quickly. "I'm fine. Seriously."

My friend's gaze told me he didn't buy it, but thankfully, he left it at that.

"If you're not, tell me."

I nodded and patted his arm gratefully.

"Let's hit the ice."

Dane guided me out of the locker room, and we passed several teammates heading in. Still no sign of Axel, which was a total relief. Jesus, this guy was taking up way too much of my headspace lately. I was surprised I could remember to skate and shoot the puck at the same freaking time.

Dane and I headed down the narrow hallway, and I was hit with the familiar wave of ammonia and sweat that lingered in the air. The atmosphere of the rink quelled some of my anxiety. I slid onto the fresh ice, a perfect plane of milky glass, and sighed with pleasure. It was weird but I always loved being the first one to break it in.

This was where I belonged.

When I was growing up, it was just me, my battered skates, and my faraway hockey dreams. Not so far off now. If I could keep my shit together and find a way to deal with

Axel. I'd had to work with players I didn't like at every level, but nothing like him.

Focus on your own game. The rest will fall into place.

I was getting so good at bullshitting myself.

The buzz of fluorescent lights and the echo of our blades scraping the ice cut through my rumination. Then I noticed Coach Banning hovering by the boards, his tablet in hand, furiously writing notes with his stylus. When he glanced up and spotted us, he nodded quickly and went back to writing. The last thing I wanted to do was disappoint him, or the team. Despite being in my favorite place, a heaviness sat on my chest, the weight of expectations. What if I screwed this up? What if…

Dane nudged me with his stick.

"As your captain, I'm ordering you to get to work," Dane quipped, and I flipped him off even though I was grateful for the distraction of his teasing.

We warmed up, and then started drills while we waited for the rest of the guys. It was a good ten minutes before our teammates joined us, and by then, I was feeling much more relaxed. Ready to face Coach *and* the most annoying forward I'd ever played with.

Or, maybe not.

I didn't need to look around to know that Axel had arrived. For some crazy reason, I was now hyper aware of him, like I'd developed 'asshole radar' or something. For sure I recognized the sound of his gait, a skating style that was heavy on the push off and long on the glide. Despite his bulk, his movement was so smooth it was almost silent, like you'd hardly know he was there until he was right up in your face. Like that night on the ice, just the two of us, grappling in this same spot.

I flushed hot but I reasoned it was just the warm-up and shook it off.

There was no way I could avoid him, and I never let

anyone intimidate me. I glanced up and watched him head in my direction. His moves were mesmerizing. I was a faster skater, but Axel prowled like our cougar namesake; powerful and ready to strike. Usually, I was the one who did the stalking on the ice, but suddenly, it felt like the tables had turned. When he stopped short, I stared into his midnight blues. Every hair on my body stood on end, my pulse beating frantically.

Whatever I was feeling, it wasn't just anger.

Oh yes, things were about to get much, much worse.

Axel

Skate past him. Keep going, don't look at him, don't talk to him.
But you have to play with him, idiot.

"Lund, Rowland, get over here!" Coach called out.

Jesus, Banning was going to make me and Jace practice together in front of our team.

This isn't going to be good.

For the first time in all the years I'd been playing hockey, I considered not attending practice and telling Coach that I was sick. Anything to avoid facing Jace again. Last night's conversation with him was playing like a loop in my head, and it sparked more questions than answers. I'd never let anyone get to me this way. Not even my family members, most of whom couldn't stand me, and hell, I couldn't stand them. And I'd had time to think about what Jace admitted and the more I thought about it the more uneasy I grew. What if Preston was lying to me all this time? What if our whole friendship was a lie?

The thought of losing my closest friend, hell, my only friend at this point, was crushing. The only thing I should be crushing right now was my game. I should be playing the best hockey of my life. Instead, I was torn up about this whole situation with Preston and Jace and unsure what, if anything,

I should say. Should I confront Preston? Or should I just stop texting him. Should I talk to Dane? He knows Jace.

Or maybe, I should just forget everything and pretend like last night never happened…

"Lund!" Coach yelled as he motioned for me to join him near the blue line. "I called your name twice. Get over here. Now!"

There were murmurs and whispers, my teammates chuckling at my complete oblivion to what was going on around me. I hauled ass and headed over to stand beside Jace, making sure that I didn't get too close, since I didn't want to risk touching him. Not even brushing against his jersey. Which was stupid, I mean, we played hockey for god's sake. It was inevitable that we'd run into each other.

Hopefully not in the shower.

And where the fuck did that come from? Thinking about Jace, naked and wet, was even more disturbing. Fucking hell.

"Let's see those passing drills. Show everyone how it's done," Banning announced as he glared at me and then Jace.

Move.

Despite the initial awkwardness and my head being fucked up, everything clicked into place when we got going. I was getting better at reading Jace's cues and he was the same with me. We passed the puck back and forth like we'd played together for years, not months. Maybe Coach had a point about the one-on-one practice time because this, here, now, there was a different kind of synergy between me and Jace. An unspoken understanding. I didn't like it, and I didn't like him, but I couldn't deny that when we pushed the personal shit aside, we played great together. Or, maybe I was just seeing things that weren't there? No, it was true because when we finished up, our teammates clapped and whistled. Even Coach Banning told us we did a great job.

Jace and I rounded the net and came face to face again. With any other player, I would have reached for him, hugged him, or slapped him on the shoulder, or the ass. But I didn't. I couldn't. We stood there frozen, inches apart, neither of us reaching for the other but not skating away either. The crackle of tension snapped like a live wire, the pulse of it making me aware of my body in a way that I'd never experienced before. Not on the ice, not off it, and not with anyone. Not even the women I'd fucked.

Holy shit.

I didn't know what was going on here, but whatever it was, it scared me.

And staring into Jace's eyes, I realized I wasn't the only one freaking out.

CHAPTER 13

AXEL

"Hug it out, guys!" Ethan shouted, breaking the silence as only he could.

Instead of doing just that, I acknowledged Jace with a sharp nod and pushed off. I heard his sigh and wondered, was it relief or exasperation? I didn't know and wasn't sure why I cared.

We got razzed relentlessly for the rest of practice.

Teammates started calling me and Jace stupid nicknames, but the one that stuck was 'Hot n' Honey'. Thank you, Ethan. What an ass. Even the usually quiet guys like Silas and Maddox got into the teasing, and if Coach hadn't been there, I probably would have given them all the finger and skated right off the ice.

By the time we got to the locker room, I was exhausted. Not just physically, but mentally. Not sure what, if anything, I was going to say to Jace when I had to actually talk to him again. I grabbed my shampoo and bodywash from my stall and headed for the shower room.

I was halfway done scrubbing up when I heard Jace's voice and my body went rigid, my dick included. Frantically, I searched for any thought that would gross me out; toenail fungus, jock itch, hemorrhoids…and nope, I was still half hard. Whatever. It's not like I hadn't seen guys with semis or erections in the shower before. I wouldn't shock anyone. It happened, especially after a practice or a game. We were all pumped up with adrenaline. It was a totally normal reaction.

Only, I hadn't been hard until Jace walked into the room and that realization was disturbing as fuck. I'd never reacted to a guy that way before. That was definitely new. New and unwelcome because it was Jace. I wasn't upset that he was a guy, I was upset because it was him. Didn't have any issue with it, it just never occurred to me that I'd be turned on merely by the sound of someone's voice. A man's voice.

I quickly glanced over my shoulder and spotted Dane and Jace on the other side, their backs to me. My eyes immediately locked on Jace's body, water sluicing down his long back and over a tight, round ass that had my cock jerking hard. Stunned, the bottle of shampoo squirted out of my hand and onto the tile floor and the resounding splash had Jace and Dane turning towards me. Jesus Christ. I bent over to quickly pick it up and faced the wall again.

Just scrub up and leave.

Thankfully, they carried on their conversation, and I recited stats in my head to calm my dick down. When I finished washing up, I wrapped a towel around my hips and prayed that my boner would stay gone. Just for the next few minutes, of course.

I scampered out of the shower room and headed back to my cubby. Ethan, Finn, and Colin were getting dressed as I walked past them.

"We're heading out for a bite and then back to my place for drinks. Join us?" Ethan offered.

"Sure," I replied, surprising myself.

Ethan smiled. "Great, because you look tense as fuck."

"I need to get laid," I admitted, and everyone chuckled.

Fuck did I ever. Then I could screw away this crazy day.

"Jace's friend Hailey was asking about you," Ethan commented with a grin.

"What? How do you know that?" I asked as I stood in front of my cubby and grabbed my jeans.

"I ran into her today."

"Is she blond, green eyes, big dimples?"

Ethan nodded. "That's her."

She was pretty, but I wasn't interested, and I wasn't one to go after someone else's girl.

"I thought she and Jace—" I started.

"Nah," Ethan waved me off. "It's a casual thing. Jace doesn't do long term."

"Right."

If—and that was a big *if*—the story that Jace told me about Preston was true, it was no surprise that he was sour on relationships. Still, the idea of sleeping with someone who'd slept with Jace…I didn't like it. At all. In fact, just thinking about him and Hailey together made me irritable as fuck.

"It's still a no," I replied as I tugged on my briefs and jeans and threw aside the wet towel. "She's not my type."

"Oh yeah, you like brunettes?" Finn blurted out.

At that exact moment, Jace stalked into the room, his dark hair slicked back. Droplets of water ran down his neck and chest, and my eyes caught on his left pec and the cougar tattoo that covered it. His biceps flexed as he reached up and ran a hand through his hair, the strands falling around his face in a messy tangle. Why couldn't I stop staring at him? This weird preoccupation was beyond my comprehension. And all logic.

"That's not what I meant," I added, ignoring the heat in my cheeks, and scowling at Finn.

"Sorry," Finn replied, nervously glancing at Jace and then back at me.

Wait. What was going on? Did he catch me looking at Jace?

"What are you guys talking about?" Jace asked as he threw me a glare and headed for his cubby.

This time when he offered me his back, his ass was, thankfully, covered. But only in a thin white gym towel, wet, almost transparent, and clinging to those perfect cheeks like a second skin. It was…obscenely hot. The curve of his ass was on full view and my cock liked it way too much. God, I needed to fuck this ridiculous preoccupation away. ASAP.

I held my t-shirt in front of me, covering my crotch, and willed my dick to ease up.

"Axel here needs to get laid." Ethan smirked. "I suggested Hailey but apparently, she's not his type."

"You mean, human?" Jace retorted.

"Haha," I bit back. "But, seriously, I don't want your leftovers."

"You dick," Jace hissed as he started towards me.

"Oh shit, here we go," Ethan announced. "Ding, ding, ding! Get ready for round two."

All the guys chuckled, but there was nothing funny about me and Jace facing off.

"What's going on?" Dane asked as he entered the room.

"Honey insulted Hot, and Hot got back at him," Ethan replied matter-of-factly while our teammates continued to laugh.

Dane was the only standout in the room, walking over to stand between me and Jace with a worried look on his face. Or, maybe it was irritation. Our captain wasn't happy about playing referee and I was skating on thin fucking ice. If I got on Dane's bad side, there was no way he'd support my efforts.

"It's fine," I bit out, staring at Jace's mouth, his full lips curled up in a pouty smirk. "It's nothing."

"Jace?"

"We're good," Jace replied quietly and then smiled at his friend. "Just the usual locker room trash talk."

More like a prelude to another tussle.

"You two need to figure out your shit. Like right fucking now," Dane demanded and motioned for us to move away from each other. "Come to a peaceful ceasefire. Whatever it takes."

I did as our captain commanded and stepped back.

"Did you hear me?" Dane asked.

"We'll work it out," I promised.

Why did I even bother lying? Everyone knew things weren't fine and how the hell were Jace and I going to work this out?

I shoved aside my mounting frustration and finished getting dressed, reaching for my t-shirt, hoodie, and parka. The usual locker room chatter quieted. I swear, I didn't let out another breath until I noticed Jace and Dane leaving.

Then I waited around with Finn until Ethan was done with his twenty-step hair routine. Like every player, Ethan was superstitious and refused to cut his hair at this point in the season. He had a longer mullet than me, but with his sleek black hair, he looked like he'd stepped out of a fashion show rather than a stinky college locker room. I couldn't care less what I looked like at this point. Glancing at my reflection in the mirror, I conceded that I look like one of those wolfhound dogs, minus the grooming. I was okay with that. The shaggier, the better.

But instead of heading into town, we headed back to Ethan's, ordered burgers and wings, and downed shots. Not the ideal post-practice combo but we didn't have a game for another two days so we could afford to let loose.

Three of us turned to ten, and then twenty, and then a weeknight party was underway.

Alcohol lubricated some of my nerves, and my tongue, and after a while, I was having a good time hanging out with my teammates. Finn laughed so hard at one of Ethan's jokes that he snorted vodka up—and then out—his nose, which everyone found hilarious, including me. Then, some of the girls from the Kappa Delta sorority stopped by, all of them friendly, pretty, and talkative. They loved Ethan, of course, the party master. I still hadn't really clicked with anyone and wondered if I was ever going to get laid again.

"The rest of the guys are heading over," Ethan declared as he sat down on the couch beside me and nudged my arm. "Including Jace."

"I guess that's my cue to leave," I said as I took another shot and slammed the glass on the coffee table.

"Seriously, what's the real deal with you and Honey?" Ethan asked.

I scoffed at the mention of Jace's nickname, but the alcohol was playing wicked havoc with my mind. Suddenly, I pictured Jace standing in front of me, naked, like he was in the shower room. But instead of water, a long, slow drip of golden, liquid honey slid down over his body, over that peach of an ass. How sweet would that taste?

"I need more booze for this conversation."

And for that image in my head.

Ethan rolled his eyes and poured two more shots. "Spill."

I took the shot, and gave thanks to clear, liquid courage.

"It's not my place to say," I announced.

"Is this about Preston?" Ethan added.

I stared at him. "You know about that?"

Ethan nodded. "Just that they dated, and it was bad. Preston treated him like crap, hurt him badly. Made him question himself."

"Preston's my best friend," I admitted.

My only friend. No way was I going to admit that.

Ethan choked on his drink and coughed.

"How did I not know that?"

"Do you know everything that goes on with this team?"

"Pretty much." He smirked as he leaned in. "Look, I don't know you that well, or Preston at all, but I can say for sure that Jace is a good guy. He might act cocky and yeah, he can be a smart-ass, but which of us aren't? I know for sure that he's been through some tough shit. He worked hard to get here. And he's nice to everyone, always friendly. If a teammate needs cheering up, or just someone to talk to, he's there. I haven't heard, or seen, a bad thing about him. Not from anyone."

That didn't make me feel any better. The longer I was here at Sutton, the more people that I talked to that knew Jace, the more I questioned Preston. I knew for sure that something had to give. One way or the other, I was going to get the truth. Even if I didn't like it. Then again, Preston was a great actor. If he'd been feeding me lines all this time, then I really was a complete fool.

"Enough about Jace," I replied, ignoring Ethan's intent gaze. "I need to forget about him, hockey, and school. I need a distraction."

"Well, let's take care of that."

Ethan waved at two of the Kappa Delta girls, the ones he'd introduced earlier as Rina and Waverley, to come join us. Ethan talked me up, flirting like mad, while I grunted a few responses and tried to make conversation. I forced myself into social mode, and made eye contact with Waverley, a cute brunette (thanks Finn) who leaned into me and started asking me the usual get-to-know-you questions.

A few minutes later, Ethan stood up and offered his hand to Rina, and they took off upstairs.

I turned to Waverley, tentatively sliding my arm around the back of the sofa, and she curled tightly into me, warm, and smelling like roses and vanilla. She gave me a flirty grin and licked her pink lips. I should've been turned the fuck on, ecstatic that this beautiful woman seemingly wanted my attention. My cock, however, wasn't impressed with this turn of events. Nothing stirred below the belt, and it made me even more frustrated. Still, Waverley looked at me expectantly, so I leaned in to give her a kiss. I'm sure once I had a taste of her, my libido would kick-start.

I was just about to take her lips when I heard a door slam and Jace's name called out.

My head snapped back like I'd been sucker punched.

"Are you alright?" Waverley asked, confusion in her eyes.

"Uh, yeah," I whispered and bit my lower lip. "Just, uh, the noise surprised me. You want to get out of here and go someplace quieter?"

"How about you come home with me?" she asked, a rosy flush staining her cheeks.

I should have said 'yes'. I should have said 'hell yes' and 'let's leave, now'. Instead, I sat there like an idiot, frozen to the couch. Why didn't I just get up, take her hand, and go? What was wrong with me?

When I didn't respond, Waverley pulled back, her smile gone.

"Or, maybe we can have another drink first," she offered, and stood up. "I'll be right back."

Judging by the annoyed look on her face, she was not, in fact, coming back.

CHAPTER 14

JACE

Ethan insisted that Dane and I drop by his place tonight.

Apparently, what started out as a few of the guys having takeout turned into a full-blown party. I didn't want to see Axel after that scene in the locker room, but I also knew that if I didn't show up, he'd win. And that wasn't happening. I wasn't going to stop seeing my friends or having fun just because Axel couldn't face me or the truth.

He's not the only one who can't face the truth.

I winced as I thought about my reaction to Axel in the shower. It took all the willpower I had not to stare at him every time we were in the same vicinity. And not in an 'I despise you' kind of way. More like, 'why the fuck are you such a gorgeous asshole'? When he dropped his shampoo, I turned around and looked at him. *Really* looked at him. Like I never did with other teammates. And the sight of his sculpted, wet body had me biting back a groan. He had a bite-able ass, thick, hard thighs, and a wide barrelled chest covered in dark blond hair. I made the mistake of letting my eyes roam longer, over those bulging biceps, and veiny fore-arms, and finally, his uncut dick. All kinds of wicked fantasies played out in my head. I knew how he smelled but now my curiosity about what he tasted like couldn't be stopped. Thank fuck the water raining down over me concealed the drool coming out of my mouth.

It was madness. Thinking about Axel like that was pure stupidity on my part.

He's a total a-hole, your nasty ex's bestie, and he's straight.

Not that I was completely sure about the last thing. I didn't miss his once-over. Or maybe he was just sizing me up and looking for weak spots in case one of our fights turned physical.

Don't even think about touching his body.

I was determined to play it cool. No way was I affected by that douchebag.

Until I walked into Ethan's house and spotted Axel sitting on one of the many couches, snuggled up next to a Kappa Delta girl. I recognized her face but couldn't remember her name. He was leaning in close, his arm around her shoulders, his mouth almost touching hers. Normally the sight of people kissing—any variation of couple, throuple, or more—would turn me the fuck on. But not now. Not them. I was confused and angry and irritated. At him, but mostly, at myself.

"This was a mistake," I muttered as Dane handed me a beer. "I'm leaving after this beer."

"What? Why?" Dane asked and then followed my line of sight. When he smiled knowingly, I glared back at him. "Get over it."

"I don't wanna," I whined and took a long sip of beer. "I want things to be how they were last year. Before that dick ever showed up."

"Poor baby," Dane teased and patted my shoulder. "But don't worry. It looks like Axel's leaving, so you don't have to."

My head whipped around again as I spotted Axel, sitting alone, reaching for his jacket. The girl he was with was gone.

Was she coming back? Then again, they were kissing—or almost kissing— a few minutes ago. Why would she up and leave so fast? Slowly, Axel put on his parka and stood up. Was he leaving alone or was he going to meet up with her?

God, listen to yourself.

I couldn't even make it through one conversation with the guy without fighting, so why should I care who he fooled around with?

Axel suddenly looked up and spotted me, and I nearly dropped the beer bottle I was holding.

Just like in practice today, facing off behind the net, we stared at each other, something wild unleashing between us. People walked by, music played in the background, and conversation ebbed and flowed around me. I had no idea what was going on.

I was angry. Turned on. Angry at being turned on.

More than anything, I was...hurt. Yes, that was it. I'd spilled my guts to Axel, showing him my vulnerability, and he still refused to believe what I said. It frustrated me that I couldn't get through to him. That he thought I was a liar and a bastard. It made me feel like total shit.

Fuck it. And fuck him.

I stalked through the room, ignoring everyone but the asshole in my line of sight.

Surprisingly, he didn't back away.

"You. Me. Outside. Now," I demanded.

Axel glared at me and shook his head.

"I don't think so."

"No? Fine. You want a public fight, I'm game."

Axel scoffed and started for the door. I followed him, but Dane stopped me on the way out.

"What are you doing?"

"I'm going to try one more time to get through to that guy. That doesn't work, then I'll talk to Coach."

"Do you want me to come with?"

"I'm good. I can handle him."

I knew just how I wanted to manhandle Axel Lund…

Dane nodded, and I slipped out of the door and back into the frigid winter air. Axel was halfway down the stairs when he stopped, pulled out a packet of cigarettes, and lit one up. I clambered down the steps and stood beside him, holding out my hand.

"What?" Axel bit out.

"Give your teammate a fucking smoke."

Axel grumbled something about 'annoying brats' but threw the pack at me anyway. I hated smoking but I needed something to do with my hands. Anything that didn't involve putting them on Axel.

I never imagined that I could want someone I despised so much. It was a new, unfamiliar, completely unsettling feeling, and one I wanted to be rid of.

I pulled a cigarette out of the pack and lit up. We continued down the rest of the stairs until we reached the gravel pathway. The wind whipped around, fat snowflakes falling on our faces. I shivered, taking a drag from the cigarette, the warmth infusing my lungs. More like burning the fuck out of them. I choked on the inhale and Axel started laughing at me.

"Fuck you," I croaked, coughing.

"Now that you're done bossing me around, what do you want?"

I scoffed. "Pfft. That wasn't bossy at all."

"Oh yeah?"

"Ask anyone I've fucked."

Axel rolled his eyes and groaned, but I didn't miss the flush that highlighted his sharp cheekbones. Snowflakes kissed his blond eyelashes, the bump on his nose, his pouty lips. Then I remembered that he was about to kiss that girl. Angrily, I admitted to myself that the blush wasn't about me, but her.

Focus, Jace.

"So, are you going to talk to me like a real teammate or are you going to continue to act like an ass?" I added.

"I don't *have* to do anything," he bit out.

"So, you still believe Preston?"

Axel paused and took a drag of his cigarette. His expression tightened as he blinked fast. Then his lips pursed together as he let out a long plume of smoke.

"I didn't say that."

His whispered admission was so low I nearly missed it.

It wasn't a win, but I'd take it.

Axel

I was out here freezing my balls off when I should have been unloading them all over...what was her name again? Whately? Winnie? Waverly. Right. Her. Yes. She was into me and that's what I should have been doing.

Not acting like a fool, again, thanks to Jace.

He was wearing his battered baseball cap, and I wished the brim was facing forward so I wouldn't be forced to look into his big hazel eyes. It was like looking into the sun. I surveyed the rest of his face and that was even worse. He had long, thick eyelashes, the dark tips white with snow, and freckles that dusted his long nose and ruddy cheeks. Dark stubble surrounded his mouth, teasing the rim of those full lips.

What would that feel like? Kissing a man?

No, not just any man. Jace. His scruff rubbing over my lips, my jaw, lower... Shit. I'd never thought of a man as beautiful before but as I stared at Jace, I realized that's exactly what he was. He was beautiful and my best friend's ex.

Oh my God.

The sexual revelation didn't bother me as much as the guy in question.

Now my balls weren't freezing at all. Despite the frigid temperature, they—and my dick—were hot as hell inside my jeans. My cock was hard and heavy. I couldn't remember the last time I'd had a monster erection. And fuck, since when did a *guy*, and a mouthy one at that, do it for me? How about *never*? My poor dick was so confused.

Well, let's be honest; he wasn't, but I was.

And what exactly did Jace mean by bossy in bed? Did that mean dirty talk? Was he into the dominant-submissive thing, or...

Stop. Don't think about fucking or Jace or fucking Jace. Or Jace fucking.

"If you want to kiss me, just do it," Jace taunted, jolting me out of my filthy daydream and tumbling me into another.

I croaked out a smoky laugh, then threw my cigarette on the ground. "Are you drunk?"

"I had two sips of one beer. You?"

"Vodka shots and a couple of beers before that."

"Well then, no kiss for you," Jace replied. His expression was playful, but his tone wasn't. "You're too drunk to consent."

"I'm not drunk, just buzzed," I argued.

"So, you say."

I shrugged my shoulders.

"Your loss," I grumbled.

He looked at me with a curiously intense expression. "For a straight guy, that's pretty flirty."

"You're pretty too," I blurted out.

Okay, I *had* drunk too much vodka. What the fuck was wrong with me?

"I think you forgot a word in there," he chuckled.

I thought about that as I stared at his mouth, his lips so fucking tempting. So fucking close.

"Nope," I foolishly admitted, the alcohol racing through

my veins, burning my worries to ash. "And don't be judgmental. I can find men pretty."

"Me?" he demanded, the fire in his eyes sparking. "You're the one who's been a dick this whole time, judging me without cause."

He had a point, but I couldn't even form words to reply.

Suddenly, I wanted to be bold, wild. I didn't want to talk, I wanted action. I wanted to grab ahold of Jace and shut him up in the most satisfying way. What would be even better? If *he* grabbed ahold of *me*. Yeah, I wanted that. I wanted him to grab me, manhandle me against the side of the house, and kiss me. Hard. And I would kiss him right back. I wanted to suck on his tongue, nip his lips, take all my frustration out on that sexy, annoying mouth of his.

I guess I couldn't hide my dirty train of thought, because Jace stared at me in the exact same way. He let out a long breath, the white puff of air curling around his face. When he licked his lips, I knew exactly what he was thinking. This was crazy. Stupid. I shouldn't be standing here, not with him.

But I couldn't walk away. I knew what I wanted, even if it scared me.

Jace took a step towards me, then another, so close, until our boot tips knocked, and his breath teased mine. Everything about Jace—his eyes, his smell, his presence—was intense and so heady I wanted to lean down and lick him. Lick every inch of skin I could find. Mark it, bite it, ruin it. Wreck him.

My heart kicked up so fast that I wasn't sure it would ever calm down.

I leaned down, closer, so fucking close.

"Not this again," a familiar voice called out.

Jace and I both startled and stumbled apart.

I was shaking, and I wasn't sure if it was from the cold, my annoyance at the interruption, or the fact that I was a barely restrained mess thanks to Jace. Judging by my painfully stiff dick, I already knew the answer. Then I remembered where I was and what almost happened and figured the interruption was for the best.

Now I had another secret to add to my list. Not so secret given the way Jace's gaze burned over me.

I reluctantly turned my head towards the street to find Silas standing on the sidewalk, staring at us with a pissed-off expression. Wearing a leather motorcycle jacket and a thick grey scarf, he'd tied his long hair up in a bun, but most of it was escaping.

"Seems I arrived just in time," Silas added as he headed towards us. "No fist fighting in the cold, idiots. You'll get injured much worse."

"We're not going to do that," I grumbled.

"Oh really?" Silas glanced between me and Jace. "It looked like you were about to lay into each other."

If kissing the fuck out of Jace was laying into him, then yes, I was about to do just that.

"We were talking, that's all," Jace insisted, his voice hoarse.

"Whatever you say," Silas snarked and pointed to the house. "I can only stay for an hour but let's have a drink together. That way, I can give Dane a reprieve from his babysitting duties."

"Funny," I retorted.

"It's not," Silas grumbled as he walked past us and called out over his shoulder. "You're both acting like goddamn teenagers in some high school drama. Just focus on hockey and put your personal shit aside. We're so close to the nationals, doesn't that mean anything to you?"

"Thanks for the advice, but stick to defense," Jace bit out. "And you haven't exactly been a role model for team spirit, either. You hardly talk to anyone, and every time Coach says something to you, you're ten seconds away from losing your cool."

Silas paused when he reached the landing and slowly turned to face us.

"It's not the same thing at all," Silas offered. "And yeah, most days I'm a grumpy bastard because I'm dealing with a shitload of responsibilities outside of school and hockey. Stuff you know nothing about. But I still do my job on the ice. I'm not acting like a fucking kid with a temper tantrum. What do we have to do with you two? Lock you both in a room until you work it out?"

Jace held my gaze.

"I'm game if Axel is."

CHAPTER 15

JACE

was joking. Sort of. Definitely.

After that near kiss—if that's what it was—I didn't want to be anywhere near Axel. We were already combustible, but touching him? No way. I wasn't ready for that kind of inferno. I wasn't into pain. Besides, he was probably just flirting with me to fuck with my head. A game that I wasn't willing to play.

Given his friendship with Preston, why should I believe anything that he said? Or did.

But Axel's eyes, his body language, it was telling me all kinds of crazy things. That he wanted me to kiss him. He was curious, and nervous too. I saw the heated once-over he gave me when I told him I was bossy. And, it wasn't a line. I liked to take charge during sex. Ever since Preston, it was necessary. I wanted, no, I needed the control. Especially with hookups. And while I was eager and happy having sex with men *and* women, there was something about being one on one with a guy that turned me inside out. There was no holding back. Sex could be slow and sensual, and then raw and rough. Always dirty, messy, and so freaking hot. And maybe it was the hockey player in me, but I was competitive, even in this. I wanted to be the best for my partner. Even group sex couldn't compare. When I had that singular attention, no one else, it was so satisfying. And when I was the only one whose name they shouted when they came? Even better.

"Are you going to stand there staring into space or are you coming inside?" Axel bellowed.

I shook my head. "I'm thinking."

"Not in this cold," Axel muttered and clapped his hands together.

"Some of us dress for it," I snarked as I forced my feet to move, heading reluctantly back to the house.

Axel ignored my comment.

The least I could do is try and play nice. I just needed to get drunk first.

Axel followed closely behind me, and I hated that I was aware of him now. The rustle of his jeans, the tobacco from his breath, and the heat that poured off his body. It was suddenly all too much. Part of me wanted to ignore Silas's request and walk away. But he was right. This thing with me and Axel was out of control. We needed to find some kind of resolution. Any kind. And I needed to put this new and ridiculous sexual fixation aside. So, I wanted Axel. So what? I wanted a lot of people. It was chemistry. Plain and simple. It didn't mean anything more than that.

And I didn't have to act on it.

That was easier said than done, especially when I climbed the stairs with Axel right behind me. I don't mean a step or two, but like, right behind me. Practically rubbing against me. The temptation was there to lean back, or better yet, turn around, shove my hands in his thick blond hair, and show him what a kiss could be. I knew it would be good. But the fact that my cock was still hard told me that one kiss wouldn't be enough.

I went to grab the door handle, but Axel reached around

me and got to it first. He held the door open, his other hand suddenly bracketing my lower back. What was happening? Why was he touching me like that? I was vibrating so hard it took everything I had to keep walking.

Reminding myself that he'd already been drinking, I reasoned his behavior was a one-off. He was out of it, presumably due to alcohol.

As soon as we stepped into the house, his hand was gone. Good. Great. I probably imagined the whole thing.

"You're back!" Dane yelled out when he spotted us. He was standing near the makeshift bar in the living room, with Kayden, Maddox, and Finn. "I'm so goddamn happy that neither of you is bleeding."

Our teammates started laughing.

"Just get us a drink," I bit back, shaking my head at my friend's teasing.

"Vodka," Axel replied. "No glasses. Bring the whole fucking bottle."

"Make that two," I stated.

Axel nudged me with his elbow. "I was going to share it with you."

"You? Share with me? You really are drunk."

"Not yet, but soon enough."

I spotted Ethan coming down the stairs, alone, his hair mussed, with a huge smile on his face. At least someone was having fun tonight.

"I told them I was going to lock them in a room until they figured their shit out," Silas announced loudly.

There were jeers and whistles at that suggestion. I glanced at Axel, who rolled his eyes.

"You're a fucking genius," Ethan replied and patted Silas's shoulder. "That's a great idea. I can put Hot n' Honey in the basement, it's soundproofed."

There was more laughter as our teammates cheered and clapped. *Motherfuckers.*

Colin offered us a bottle of vodka and two glasses. Without pause, Axel poured two very large shots, then offered one to me. I downed mine and asked for seconds.

"You guys won't be laughing if we don't make it out and miss our next game," Axel retorted.

"Only for tonight. Then we'll let you go in the morning. That still gives you a day to prep for the game," Ethan quipped.

"Okay, okay, the joke's over," I said as I reached for another shot. "Go back to the party."

"It's not a bad idea," Maddox muttered, and glanced at Kayden. "Coach forcing us to share that hotel room on the road got us talking. It could work."

"You mean, it got *me* talking." Kayden smiled at him. "You ignored me, remember?"

"Oh, yeah." Maddox nodded. "But, eventually I caved."

"That's what you're calling it?" Kayden teased. "Ouch."

"You know what I mean," Maddox grumbled and put his arms around Kayden.

Judging by the kiss Kayden laid on him, he did.

"Listen up!" Dane announced, jumping up on the couch and waving his hands in the air. "As the Cougars' captain, I'm ordering Jace and Axel to either shake hands now or share a room for the night!"

The whistles, laughter, and comments got louder.

"So not funny!" I called out.

"So not joking!" he shouted back.

Instead of fueling the fire, I offered my hand to Axel. When his bigger palm gripped mine, all that electricity between us jumped to life again, kick-starting my pulse. I nearly ripped my hand away but forced myself not to react. I could do this.

Physically, Axel was the bigger man, but right here, right now, I was better.

The joke was forgotten, but tonight? I needed a lot more than vodka to erase Axel's touch.

Axel

I woke up disoriented, feeling like someone put a jackhammer to my head and was working it full blast, drilling into my skull. Shit, I was never drinking vodka again, or at least, not that much.

I reached into my pocket for my phone, and when I pulled it out and tapped on it, I realized it was just after three in the morning. I didn't remember walking back to the dorm, but I must have if I passed out on my bed.

Only, the bed felt different. And the room was in total darkness, except for a tiny window at the far end.

Wait, that couldn't be right.

I tapped the flashlight feature on my phone and started scanning around me. This wasn't my bedroom. What the fuck? This wasn't any room in the dorm. Then I heard it. A snore. There was someone else in here with me.

Where was I? And who was that?

Memories of the night before came flooding back, everyone teasing me and Jace about locking us in a room until we sorted out our shit. There were more drinks, and laughter, and then…

Fuck, they didn't. They wouldn't. Would they?

I scanned again, doing a full 360 this time, and sure enough Jace was lying on the far side of the king-sized bed, sprawled out on his stomach, hugging a pillow. Then recognition hit me. We were in the attic in Ethan's house. The space for extra crashers.

So, not the basement but still, did they lock us up here?

Instead of freaking out, I quietly got up and located the door. There was a switch nearby and when I flicked it on, the room flooded with bright, white light.

"What the fuck?" Jace grumbled as he sat up, his hair sticking up on end.

Holy shit, how'd we gotten up here? What did it matter, as long as we could get out.

I reached for the door handle and jiggled it. Phew. It wasn't locked.

"Don't tell me they really—" Jace started.

"Yes, they did. Serves us right for drinking so much. But we're in the attic, not the basement, and the door's not locked."

Jace sat up, stretching, his white t-shirt riding high, exposing his taut abs. I licked my lips. Fuck I was dehydrated.

"Thank God for that."

"Grab your stuff. I'll walk you back to the dorm," I offered.

Wow, I was so polite. I was obviously still drunk.

I padded back to the sofa, slipped on my boots, and reached for my coat.

"You go," Jace replied, running a hand through his hair. "I'm gonna raid Ethan's fridge as payback and then go home."

He slid off the bed and walked around it, sleep-rumpled, his tight jeans riding low on his hips. My eyes couldn't look away from the tease of sleek skin and tight v-lines.

"Axel?"

"What?"

"Are you hungry?"

Now? I was fucking starving. Only, it had nothing to do with food.

"Um, yeah," I finally replied. "But first, I need water. My mouth tastes like stale booze, and it feels like I've been chewing on sandpaper."

Jace grimaced. "No wonder you never get laid."

I gave him my best finger.

"We gotta find a way to get back at the guys," I suggested. "But I'm too hungover to think of something. Give me a day or two and we'll get them back good."

Jace gave me a wicked grin.

"Oh, we'll think of something, alright. In fact, I already have an idea."

"What?"

Another grin but this time, with a wicked wink. "Just play along."

"Oh God," I groaned.

I knew whatever Jace had planned in that mind of his, it wasn't going to be good.

"You've got quite the porn star moan," Jace teased. "It's very distracting."

"Shut up."

"Hasn't anyone told you that before? Do it again."

"Knock it off."

Jace sauntered up to me, his steps sure and confident, his eyes brimming with mischievous carnality. I don't know why I didn't notice it until now. The guy had raw sex appeal, and he fucking knew it.

"I say we give Ethan a good, hard lesson. One he won't soon forget. Follow my lead."

"What do you mean?"

"Get back on the bed," he demanded.

My cock jerked at the order.

"Grab the bedframe and shake it as hard as you can so it bangs against the wall. Moan like you did before, but louder, and say some dirty things. Like 'harder, more', and 'oh God, don't stop'."

"Jace," I groaned.

Despite the alcohol-induced headache, my cock filled so fast I was about to pass out again.

"Just like that."

Jace got down on his hands and knees on the floor beside

the bed and I stared at him in confusion. Confusion and lust, my eyes lasered to his pert ass, sticking up in the air in obscene invitation.

"What are you doing?" I asked.

"There's an air vent on the floor," he explained as he moved a couple of boxes to the side. "I want to make sure nothing's covering it so the rest of the guys in the house can hear us, nice and clear."

When he popped up again, he slid onto the bed and beckoned me to join him with one finger.

"Now we're ready."

Was I ready? No fucking way.

CHAPTER 16

AXEL

J ace grabbed the slatted wood headboard with both hands and started banging it against the wall, rocking the bed back and forth. A loud crack reverberated as the wood hit the wall, like a player slamming into the boards. In this space, with nothing except a bed and a few boxes, everything echoed loudly. And I was pretty sure that thanks to that air vent, everyone else in the house heard the racket.

"Oh God, oh fuck, yes!" Jace moaned loudly, moving faster.

Every time he shook the bed he rocked his hips, and I could so easily imagine what he'd look like naked in the same position. With me underneath, my legs wrapped around his slim waist as he pounded me into oblivion.

Whoa.

I'd never been on the receiving end, but suddenly, my ass clenched tight at the very idea.

"That's it," Jace growled. "Touch me right fucking there. Don't stop."

I had to be hallucinating because it sounded like Jace was having sex in this bed. With me. Every part of my body was on fire, and I was sweating like mad, my pits soaked, my face flushed, perspiration trickling down my hairline. The only other time I got this hot was after the end of a game with all my equipment on.

Jace turned to me and licked his lips and without thinking, I slowly slid onto the bed and joined him. Hoping like hell that he was so involved with his 'performance' that he wouldn't notice the very huge bulge in my jeans. When I glanced over, however, I could tell he was in a similar state.

My mouth was no longer dry.

I grabbed the headboard and added my weight to it, rocking back and forth, the loud slam as it hit the wall almost deafening. The noise didn't help my hangover, but it sure as fuck would wake everyone in this house.

"I want to eat your ass," I moaned before I could stop myself.

Jace's face flushed but he didn't stop moving.

"Do it," he demanded as he locked eyes with me. "Fuck me with your tongue."

The filthy fantasy played out in my head as I reached down with one hand to palm my covered dick, rubbing hard, desperately needing friction. Instead of staying where he was, Jace moved and kneeled behind me, his crotch to my ass, his arms bracketing mine as we both held on to the headboard like a lifeline, knuckles stark white with strain.

"I'm going to lick every inch of your gorgeous body," he replied, his hot breath teasing my ear.

Jesus, he was good at this. I almost believed that he really wanted me.

My body locked up tight, pleasure spiraling, running hot in my veins. For me, this wasn't acting, it was real. I canted my hips and rubbed my ass against Jace. Against his hard cock. Oh man. This was real, alright. It didn't feel strange like I was expecting. If anything, it turned me on and made me flush all over.

"I'm gonna kiss and suck and bite," he continued. "Leave

you with marks, make sure everyone knows that you're mine, and only mine."

A violent shudder wracked my body.

Why was that the hottest thing anyone had ever said to me?

"Jace," I growled deeply, rocking my hips.

Jace humped my ass like a man possessed. I should've been freaking out. What did I know about fooling around with a guy? But it felt entirely natural to grind against Jace. Sexy images bombarded me, raw and dirty, and once I started, I couldn't stop.

The heat of his body enveloped mine, the heady smell of our sweat and arousal. I closed my eyes and dropped my head forward as he writhed and moaned against me, his hot breath teasing my neck. We hadn't kissed but already it was the best sex I'd ever had. And when his hands moved to interlock with mine, my climax threatened to let loose.

This was supposed to be a prank on Ethan. Once again, the joke was on us.

"I'm almost there, Jace," I said breathlessly. "So close."

"Come for me. Do it now."

"Jace. Oh God, oh fuck."

I undulated again, and the movement had me pushing against the headboard as I came hard, wet, sticky cum filling up my briefs.

Jace let out a loud moan, and I felt his body stiffen behind me. He gripped my hands tighter as he whispered my name in that filthy, raspy voice of his.

"Axel. Fucking hell."

I could hardly breathe, gasping for air. Did both of us win this time? It sure as hell felt like it.

We stopped pushing the headboard against the wall, but our hips kept moving, rubbing against each other. And then there was just the sound of our heavy breathing and the squeak of the mattress underneath us.

"Are you done now, you assholes?" someone in the house roared.

Jace and I both burst out laughing. Since he was still behind me, I felt the vibration of his laughter settling into my back, my body lax and lazy with pleasure.

"Looks like the plan worked," I admitted.

There was a bang, and a strange voice echoed from the air vent. "Did someone break into the house, or did they just break one of our beds?"

"Mission accomplished," Jace chuckled as he slowly let go of my hands and slid back.

I shivered at the loss of contact, unsure how I was going to talk my way out of what just happened. The joke that went too far. It was the first time I ever fooled around with a guy, and it wasn't funny in the least. It imploded what I thought I knew about myself.

Would I do it again?

I turned my head and found Jace staring at me with those intense green-gold eyes. His stunning face was close, his cheeks a gorgeous shade of pink, his eyes bright with pleasure. Without thinking, I angled my head and leaned back, tasting his soft lips, wanting to kiss him more than I wanted to breathe.

I had to know if this was real, or an alcohol-induced dream.

When his hot tongue slid against mine—bold and sensual—and his scruff teased my lips, there was no question.

I was walking a dangerous line before, but I was in even deeper trouble now.

Jace

I'd once been told by my high school science teacher that my smart-ass jokes were going to get me into a world of trouble.

I didn't believe it then, but I sure as fuck knew it now.

What started out as a simple prank to get back at Ethan turned into the hottest fake—not-so-fake—orgasm I'd had in forever. Not to mention that kiss. Axel's mouth took mine without hesitation, stealing the remaining breath from my body. There was something urgent and primal about the way we kissed. It was rough and messy and possessive, like neither of us was going to survive if we stopped. I cupped his face, feeling the scratch of his scruff under my palm, then slid it into his thick hair and tugged, angling his head, shoving my tongue deeper into that wicked mouth of his. The low rumble of his responding growl had my cock jerking hard.

Suddenly, over the furious rhythm of my heartbeat, I heard the stomp of footsteps.

Someone was coming up the stairs.

Shit.

Axel nipped my lower lip, gave it a teasing lick, and then pulled back. The loss of contact had me shivering hard. I was finally able to take a full breath. Not that I wanted to breathe or needed to. I'd willingly forego oxygen for another taste of Axel's mouth. Or, to watch him come again. Hearing and feeling Axel unleash was unexpected and so incredibly hot that I came in my jeans embarrassingly fast.

What the fuck do I do now?

I watched him slide off the bed in one smooth move, like he wasn't affected by our kiss at all. Like he kissed a guy every day. And me? I was so fucked out by what had just happened that I nearly tumbled off the bed and onto my ass.

A loud knock at the door had me scrambling to move. Luckily, I didn't land in a tangled heap on the floor. Instead, I reached for my jacket and pulled it on. Then I noticed Axel did the same, covering up the wet stain on the front of his jeans. Fuck, I could smell his musky cum, and I wanted to shove him back on the bed, yank those jeans down, and lick up every drop.

The door opened and a grumpy, rumpled-looking Ethan came barreling into the attic, dressed in white briefs and a stained Cougars t-shirt.

"We should've locked you in the goddamn basement after all," he announced, running an agitated hand through his long hair.

"Did you enjoy the show?" I quipped, thankful that I was able to form words again. "Did your frat bros like it too?"

Ethan gave us two middle fingers.

"Half of them came knocking on my door. I'm gonna get reamed out at the next meeting," Ethan replied with a sigh and then paused, staring at me. "Your show was damn realistic, by the way."

"Watch a lot of gay porn?" I teased.

"I watch a lot of porn, period," he quipped as he looked at me and then Axel, his narrowed eyes ping-ponging between us. "Smells like cum in here."

Fucking hell.

"That's the bed," Axel replied quickly. "You guys probably never wash the sheets."

Ethan shook his head. I wasn't sure he was buying Axel's explanation.

Instead of worrying about it, I crossed my arms and faked boredom, giving a huge yawn.

"Well, we're gonna head back to the dorm and get some sleep," I declared.

Ethan rolled his eyes. "It's almost four in the morning. Just sleep here and I'll feed you breakfast in the morning."

"You're not going to put laxatives in our eggs or anything like that?"

Ethan walked up to me and flicked my forehead. "We have a game coming up. Don't be dumb."

"But afterwards?" I asked.

"Then, fair's fair," Ethan quipped, and I glared at him. "Kidding."

He wasn't. Just like his frat bros and hockey teammates, Ethan was competitive as fuck and wouldn't let things go. Payback was coming, one way or another.

"So, have you made up now?" Ethan smirked. "Did forcible confinement work? Are you best buddies?"

I glanced at Axel, but he gave me a look that I couldn't quite interpret. In his eyes, I saw a mixture of surprise, confusion, and tension, all at once. I had a feeling that I looked very much the same.

What the hell had we done?

"Not best, but we're still breathing, so that has to count for something," Axel responded quietly, never losing eye contact.

Speak for yourself. How could I breathe after that kiss?

"Good." Ethan grinned and made his way back to the door. "Now get some sleep. Fuck knows we need it."

"I'll grab the couch downstairs," Axel replied, following our teammate.

That was a smart idea. Space. Distance. Axel and I needed all that and more. And we didn't need a repeat of that incredible, but incredibly stupid, kiss. I could chalk it up to too much drinking, but I was never one to lie to myself. Both of us wanted it. I think? I certainly did. Maybe it was just curiosity for Axel. Or, worse, maybe he was playing a game with me that went far beyond the rink. Was his reaction an act? Was he trying to get close just to toy with me? The idea that Axel could be as manipulative as my ex had my stomach clenching hard.

Stop angsting. It was just a kiss. No harm, no foul.

And erections don't lie.

It didn't change anything.

It didn't mean anything.

I'd had plenty of kisses. And none of them left me feeling anything more than pleasure in the moment. It was done, over. There was nothing to worry about, and nothing to replay.

When Axel left the room, I should've felt relieved. Instead, a gnawing ache nagged at my chest. It was probably just too much booze. Or the stale air up here.

I threw off my jacket and lay back down on the bed. But sleep, unfortunately, didn't come as fast as I did.

CHAPTER 17

AXEL

wo days later, game day

I kissed Jace and I liked it.

Two days after that kiss and I was still walking around in a daze; horny, frustrated, and just plain confused. No matter what I was doing—working out in the gym, taking notes in class, studying in the library—my attention inevitably strayed back to that night at Ethan's. I couldn't *stop* thinking about that kiss. I couldn't forget how Jace tasted, how he smelled, the sounds he made when he came.

All because of a stupid game. A prank gone wrong.

The joke was completely on me. The way Jace wrecked my mouth, and my control? It was, without a doubt, bar none, the hottest sex I'd ever had. Fuck, I'd been drinking but apparently not enough, because every second of that night was clear in my mind, replaying over and over until it became an obsession. I'd jacked off to the memory of it so many times over the past forty-eight hours that I had new calluses on my hands and sheets that required twice daily washing. It even distracted me from the reality that I was going to face off against Langston, my former team.

I needed another taste of Jace, and feverishly wondered if

he felt the same. Or was he out with someone else? Hailey? The thought of him kissing her, even worse, fucking her, had my blood boiling. I'd never been one to let my cock make decisions, but he was all I could think about, and I didn't want to share.

What the hell is wrong with you?

A lot. A lot was wrong with me. Fucking around with my teammate for one. I remembered my initial reaction to seeing Kayden and Maddox together.

I'm such a hypocrite.

And what would Preston say if he found out? Then again, did I care what Preston thought? He and Jace weren't together, and they hadn't been for two years. And if Preston lied to me, like Jace said he did, what did his opinion matter?

I was so confused that I didn't know what to believe anymore. I texted Preston but I didn't get any more clarity.

> Axel: You need to tell me the truth about you and Jace.

It took Preston hours to respond and the longer I waited, the more my stomach churned.

> Preston: You know the truth.

> Axel: Do I?

> Preston: Of course. He treated me like shit. What more do you want?

> Axel: Apparently you left some things out. You cheated on him? Gave him an STD?

> Preston: Is that what he said? And why the fuck do you believe him?

Axel: I didn't say that I did, because I can't imagine that you'd lie to me. But I don't think you're telling me the whole truth, either.

Preston: This is so fucked up.

Axel: Jace gave me a lot of details about your relationship. I'm not sure that anyone's that good a liar.

Preston: And you're the best judge of character?

Axel: I have enough experience, remember?

Preston: Bestie, come on. Think about it. Are you seriously questioning reality? You sound as paranoid as Jace. Jesus, you know me.

I thought I did. And reality? The only thing that was real to me was that kiss with Jace.

Axel: I've got a game to get to. Call me later so we can talk.

I reread the texts and my doubts about Preston intensified.

I put my phone away and my mind wandered back to Jace. I didn't care if kissing him was wrong or the worst decision I've ever made. I wanted to do it again. I wanted it more than anything else. Which was strange because the only thing in my life that I was obsessed with was hockey. Everything else came second. And to be honest, everything else wasn't much. I didn't have healthy relationships with my family, I was suspicious of other people's motives because I figured they wanted to use me to get to my family, and I didn't have close friends outside of Preston.

I didn't have much of anything in my life *except* hockey.

But things were shifting, something was changing.

I was getting to know my teammates here at Sutton. And I liked them. Real friendships were within reach. And I was starting to see Jace in a way I never imagined and my sexuality too. I didn't know how to deal with it, or him, but there it was.

Transferring colleges wasn't just changing schools. It was changing me.

Jesus, maybe I should switch from economics to philosophy.

I should've been focused on preparing for today. But after that weird exchange with Preston, I didn't know how to get my head back to where it needed to be. Even my usual pregame routine of carbs, hydration, and replaying my opponents' weak spots only helped so much. It didn't bring the calm it usually did.

I hadn't seen or spoken to Jace since that night, but with every passing minute, my restlessness grew. Instead of getting my head in the zone, where it should be, I was thinking about sex.

Not a great way to prepare for a game that had so much riding on it.

My nerves cranked higher the moment I stepped out of the dorm and reached the stratosphere when I entered the rink.

The locker room was already packed by the time I arrived. Some guys, like Maddox and Silas, kept to themselves, headphones on, getting themselves psyched up. Others, like Dane and Ethan, talked and joked around to lighten the mood.

I hadn't spotted Jace yet, but explosive anticipation flared in my veins.

I nodded at Dane, trying my best to stay cool, but failing miserably, jumpy as a rookie in a tight jock on the first day of practice. Standing in front of my stall, I threw down my backpack and reached for my gear. Once I was padded up, I sat down and tied on my skates. That was my fixation. All hockey players had them. For me, I had to have red laces. The first hockey team I ever joined had red and white jerseys and for home games, all the players wore red laces. Ever since, it was my thing. No deviation. If I didn't have them, I'd hunt down every equipment store in the country to find them. Was it rational? No, but this was hockey. There was nothing normal about speeding around a confined icy surface on razor- sharp blades.

I heard a door open and then Jace's laughter before he stalked across my line of vision like the predatory animal we were named after. A shiver ran through me as I did my level best to make casual eye contact, but not for too long. My gaze traveled over his body, taking in the simple outfit of Doc Marten, tight jeans, and a black t-shirt. He looked damn good, and worse, I knew that he tasted even better.

Jace nodded and reached for the baseball cap on his head, and I stifled an unexpected grin. I had red laces; Jace had his ballcap. Backwards, of course.

He gave me a knowing smile. I fought hard, but lost, when I fucking blushed. Right there in the locker room, surrounded by my teammates. Then again, the crimson cheeks could be explained away. Every player in the room was wound up tighter than a wrapped dick.

"Please tell me you're not about to start arguing with Jace again."

I glanced to my right to find Kayden giving me a concerned look. The gentle giant was worried.

"We're fine," I assured him.

"You don't look fine. More like you're about to explode."

It was already too late. I came in the shower this morning, shouting Jace's name.

"It's hot as hell in here," I explained, looking away, hoping Kayden wouldn't notice the heat in my face and neck. "I mean, the heat's cranked up. I'm sweating through my pads."

I reached for my jersey, but it took me three tries to get it on. Good God, I was acting ridiculous. I needed something, anything, to distract me from Jace. Gloves, where were my gloves?

"Are you kidding? It's like a meat locker," Kayden rubbed his hands together. "This entire building has next to no heating, never mind the rink. Every time I take a shower, I nearly freeze my balls off."

"I guess I just run hot."

Kayden stared at me, and I shook my head.

"What?"

"You seem different today," he mused.

"I don't know what you're—"

"What's different?" Dane called out as walked up to us.

"Axel." Kayden pointed at me. "Something's up but he won't share. And he's about to break a hole in the floor with his skates."

I didn't realize I'd been popping my knees. Dane sat down on the bench opposite me and tapped one.

"You alright?" he asked as he leaned in.

I nodded. "It's nerve wracking facing my former teammates. But I'm fine."

It wasn't a lie. I was nervous, but also excited. Because I knew exactly how they played and how to play them.

"Everything good with you and Jace?" Dane added.

"Yep," I replied quickly, reaching for my water bottle, and glanced over at Jace.

Bad timing. Jace was getting undressed. In the past, I made it a point to never look at him when that happened. But I couldn't look away now. It was like watching a strip show, and I was helpless. Helpless and hyperaware of every ridge, muscle, and curve of his lean body. He slid his jeans down and revealed that pert ass, his tight cheeks framed by a black jock. I nearly swallowed my tongue along with my water.

"Maybe he's been punking Ethan's frat again," Kayden offered.

His comment was the distraction I needed, but fuck, I was

never living that down. I turned to Dane and Kayden and shook my head.

Dane gave me a wild grin. "You and Jace woke up the entire house. You're legends."

I groaned and held my head in my hands.

"I can't believe I let Jace goad me into doing that," I admitted.

Was I talking about the prank or the kiss? I wasn't sure I could tell one from the other.

"He's a very persuasive guy," Dane quipped. "And I'm glad to see you're not automatically arguing."

I nodded.

"It's always better to kiss and make up, right?" he added.

I lowered my eyes. *Don't think of kissing or making out or sex.* But it was too late. My dick was half hard from the moment I spotted Jace, and this was not good. Sitting with an erection while wearing a sports cup was damn painful.

"I just want to get out there and win this game," I croaked.

"That's what I want to hear."

Dane playfully smacked my leg and stood up. He started to walk away but paused and looked over his shoulder.

"If you ever need to talk, about anything, hit me up."

I shouldn't have been surprised, since Dane was friendly with everyone, but I was.

"Thanks."

He quietly padded off in the direction of his stall and I finished getting ready.

I wasn't as shaky as I was earlier, or as distracted. I double- checked my skates and my stick, ensuring everything was just how I liked it. Reminding myself that I had a job to do, and a position to fight for, I focused on my breathing and let everything else fade away.

By the time I headed out of the locker room, I was feeling pumped, ready to take on anything. Including Langston. I lined up in the hallway ready for our big entrance, as one by one, my teammates joined in. The rumbling echo of the crowd calmed me. Home games were a huge thing here at Sutton. Not as big as our football team, but still, the Cougars always packed the rink.

Today was no different. But it felt like it. Like I finally belonged.

Coach exited his office and walked by us, inspecting each player, and then letting out a sharp whistle to calm our chatter.

"I'll keep it short and sweet," Banning started as he crossed his arms, hugging his tablet to his chest. "Be intentional with every play. I want to see your best and nothing less."

"Yes, Coach!" we replied in unison.

Banning motioned for us to get our asses moving. I was at the front of the queue and when I looked around, I spotted Jace at the back, talking to Finn and Kayden. Part of me wanted to walk back and say something but the bigger part told me to face forward and keep walking. I didn't know what, if anything, I should say to him. Nothing, unless it involved the game. This was not the time or place to let personal feelings get involved.

Oh God, the fact that I even used the word 'feelings' had me shaking my head. I hadn't even started playing and already I needed a time-out.

One by one, we filed onto the ice to start our warm-up. Surrounded by the buzz of the hometown crowd, I finally settled into my game- day zone. My head, my body, my heart; everything synced. I was ready to get this done. To play the best fucking hockey I could.

I had something to prove, not just to the Cougars, but to myself.

Langston's roster filed out, and I skated over to say hello to the guys that I used to play with. It wasn't as awkward as the first time we'd faced off, but the tension was there. Now there was more at stake, a semi-final place on the line, and our future as professionals too. Coach said it right; we had to give our best and nothing less.

After the warm-up, Banning rounded up our team. When he announced the first line, I bit back my frustration. Jace was center line, and I was off to the box until my turn. But I refused to let it get to me. Jace offered me a questioning look as he made for the ice. For once, I didn't glare at him. Instead, I offered a hint of a smile. I was trying to be encouraging. Team spirit and all that crap.

Or, so I thought. Jace tripped and nearly fell head over skates.

Teammates looked at him with concern, but he waved them off, skating away and taking up his position.

"Did you see that? The best skater on our team nearly tumbles just before the game," Ethan said to me, his tone shocked. "Fuck, please tell me that's a fluke."

When the ref blew the whistle, Jace exploded into action, as smooth and confident as always.

The only thing better than watching him play is sharing the ice.

No, scratch that. Kissing Jace was better.

That surprising realization hit me harder than any boarding ever could.

CHAPTER 18

JACE

think I broke Axel.

Worse, I thought maybe he broke me too.

I was nervous walking into the rink today, but not in my usual way. Instead of struggling with the urge to puke, I was jittery and confused, a menagerie of butterflies fluttered away in my stomach. Or maybe it was a whole flock of baby birds. I felt like a high school kid on the first day of class, wondering where to go, who to talk to, and if anyone would sit with me during lunch. Not that I doubted my ability to find my footing. But everyone had nerves, even confident players like me.

No, this wasn't my usual pre-game anxiety. It wasn't about hockey.

It was about Axel.

He was staring at me, not scowling, and it seemed like no matter where I moved, his eyes followed, tracking me. When he smiled earlier, I was so shocked that I tripped, like I was performing a comedy skit. I hadn't been that clumsy since, well, since I put on my first pair of skates. Oddly enough, I didn't mind being hunted by his gaze. In fact, I really liked that I had all his attention. I was nervous in a good way, anticipation flooding my veins and making me almost giddy with excitement.

That was screwed up. I shouldn't be reacting to him this way. Or, at all.

I'd been a good boy and avoided texting Axel these past two days. Even though my fingers itched like mad to do just that. And I kept my distance in the locker room, not knowing what to expect. Or, how to act. How he'd react. My usual cocky confidence was sitting on the sidelines, and it made me restless.

Was Axel as fucked up over that kiss as I was?

I'd said nothing to Dane or Kayden or any of my friends about what *really* happened in that attic. They'd all heard about the joke and assumed that Axel and I had finally come to a truce. How could I tell them that I hadn't been faking when I didn't even believe it myself? The whole incident at the frat house was like a hazy, fevered sex dream. It had to be. Axel was straight. He hated my guts. Anything that happened between us should be dismissed due to alcohol, experimentation, and a prank gone too far.

Yes, that's all it was. Forget about it.

That's exactly what I intended to do. And did.

We have a game to win and that comes first.

That was the last thought I had before the puck dropped in front of me.

I was conditioned to react decisively. Hockey was a skill and an instinct. You couldn't have one without the other. There was no time to second-guess yourself because things moved fast.

Unfortunately, not fast enough.

I didn't win the face-off. But it didn't put me off my stride. If anything, the sting of loss had me fighting back hard, delving into the fray with Langston's best forwards, Joliet and Kourinko. Joliet was all power and finesse, a total natural who made every shot on goal look easy. Kourinko, on the other hand, was big and bold, and he didn't hold back when it came to fighting for possession. They were the reason Langston was number one in the college rankings last year. But not anymore. We had an aggressive offense, more shots on goal, and a defensive lineup that was getting better with every game.

Kourinko took control of the puck, but I was all over him, and Dane launched into the fray with me. We battled it out, and when I finally wrenched the puck out from Kourinko's control, I didn't waste time hauling ass down the ice. My best effort wasn't good enough, though. I neared the net, but was suddenly blocked by Delacourt, one of Langston's d-men. I managed to sneak around him, and his teammate, Whitman, and spotted my opening.

I took the shot, fast, but the goalie was faster. Fuck.

I skated around their net and slammed my stick on the ice in frustration. Until Dane met me on the other side and gave me a cautioning look. Losing my cool wasn't playing smart. The fact that I was already hyped up and we'd just started wasn't good.

Neither side scored during the first period.

It was twenty minutes of pure frustration. Back and forth, but with no headway on either side. Tension grew thick and heavy when, near the end of the period, Kourinko cross-checked Silas into the boards. They nearly came to blows, until Dane intervened.

During the second period, Axel and I had our chance to play on the same line.

His size alone was intimidating, but it was his knack for finding the openings that made him a star. Less than a minute after the ref blew the whistle, Axel managed to grab ahold of the puck and when he was about to get crushed by Whitman, he shot it to me in a pass that I could only describe as beautiful. Even I could admit the asshole had talent.

Too bad the same couldn't be said for me in that moment because my shot sucked.

No goal.

When intermission was called, we took our break, rehydrated, and regrouped. Coach Banning didn't hold back when it came to his analysis of the game so far.

"Rowland, Lund, nice plays, but I want you to see them through," Banning explained. "Remember what we talked about in practice. No stalling near the net. Hesitation kills momentum."

I wanted to argue and tell him that I was busting my ass, but I was cocky, not dumb. And Coach had a point. Something was off with me. I was so intent on the team winning that I wasn't focused enough on my own plays.

"The same goes for all of you. It's a tough game but we've got this, let's see it through," Banning looked around and locked eyes with Silas. "And a reminder, don't let guys like Kourinko goad you into a stupid fight. The last thing we need is Langston on a power play. Understood?"

Silas bit his lower lip and nodded, glaring back at our coach.

"I didn't hear you?" Banning added with a raised eyebrow as he looked around the room.

"Yes, Coach!" everyone called out.

Coach finally smiled. "Good. Now go get your spot in the semi-final."

Fucking right. Langston was going to play their last game of the season. We'd knock them off their pedestal and then some.

I headed into the third period with renewed fire in my veins. Every play was fast, hard, and brutal. Fighting for the puck, fighting for an opening. Thankfully, no actual fighting. I finally got my chance with ten minutes remaining, after another incredible pass from Axel. I took my shot, and watched it whiz through the goalie's knees. It hit the net so fast it boomeranged and bounced out just as quick. But I didn't miss it and neither did the crowd. The roar of student cheers bombarded my ears.

The buzzer sounded and I glided around the net, then raced back to center ice to celebrate with my teammates.

And the first player to pull me in for a hug? It was the last person I expected.

Axel

The rush of witnessing that goal, even if it wasn't mine, was heady.

So was the guy who scored it. The sheer joy in Jace's smile, the way it lit up his entire face, I couldn't look away. And I surprised myself by grabbing ahold of him and hugging tightly, both of us panting hard, sweat soaked, and exhilarated by that play.

Was I frustrated that I had another assist and not a goal? Yeah, of course it bothered me. But the fact that we were up by one, against my former teammates, was still sweet. And watching that goal? It was a highlight I'll never forget.

I never really clicked with the guys at Langston. Probably my own fault. I never wanted to be there in the first place. Because I knew that I hadn't earned that spot. People there respected me, but it was because of my family history with the school, not because of how I played. But things were different here. Due, in no small part, to playing with Jace. Maybe Coach had the right idea.

It appeared that I'd been wrong about Jace, like I was about so many things.

If I was wrong about Jace, then I was wrong about Preston. I had to talk to him, and soon. Even if it hurt. Even if it meant letting go of someone I thought was my friend. I couldn't stand to be lied to.

Still, a part of me told me to hold back. Be cautious. Just

because Jace was getting to me, didn't mean I had to give in. To him, or these crazy feelings he was inspiring. Feelings that offered nothing but confusion and more questions.

When it came to hockey, I thrived in the offensive mindset.

When it came to everything else in my life, I tended to lean into my defensive instinct.

But I didn't know what stance to take when it came to this unexpected play going on between me and Jace.

The game ended with that one goal. When the final buzzer rang out, everyone on the team crashed into each other to celebrate, me included. Most surprising of all, Maddox. I'd never seen our goalie smile like that before and I wasn't sure if it was good or kind of scary. Maybe a bit of both. The crowd was wild, and the music got louder, with Julian, Ethan, and Sean busting out dance moves on the ice, making everyone laugh. Dane encouraged us all to wave to the fans while our opponents looked on at us in disbelief. Winning any game was a high, but at this point in the season, it was surreal.

The celebration continued in the locker room, with guys spraying each other with bottles of water and electrolyte drinks. The place was a soggy, sticky mess, our stalls included, but no one cared.

We showered, changed, and gathered in the lounge for our post game scrum.

The lounge was small, not enough seats for the entire team, and since I was one of the last ones in, I stood beside Silas at the back. Jace and Dane were side by side, their heads together, talking in that way that close friends did. A pang of jealousy hit me, but I shoved it away. These weird feelings I had every time I looked at Jace had to get gone.

By the time we all got settled down, waiting for Coach, the post game euphoria had calmed a bit, and the reality that we were one step closer to the national championship settled in.

"Sorry for the delay, guys," Banning offered as he entered the room and moved to stand at the front. "I was just on the phone with the college president, who by the way, extends her congratulations to all of you on this win—"

Everyone started clapping but Coach motioned for silence.

"—I'm not done yet," Coach chuckled and glanced around the room. "I want to take this moment to officially announce that Dane St. Pierre is your permanent captain. Dane stepped into this role in September and has proved, far beyond my expectations, that he deserves that title."

Everyone cheered and clapped.

"And, as you know, I've also been considering the candidate for the center position for months. Every forward on this team is outstanding, so my decision wasn't made easily or lightly. But I'm happy to announce that Jace Rowland has earned the spot. Let's give Dane and Jace our full support."

What?

My elation evaporated as blood pounded in my ears, until my heartbeat was all I could hear. Shock didn't begin to describe how I was feeling. I was furious—at Jace, at myself, at Coach. I heard my teammates clapping and calling out, but I couldn't move.

"Settle down, I'm still not finished," Coach continued with a wry smile that made me want to punch something.

The wall behind me would be a good start.

Instead of giving in to that urge, to the rage, I crossed my arms and lowered my head, not wanting to look at anyone. Humiliation had my cheeks running hot. No matter where I went, or what I did, I was never good enough. I don't know why I thought that things were starting to go my way.

If anything, Coach's announcement confirmed what I knew but didn't want to face.

"While I know that titles have their place, this is still a team sport. We don't win as individuals. We're only as strong as each other," Banning insisted and something in his tone made me finally look up again. His gaze was imploring but my brain refused to hear him out. "There's no second best in this room. We win together or not at all."

Coach's comment sparked an unwanted memory.

You're the first born but you'll always be second best.

It turned out, my mother was right.

I was a good player, but not a great one. The spot I'd been working towards, dreamed about, obsessed over, it wasn't mine to take. It was Jace's. I could accept it and move on or fight against it and let the chips—or, in this instance, pucks—fall where they may.

Steeling my resolve, I looked around the room and locked eyes with Jace.

Fight it is.

CHAPTER 19
JACE

Me? Center line? I was so proud I wanted to run around campus doing cartwheels.

Like Dane, my role on the team was now official. There was responsibility and a shitload of pressure since I was someone other players relied on, respected, and trusted to lead us to the next level. Not that they didn't already do that, but Coach's confirmation solidified things. It meant a lot.

It was also kind of scary. I didn't want to let anyone down or fuck this up.

And I also knew that the tentative truce between Axel and I was now in jeopardy.

After Coach gave his analysis of the game, he called a close to our wrap-up discussion. Everyone on the team came up to Dane and me to offer their congratulations.

Everyone except Axel.

His fury was as clear as those deep blue eyes of his. Not that I could blame him. If I was in his position, I'd be pissed too.

Give him space and time. He'll come around.

Instead of listening to my inner voice, I made a beeline for Axel, but he was already leaving.

"Axel!" I called out.

He kept walking, faster, stalking towards the exit like he was marching off to war.

"Let him be," Dane warned me, tapping my arm.

"But I just want to—"

"Jace, you'd be the same. Come on. Let him go for now."

Dane was right. It was smarter to let Axel deal with the news on his own. It didn't stop me from tracking him, though. Axel slapped the door open with a bang, and just as quickly, he was gone.

I turned back to my friend.

"I'm heading to the dorm," I muttered.

"What?" Dane looked at me like I'd lost it. "Who are you right now?"

"I'm a forward who's tired as fuck."

"No way. School party crawl. All the frat and sorority houses are hosting parties tonight to celebrate the win," Dane explained and gave me a knowing smirk. "Literally everyone on campus will be there. You've gotta show up."

"Fine," I grumbled.

Dane stared at me like he didn't know who I was. Then again, I never turned down a party. And after today? I must be coming down with something.

"Come on Honey, stop thinking about Hot."

I rolled my eyes at those nicknames, even though secretly, I kinda like them.

"Who says I'm thinking about *him*?" I scoffed and shook my head. "I mean, I'm happy as fuck. I just don't want Axel to disrupt the vibe of the team. That's all. Things were moving in the right direction a few days ago—"

Yeah, when I had my tongue down Axel's throat.

"They still are," Dane insisted, patting my shoulder. "Just give him a couple of days to absorb the news and calm down."

I shrugged, unconvinced.

"Jace," Dane warned.

"What?" I said innocently.

I had to talk to Axel. Right now. Or things would only get worse.

"Don't give me that look," Dane sighed. "You're going to talk to him, aren't you?"

"No. Maybe." I ran a nervous hand through my hair. "I don't think so."

"Fuck."

"Relax, Captain. It's all under control."

Dane shook his head. "Yeah, like those words don't make me nervous at *all*."

I said my goodbye to Dane and headed off to the dorm.

When I got to my room, I dropped off my bag. My stomach growled up a storm, so I grabbed a protein shake from my fridge, downed it in record time, and then chugged another one for good measure.

I was pretty sure Axel went back to his room. It was fine. We'd have it out, he'd yell at me, and then it would be done. He'd have to deal with it. I wasn't going to let this fuck up the team.

Jace: We need to talk.

Axel: Nothing to talk about.

Jace: I'm headed to your room.

Axel: Don't.

Jace: Don't be an ass.

Axel: Fuck off or I'm blocking you.

Okay, I'd try another tactic.

Jace: There's a party crawl going on to celebrate our win. You have to come. Everyone on the team will be there.

Axel: I don't have to do anything.

Instead of responding, I shoved my phone in my pocket and headed for the elevator. The ride to the third floor seemed to take forever. Kayden's room was 333 and I'd found out through him that Axel was in 339.

When I arrived at Axel's door, I raised my hand to knock and noticed that my hand was shaking. Weird. I rapped on the door twice and waited.

And waited. I rapped again.

And waited.

I was about to knock for the third time when the door opened, an irate Axel staring back at me.

"Get lost," he replied and slammed the door in my face.

I knocked again. "I'm going to camp out here until you talk to me. Or, until you come and party with us."

A minute passed. Then two. Five.

I sat down on the carpeted hall floor and put my earphones in, listening to some tunes while I waited. And waited.

Ten minutes later, the door cracked open again. Axel had his jacket on and stared daggers at me.

"I'm going for an hour. For the team," he declared with a scowl. "But that's it."

"Fair enough," I replied and stood up.

Axel closed and locked his door, and we made our way silently, awkwardly, to the elevator.

"You played amazing today—" I started.

Axel slammed the elevator button so hard that I worried he might have broken it.

"Really? Do you hear yourself?" Axel grumbled.

"What? It's true. I wouldn't have scored without that pass. You—"

"I get it," he bit out. "You're the best forward on the team, and I suck. I get it."

"You don't suck."

"Well, I'm not a first line forward, am I?" he groused.

"No, but you're still one of the best around. You're making a difference on our team. You've got so much potential."

"You don't know that."

"I do know that," I said with a confident smirk.

Axel scowled. "Always so fucking sure of yourself."

"I have to be, or I wouldn't get anywhere. Fuck, I'd still be stuck back in Hillington if I didn't believe in myself and work my ass off. Not all of us are born with a tuition fund and every advantage in life."

The elevator doors opened, and I stepped inside first, Axel following.

Honestly, I was surprised. I expected him to stand there and let the doors close on me.

"Money doesn't matter when it comes to hockey. Either you've got the skill or—"

"Are you kidding me?" I snapped. "Equipment, lessons, travel. You bet your rich, spoiled ass that it's about money. Most guys like me can't afford to play for a month, never mind for years. My aunt sacrificed a lot for me to get here and I work my ass off. I earned that spot. I'm sorry that you can't deal with it, but maybe if you can't, you're not worthy of our team."

Axel let out an angry growl and came at me.

We collided against the wall of the elevator, his bigger body enveloping mine. A different kind of heat rolled through me when our hips collided, a need so intense that it seared my skin like a brand. I glanced up at his midnight blues and there was no mistaking what I saw there. Fuck, why did this asshole turn me on? I was grateful that I had a solid wall to hold me up because suddenly my knees were shaking, and my hands too. My head was fucked up and my dick so hard I was straining against my jeans.

And I wasn't the only one.

Axel's mouth hovered over mine, his hot, minty breath kissing my face.

"Don't let your frustration ruin everything. Deal with it and move on. Focus on your game, not trying to outplay everyone," I whispered as I glared at him, willing him to see sense. Willing my body to do the same. "The problem isn't me."

He stared into my eyes, electricity snapping between us.

"The problem is definitely you," he admitted and slammed his mouth over mine.

There was anger in that kiss, frustration mixed with lust, both of us desperate as we ate at each other's mouth. His callused hands slid into my hair and gripped my neck so tightly I'd probably have bruises tomorrow. I moaned at that thought and reached for his hips, pulling him in as close as we could get. The kiss went on and on, punishing, brutal, and so fucking hot. I snaked my tongue around his and sucked hard, teasing him, and he let out the filthiest moan I'd ever heard.

Without pause, I reached down and cupped his bulge, feeling the weight of his hard dick in my palm. He might be pissed at me, at the situation, but there was no denying he wanted me too. And when he touched me, all my reason and logic were blown to hell.

"I don't know how to play this game," he groaned and canted his hips, pushing his dick into my hand. "Fuck, Jace. Fuck."

"Not a game," I whispered and gave his lower lip a not-so-gentle nip. "And yes, fuck is right. But don't worry, like with everything I take on, I'm really great at what I do."

"You arrogant ass—"

I kissed him back, hard, cutting off his words, taking possession of his mouth the way I needed to, not letting him up for air as our tongues tangled, until I was full-on fucking his mouth.

"My room," I demanded when the elevator pinged. "Now."

Thank God my room was on the first floor.

When the doors opened, I grabbed Axel's hand and surprisingly, he let me. Every step towards my room felt like an eternity, until finally, with sweaty hands I reached into my pocket for my key. Axel pushed his hips against my ass, rocking into me, his hard dick the only thing I wanted. If I didn't get this door unlocked in the next five seconds, we were going to hump each other to orgasm in the freaking hallway.

"Jesus," I muttered as I pushed open the door, and we tumbled inside.

"This is just sex," Axel confessed with a hard scowl. "We can fuck it out of our system."

I closed the door and leaned against it, my lips sore and swollen.

Licking them, I tasted Axel. It was heady. Too good.

I nodded. "That's the only thing I want."

The moment the words left my mouth I knew it was a lie.

"I've never…I mean, with a guy," he admitted and swallowed hard. "I don't know—"

"If you want to fuck me, I'm down for that," I replied and started stripping off my clothes. "Or, we can do other things. Whatever you need, however you're comfortable."

He nodded quickly but said nothing.

"We have regular physicals, and my last test was negative," I reassured him. "I've got the results here. I'm also on PreP. I thought you should know."

His gaze met mine and he nodded, licking his lips.

"I'm negative too. I always use condoms."

I threw my jacket aside, my t-shirt, toed off my boots, and kicked off my socks, until I was standing in nothing but my jeans. My confidence soared as Axel's eyes roamed over me with hungry heat. I yanked on my zipper and shoved my jeans down and off, leaving me bare except for my black jock.

"Take it off," Axel groaned. "I want to see all of you."

I complied, but took my time about it, teasing him. When the cool air finally hit my heated skin, my cock slapped hard against my stomach.

"Jace," Axel whispered. "Holy shit."

Without pause, I knew what Axel needed. He was all caught up in his head.

I dropped to my knees in front of him and his sharp inhale told me my instinct was right. I was going to suck his stubborn brains out of his gorgeous cock and leave him begging for more.

"Lose the jacket and lean against the wall," I commanded.

He did just that, throwing off his navy parka, revealing a tight grey t-shirt that stretched across his broad chest, and jeans that molded to every inch of those sculpted thighs. Axel loomed over me, fit as fuck, hard all over, intimidating to some but not to me. I was always amazed that someone so big could be so agile, but he proved it every time he stepped onto the ice.

Now, he hardly moved at all.

Instead of stripping down, he stood rigid, hands fisted by his sides, like he wasn't sure what to do. No, not that. He was nervous.

Duh, Axel's never been with a guy before.

His midnight blues were dark, vulnerable, and the power of that look hit me like a wicked cross-check. Axel sparked a possessiveness that I didn't even know I was capable of. I loved attention—giving and receiving—but there was something about Axel, fuck, I wanted all of his. And only his. To protect whatever this was between us. To make it good for him.

Because, for some unfathomable reason, it felt like he was already mine.

CHAPTER 20

JACE

Why was Axel fully clothed and me completely naked, the sexiest thing ever?

I reached for his zipper and undid it, taking my time, watching his eyes glaze over and his chest rise and fall, like he'd just raced down the ice at full speed. When I pushed his jeans down to sit low on his hips and reached inside his briefs, taking his hard, leaking cock in my hand, he let out the filthiest moan. His uncut dick was heavy, covered in thick veins, and my mouth watered. Axel was a huge man, and his dick was perfectly proportioned to the rest of him. My ass clenched just thinking about riding him. I slid one experimental hand under his t-shirt, running my fingers along his abs, hot skin and firm muscles quivering with every stroke.

"You don't need to—" he moaned.

"Yes, I do," I insisted.

Leaning in, I buried my nose in his blond pubes and drew in a deep inhale, taking in the scent of musk and the citrus bodywash that lingered. Fuck, he smelled delicious, and I couldn't help but give his taut v-line a teasing lick, tasting salt and something uniquely Axel.

One taste wasn't going to be nearly enough.

"Fuck, that's hot."

His appreciative groan had me glancing up, his dark eyes glazed with lust. I turned my head and licked the base of his cock, tracing a long vein with my tongue, feeling his pulse jump, my own heart racing in time.

"Good?" I asked him as I continued to lick my way down his cock, noting the way his breath hitched, his muscles quaked, his cock jerked.

"Meh," he croaked in a breathy whisper. "A blowjob's just a...b-blowjob."

Judging by his fumbled words, tense posture, and heated eyes, he was so full of shit. I let out a dirty laugh, determined to prove my point.

"I haven't even started yet," I replied smugly. "And you've never had your cock sucked by me before. Hold on to my hair. Or the wall. Either way, grab something, because your knees are about to give out. It's your only warning."

Axel shook his head.

"So fucking cocky," he muttered, licking his lips, his eyes sparking fire.

"Damn right."

I loved sucking dick. I leaned in, holding the base of his dick in one hand, and slid his cock into my mouth, inch by inch. And there were a lot of inches. Axel smelled amazing but he tasted even better. I swallowed, taking him down, down, deeper, until my throat was stuffed full of his fat dick.

"What the fuck?" he groaned loudly and gripped my hair like he was reaching for a lifeline.

I'd have a sore throat tomorrow, but it would be worth it. Giving head was such a rush.

When I hummed my pleasure, Axel's cock pulsed in my mouth. My cock jerked hard in response, and I wanted to touch myself, but that would have to wait. First, I was going to suck all that strain and stress from his body. Still, that didn't mean I couldn't have fun and tease him while doing it.

I popped off his dick and leaned back on my heels.

"Had enough already?" I quipped and licked my swollen lips.

His answering glare made my cock even harder.

"Suck my dick," he growled.

His husky demand made me laugh again, lighting up every pleasure point in my body. He was still holding tight to my hair and looking down at me with a fierce gaze.

I wasn't sure if he wanted to kiss me again or shove me away for good.

He tugged my hair, pulling me in closer, and I got my answer, leaning in and swallowing him down again. He grunted and swore, and then I hummed again and he lost it.

"Jesus Christ," he whimpered. "Jesus fucking Christ, Jace. No one's ever…shit."

The sounds he made, filthy and provocative, had my own cock leaking furiously. But the only thing I needed was to watch Axel fall apart. My orgasm could wait.

I kept licking and sucking, taking him deep, until I was sure I was going to pass out from the lack of oxygen. But what a way to go…

"Don't—" Axel whimpered.

What? Did he change his mind?

"Don't stop," he rasped. "Don't you dare fucking stop."

Yes, fuck yes. Goosebumps popped up all over my skin. I sucked harder, my eyes watering, saliva slipping out of the corners of my mouth. I was a man possessed, cradling his balls with my hand while I took him deep down my throat, so deep I'd probably be unable to speak for days, never mind tomorrow.

"Jace…you…oh God," Axel roared, punching his hips forward, his hands taking control of my head. "Motherfucker, I'm going to come."

I moaned, the sound muffled by his dick.

"Pull off if you don't…don't want my load," he panted.

Want it? No. I didn't want it.

I needed it.

Axel

Nothing prepared me for Jace, on his knees, sucking my cock.

I didn't recognize the raw, animalistic sounds coming out of my mouth. Or the desperate craving I had to rub my body all over Jace's, until we were sweaty and covered in each other's cum. Was this what everyone was bragging about when they talked about sex? I'd never wanted to kiss anyone like that, totally and completely consumed. Like if Jace stopped touching me, I would fucking die or something.

That gorgeous, smart-ass mouth of his was my downfall, but fuck it, I was ready for the ride.

And Jace knew exactly what he was doing, sucking my dick with abandon. But the realization about *why* he was so good at this made me pissy as hell. Picturing him going down on another guy had me biting back a possessive growl.

Until lust overwhelmed me, and I couldn't think at all.

I just needed more of his hot, wet mouth, and his tormenting fingers.

His bright eyes hid nothing. The cocky asshole knew exactly what he was doing to me. And the things I wanted to do with him? I didn't have any experience in hooking up with guys, but it didn't seem to matter. Just like in hockey, I let my instinct guide me.

My instinct, and Jace.

Jace slid his warm hand under my balls, over my taint and then my ass, making me shiver, teasing my hole but not going any further. A frustrated snarl rumbled out of my chest. I snapped. Or, rather, my knees did.

Yep, Jace was right, even though I wasn't going to give in and admit the truth.

Thankfully, when my knees gave out, I had the wall to support me.

"Touch me there," I demanded. "Do it."

I wanted him to touch me everywhere. My cock, my nipples, my ass. Fuck, I'd played with my ass before, but the thought of Jace's fingers there? Inside me? Yes. I wanted that. His tongue. Maybe even his cock. The fantasy of Jace fucking my ass was so freaking hot that my entire body went rigid, my climax just within reach.

It was too damn fast. But so damn good.

And when he rubbed his rough finger over my sensitive hole, teasing the rim, I was done. Gone. Finished. I came down his throat in a heated rush that had me shaking uncontrollably. He'd bested me again, but this time I was too satisfied to feel bad about it. I reveled in the pleasure, the orgasm slamming into me, hitting me hard. All I could do was scream Jace's name and let him pull me under.

"Yes," I panted, gasping for air. "Yes, fuck, yes."

Then I realized I was still holding on to Jace's head, running my hands through his soft, thick hair. Slowly, reluctantly, I let go of him as my cock slipped out of his mouth, my cum dripping down his chin, over his scruff. Jace was hot as hell, but he looked even more gorgeous with my cum painting his face.

The support of the wall was no match for that orgasm, and I slid down, until my bare ass met carpet.

Normally after sex I just wanted to walk away. But this was different. *I* was different with Jace. It felt like I'd barely scratched the surface of what sex could be like, and now that I finally found out just how good it could be, I didn't want to let go.

"Kiss me," I whispered to him.

Jace shook his head, but I ignored that and reached for him, cupping his face.

"What, *now* you're shy?" I quipped, drawing a small grin out of him.

"Never," Jace admitted and licked his lips.

Fuck, he was tasting *my* cum. That was so hot.

"And?" I demanded, cupping his jaw, leaning in until our lips brushed, setting off sparks I couldn't control. "What? You think I'm going to freak out? That I don't want to kiss you?"

"Cum isn't for everyone."

I barked out a laugh, and since when did that happen during sex?

"I can't speak for them. Only for me," I returned and nipped his lips. "Kiss me, goddamn it."

Jace finally gave in, straddling my lap, mauling my lips. Tasting myself was sexy. Sexy and addictive. Just like the man in my arms.

His hard cock brushed against my abs and shit, he hadn't come yet? This was another reason why I had a lousy track record in the bedroom. I was selfish.

Not that I wanted to be that way now.

I ran my hands down his neck, over his smooth back and cupped his ass, pulling him in tight, roughly, needing him closer. Needing him all over me. His chest teased my nipples, and he rubbed against me, rocking his hips, my cock half hard and getting harder. He shuddered and writhed, and I wanted to see him come. I wanted to taste him too.

"That's it, Honey, come all over me," I moaned, unable to stop the words from spilling out of my mouth.

Honey? God, I really was fucked up. That goddamn nickname was stuck in my head but apparently not in my mouth. I thought for sure Jace would laugh. Instead, he launched himself at me and ravaged my lips, making my eyes roll back in my head. We humped frantically, my back slamming against the wall, the sound loud, but our mutual groans even louder. He dug his hands into my shoulders and rode me, our cocks rubbing together, our sweat and the smell of cum inten-sifying.

I need more, I need more. I need…Jace.

"Fuck, Axel, fuck," Jace chanted, rutting harder, his body undulating, straining close.

Not close enough. I buried my face in his neck, inhaling the sharp scent of my cum combined with his sweat. So deli-cious. I licked and bit his shoulder, sucking hard, marking him as he jerked and shuddered. Holding on tighter, I wrapped him up in my arms, feeling protective and posses-sive all at once.

What the fuck was he doing to me?

"Come for me, please, please, come for me," I begged, so far gone that I didn't recognize myself.

"Axel!"

Jace's hot cum lashed my skin and my cock jerked in response.

The first orgasm was intense. The second one totally ruined me.

Ripples and aftershocks rolled through my body, both of us a sticky, completely debauched mess.

I didn't let go of Jace, though, loving the feel of his weight on me, and the smell of our sex. He didn't seem keen to move either.

"Holy fucking shit," he whispered. "What the hell was that?"

"You're asking me?" I panted.

"You're the only one here," he quipped, kissing my neck the way I had his, the gesture making me clinch him hard again.

"I don't know," I paused and looked into his eyes.

I was so fucked.

"I really don't know."

CHAPTER 21

JACE

expected Axel to bolt from my room before the cum dried between us. Or, when he caught his breath.

Whatever came first.

What did he do? He gave me a deep, dirty kiss, slapped my ass, and ordered me to get the shower started.

"Say what?" I huffed as I stared into his eyes.

Those deep, dark blues were dangerous, and my chest tightened.

"After a hockey game, a fight, and two orgasms, I have no brain cells or energy left. The least you could do is help me shower and offer me food," he grumbled. "I'm fucking starving."

I was shocked and amused and couldn't help but laugh at his statement. Typical hockey jock.

"I'm in the same boat," I returned. "Who's going to help me shower? Or feed me?"

He raised one blond eyebrow.

"Okay, sure, well...I...I just—" God, I was fumbling over my words. "I wasn't expecting you to want that."

Like, at all. Most of my hookups were quite happy to leave once we were both satisfied. I made it clear I didn't do repeats, and I never had any desire for post-sex snuggling, eating, or sharing a shower. And given that Axel didn't fuck around with guys, I figured he'd be all too eager to forget this ever happened. Instead, he didn't let go, his massive arms wrapped around me like a python. And even more strange, I didn't have any desire to move away.

"I didn't expect to want it either."

His quiet admission gave me goosebumps and left me momentarily speechless.

He kissed me again. A long, slow kiss that made me feel like I'd been drugged. Why did he have to be so damn good at that?

"Did you hit your head while we were frotting?" I teased when he finally let me come up for air.

His body stiffened. "If you want me to go, I'll go."

I shook my head.

"I didn't say that."

"Then feed me."

He swatted my ass. Hard.

"Save the rough stuff for another day," I quipped.

"I barely survived this one."

He squeezed my ass cheeks.

"If you don't let go, I can't reach for my phone," I suggested. "No phone, no food delivery."

Axel's stomach rumbled loudly. I was about to make a snarky comment when he gave me a quelling look. Ignoring my urge to poke the beast, I gently pulled back and winced as we separated. Drying cum and body hair wasn't a great match. I regularly shaved off my pubes and chest hair, but I'd been too busy lately to manscape.

"Are we going to talk about it?" I asked, boldly meeting his gaze.

"Talk about what? You swallowing my load? Me being bi? Center line? Preston?" Axel replied. "I need food first. I'm too hungry to think, never mind talk about all of that."

Axel shook his head as he stood up to his full height, and fuck, what a gorgeous view. I noticed a few scars and I wondered how he got them. They looked like old hockey injuries. Then there were the dark bruises from our game, and the marks I'd left. My eyes traveled lower, to his taut v-lines, all leading to that gorgeous cock and heavy balls. And those thick thighs? Fuck, I wanted them wrapped around my head while he sat on my face and I ate his ass.

"Fuck, Jace, the things that come out of your mouth."

Despite Axel's claims of hunger and sex exhaustion, his cock grew stiff, and he quickly gripped the base. His recovery period was impressive.

"What?" I asked, completely distracted, and probably drooling. "Did I say that out loud?"

He quickly nodded.

"And? You don't want me to eat your ass?" I stared at him.

"Jesus, don't say that. I'm gonna pass out if I come again," Axel replied as he stroked his hardening cock. "Fuck it. I don't care. It's worth it."

"Sit on my face."

"Ngh."

I lay down on the floor and crooked my finger at him.

"Come on, haul your hot hockey ass over here so I can suck your hole."

Axel shuffled quickly, standing over me, offering me his ass. His legs shook as he slowly kneeled, his hairy thighs bracketing my head. I gripped his ass cheeks and spread them, sticking my tongue out, going directly for his tight hole.

"Oh God, oh fuck," he whimpered as he pushed his ass onto my face, begging for more. "You play dirty, Jace."

He didn't know the half of it.

I bit back a chuckle as more of that musky, addictive taste hit me. I circled his hole, teasing the sensitive rim. I licked down, over his taint and back up again, pushing the tip of my tongue into his hole. He tasted so good, addictive. My cock pulsed hard and heavy again, precum leaking out of the tip, down my cock and balls.

"More," Axel moaned. "Please, more. Don't stop. Fuck, don't stop."

I continued to lick and suck on his hole, clamping his ass cheeks tight as his hips jerked in response.

"Use my cum to jerk yourself off," I rasped.

Axel's rough palm gripped my dick, and he started stroking me off. I nipped one of his ass cheeks in retaliation.

"I said you, not me," I moaned, distracted.

He removed his hand from my cock, and I grunted in frustration. Me and my big mouth.

"Now your cum's all over my cock, Jace," Axel groaned. "I can't…it's so hot."

His ass cheeks flexed and he jerked his hips faster, harder, his moans getting louder.

Jesus Christ, Axel was using my cum to get himself off. Never mind him, I wasn't going to last at all. I licked his hole again, pushing my tongue inside of him, fucking him with it as he keened and shuddered.

"Yes, yes, yes," Axel chanted as he sat on my face and rode me. "Jace!"

My body locked up tight, pleasure spiraling out of control. I didn't even need to touch myself or for Axel to touch me. I came hard, hands free, the orgasm crashing through my body, fierce and unrelenting.

Axel was right there with me, shouting my name, coming all over me.

He fell forward, collapsing on my legs for a moment, then rolling sideways. I was dizzy after two orgasms, and completely breathless. And when he crawled up my body, face to face this time, that feeling intensified. Oh God, what the fuck was happening? He stared down at me, his cheeks flushed, his eyes glazed. Shock and tremors ran through my body when he leaned down and kissed me.

I wasn't expecting that. I wasn't expecting any of this.

"Looks like I'm not the only one who plays dirty."

———

Two hours later, we lay facing each other, sprawled out on my bed, in a post-sex, post-nap, post-carb coma.

I'd ordered Axel into the shower while I ordered the food. I needed some distance. Space to think about what we'd done and why I wanted to do it again. My resolve to think of this as sex and only sex was wavering, hard, and I only had myself to blame. I should've known this had disaster written all over it. Fighting like Axel and I did, all that passion had to go somewhere. And, oddly enough, it wasn't spent. In fact, it felt like just the beginning.

No. I wasn't going to let myself be affected.

Draw a line and do it now. Time-out.

After eating, we both fell asleep and then woke up an hour later. We downed a couple of protein shakes and a gallon of water.

"We should make an appearance at the party crawl," I suggested.

Axel reached out a hand and ran it through my hair, massaging my scalp. He was full of surprises. Surprisingly gentle for such a big, gruff guy. His touch was so good that I almost purred.

You're acting ridiculous. Stop letting him get to you like this.

"In a bit," Axel offered. "I'm sure it's just getting started."

"Are you trying to avoid your teammates? You can't and you shouldn't."

"I know."

"Are you still pissed about Coach's decision?" I asked.

His hand stopped, but he didn't let go.

"I'm not pissed," he grimaced. "Okay, I'm pissed. And frustrated. I came to Sutton with something to prove and now—"

"Prove what?"

He bit his lower lip. "That I can make it on my own. That I'm good enough to leave my old life behind. That I'm not second best in hockey, or anything else."

"You're not second best."

"I know that, somewhere, in here," he tapped his heart. "But in my head, I'm still struggling. I was never great at school, and my parents didn't shy away from making it known that I was a disappointment."

Axel shook his head. "Like they should talk. My family's fucked up. And I hate Redgewick. Couldn't wait to leave. And I'm never going back."

"Fucked up? How?"

Axel sighed and rolled to his back.

"Let's see, my dad works eighty plus hours a week and then parties the rest of it, my mom is ruthless and fucks anyone and everyone in some twisted game to get my father's attention, and oh yeah, my brother has a pill and gambling addiction, and he despises me."

"Whoa, that's a lot," I replied, dropping a comforting kiss on his shoulder.

What was I doing? *Stop it right now.*

"Why does your brother hate you?" I asked.

Axel turned his head and stared at me. "I can't believe I'm telling you all this."

"You can't resist me. No one can."

He rolled his eyes.

"There's that huge ego of yours."

"Well, I am the highest scorer on the team."

"I'm catching up," he bit out.

"Catch me if you can," I teased him. "Now tell me. I swear I can keep a secret."

"Really?"

"Who am I gonna tell?"

"Dane, Ethan, Kayden, Colin, Finn, Silas, Sean—"

"I'm not going to tell anyone." I made a zipping motion over my lips. "I swear."

"Swear on the cup."

"My cup?" I pointed to my dick.

"Hockey, Jace. THE cup."

"Fine. I swear on THE cup."

That was serious shit right there.

Axel rubbed a hand over his face. "He hates me because I'm…I'm actually his half brother. And I guess, his cousin."

"What? I don't understand."

"I'm a Lund, but the father I grew up with isn't my bio dad. His brother, my uncle, is my real dad."

For the first time in my life, I had absolutely nothing to say.

"Yeah, it's fucked up," Axel muttered and ran a hand over his jaw. "I told you."

"You mean your mom and her brother-in-law—"

Axel nodded.

"Holy shit."

"I found out a year ago. I always felt different, but I finally knew why. They don't want it public though. That would sully their reputation."

"Oh my God," I whispered. "No wonder you wanted to get out of Redgewick."

He nodded. "My family didn't want me to come here but when I told them I knew about my real father, well, let's just say it bought me time. I get access to my trust fund when I turn twenty-one. Nothing they can do after that. And they can't touch that money. My grandfather put it in place when I was born."

"Why would they need to touch it? Don't they have enough?"

He sighed. "Not anymore. I mean, yes, when I was growing up. But they're spending more than they make. They have lots of houses and cars and expensive vacations but it's all for show. Most on borrowed money. They've got massive debt and it's getting worse."

"How do you know that?"

"They were arguing about it last year. Thankfully, I have enough money to pay for my tuition until I graduate. My grades weren't good enough for a scholarship to any school."

"I don't know what to say. It's like something out of a TV drama."

"Unfortunately, for me, it's all too real."

"Reality sucks sometimes."

His phone buzzed.

Axel picked his phone up and swore.

"What is it?"

"I have to take my meds."

"Oh."

"I'm on antidepressants. Have been since I was fifteen. It's not a cure, but it helps."

"Do you see a therapist?"

"For a while I did," Axel admitted. "He was okay, but then my mom slept with him, and I really didn't respect him after that."

"Oh my God, are you serious?"

"Unfortunately. I got suspicious when my mom insisted on picking me up from his office after every appointment. Usually our housekeeper, Kelly, drove me to stuff like visits to the doctor. Anyway, the last time I was there, I had to use the bathroom and when I came out, I saw them kissing. I didn't say anything, but I couldn't trust him after that. He was prob-ably telling her all about my sessions. I wouldn't put it past them."

"That's disturbing. On so many levels," I admitted. "Shit, Axel, I'm so sorry."

I couldn't imagine that. I thought I struggled growing up, but it sounded like Axel was worse off. At least I had my aunt in my corner. No wonder he didn't trust anyone.

"I'm used to their chaos," he admitted quietly. "Let's change the subject."

He sat up and ran a hand through his shaggy blond waves, his face suddenly devoid of any emotion. I recognized the look. It was his game-day face, his jaw clenched in determination. I fought the strange urge to hug him, to reassure him that everything would be okay. With my friends, that was normal. With my hookups? No.

"You don't have to worry about sex," I blurted out and he gave me a questioning look. "I mean, I told you about my results. Given what happened with Preston, I take my health seriously. I know I joke a lot, but not about this."

His gaze met mine and he nodded, licking his lips.

"Same. Even though I haven't fucked around that much lately."

The image of Axel having sex with someone, anyone other than me, sat like a heavy weight in my gut. Jealousy? Fuck yes. The feeling was both unexpected and unwelcome. This was sex. Only sex. It had to be. And yet...

"Cool," I bit out and made to roll away.

But Axel's reaction time was faster than mine, snaking his arm around my waist and pulling me in tight to his body. The kiss he placed on my neck was also unexpected, but if my racing heart and hardening dick were any indication, very welcome.

"You said you wanted to talk. I'm talking," he whispered, moving up my neck, nipping my earlobe, making me groan. "The last time was just over two months ago. She was—"

"I don't need details, alright?" I snapped.

He chuckled, the husky sound making me shiver.

"Ooh, touchy," he quipped softly as he kissed my jaw. "Same goes."

"It shouldn't matter," I confessed.

"No, it shouldn't."

But it did. I knew it did.

Still, we lay silent, like neither of us could believe or wanted to admit that something surreal was going on here. There was a heaviness in that silence. A warning that I ignored.

"What about Preston?" I asked him.

Axel's body tensed up. "I need to call him. I want to know why he said what he did about you."

Did that mean Axel believed me?

"I think it's time to get dressed and join our team at the party," Axel finally offered.

I wanted to stay here, and fuck everyone else. Or, in my case, only Axel.

Instead of giving into that craziness, I shoved it aside.

"Try and control yourself when we get there," I teased him, grabbing hold of the out he'd lobbed at me. "Everyone flirts with me. I can't help it."

"Yes, I know," he replied and swatted my ass. "But I make no promises."

CHAPTER 22

AXEL

The party crawl was the biggest college event I'd ever experienced. It seemed like the entire student population from Sutton and the surrounding towns was out here tonight celebrating our win. Music blasted from all the frat houses on the block, and the sororities too.

We met up with the rest of our team at the Delta Beta Ki house, the biggest frat on campus. There was beer pong and funnel contests, and every other drinking game you could imagine going on. I was surprised to see Silas in the crowd, talking with Maddox, Kayden, Finn, and Colin. Ethan was standing in the center of the makeshift dance floor, the main living room of the house, along with his frat brothers.

Jace and I had arrived separately, of course, with me trailing a good five minutes later.

When I'd entered the house, though, Jace was right there, talking to Ethan. I passed by them, overhearing our teammate pointing out Jace's giant hickey and speculating on the source. I scurried off to the kitchen and gratefully accepted a shot of vodka and a beer chaser from Jackson, Dane's boyfriend.

Jackson was the quieter of the duo, but just as friendly,

and sometimes fiery to boot. I got into a heated conversation with him about rowers vs. hockey players and who was the better athlete. Hockey players, no question. I was right, of course, but Jackson held firm and suggested that we have a friendly competition between groups to prove his point. I agreed to that, but only after nationals. Then we continued talking about the hockey season so far, and I was incredibly grateful for the distraction.

Not that it worked for long because inevitably my gaze scanned the crowd for Jace. I didn't want him out of my sight, which was all kinds of fucked up. It took everything in me to stay where I was and not follow him. Not reach for him. I wanted him right here, beside me, warm and real and…mine.

Do you hear yourself? Jesus, sex with Jace melted what was left of my brain.

And it rankled that he didn't appear affected in the same way at all, smiling and laughing as he made his way around the room. Like he hadn't just given me the most intense orgasms of my life. Then again, he hooked up a lot.

Maybe I was just another notch in his hockey stick.

Jace certainly knew everyone here. But I didn't like the fact that some of the guys and girls got up in his personal space. I bit back the possessive urge to intervene and tried to focus on my conversation. Thankfully, the beer was kicking in, and I was starting to relax. I was just tired and out of sorts because today was an anomaly—the game, the fucking, the talking. It was all too much at once.

Everything was fine, though, and I was under control.

Until I spotted a preppy looking guy making his move on Jace. Suddenly, the stranger wrapped his hand around Jace's bicep, and then accidently (or maybe not) spilled his drink on him.

My first thought was *get your fucking hands off him.*

And then *oh my God, Jace is wearing my t-shirt.*

No wonder I kept pulling at the neckline of mine. It was

too small. Shit, I'd accidently thrown on Jace's shirt and he'd put on mine. Despite the chill of the cold beer in my hand, I was sweating something fierce. Knowing that Jace was walking around in my shirt, smelling like me, was such a turn on. I casually dropped my head and sniffed my shoulder. Yup, I smelled like him, spicy and delicious. Swapping t-shirts was like marking each other. It was probably a simple mistake, but it didn't feel like one. It was fucking hot.

Don't get a boner.

Then I gave myself an eye roll. *You're acting like an idiot. Calm down.*

Easier said than done because my jeans were getting tighter by the second. And when Jace pulled his arm away from that eager stranger? I gulped down the rest of my beer in relief.

"Are you okay?" Jackson asked me. "You're not coming down with a bug, are you?"

"Uh, no. I just…uh…ate too much after the game. I need to sweat it off. Or, drink it off," I replied and held up the empty bottle. "Pass me another beer?"

Jackson gave me a quizzical glance, then handed me another drink.

I was about to take my first sip when Jace glanced over, and we locked eyes. Intense heat crawled up my neck and cheeks. I was burning up, like I'd been sitting in a sauna for hours. Jace licked his lips and all I could think about was the way he'd feasted on my ass. I'd never had a rim job before and riding his face was the hottest thing ever.

I took a long pull of beer and swallowed down my lust.

Until that stranger leaned into Jace again, distracting him. Unfortunately, I couldn't swallow down my temper.

"I'll be right back," I said to Jackson and set my beer aside.

I stalked across the room, every step ratcheting up my heartbeat, the rushing sound filling my head, until I saw nothing but Jace.

It was obvious that the guy flirting with Jace was drunk and handsy. Jace was doing his best to get the guy to back off, but whoever this asshat was, he wouldn't take a hint.

"Go find a room and sleep it off," I announced when I reached them.

"Who the fuck're you?" the stranger hissed, glaring up at me.

"It doesn't matter who I am," I barked, staring down at him. "Clearly, Jace doesn't want you touching him. Back off."

Jace scowled at me. "I can handle this, fuck you very much."

"Really? It doesn't seem that way," I bit out. "He's got his hand on your arm and my…I mean, *your* t-shirt is wet thanks to his drunken accident."

"You guys are t-talk…t-talking too much," the stranger slurred. "I wanna get laid. Did you hear me? I came all the way from U of V, and I want to get laid. C-come on, Jace, fuck me. Come on."

Jace wrenched his arm away and shook his head.

"I told you, I'm not interested, Lorquin," Jace replied. "You're drunk."

"Lorquin?" I chuckled.

"You're one to talk about names, *Axel*," Jace snarked.

"Right back at you, *Jace*," I returned.

"But—" Lorquin interrupted.

"No!" Jace and I yelled at the same time.

"W-wait a minute," Lorquin tapped my arm. "Axel? A-Axel Lund? The forward? S-so hot. I know you."

"I don't think so," I bit out.

I'd never met this guy in my life.

"Ha!" Lorquin smacked his forehead. "Ow, that hurt."

"Get lost," I repeated.

"No! I mean, I d-don't know *you*. But, I know of you. And Jace here. That's why I want to fuck him. Because of P-Pearson. Preston. Too many p's in that stupid fucking name," he mumbled. "What was I saying?"

"What are you talking about?"

"Preston. My f-father, Luke Bane, works with his father. They're like this." Lorquin tried to cross his fingers, several times, but he didn't succeed.

If I wasn't in such a bad mood I'd laugh my ass off because Jesus, this guy needed to sober up. Still, the mention of Preston certainly had my attention.

"Preston's a lying l-little shit. Did you know that? He uses people and then dumps them," Lorquin muttered and sneered at Jace. "Like Jace here. He f-fucked you up good, didn't he? P-Preston told me you were an easy bitch to c-control. I thought you'd be a sure thing when I got here. Why aren't you easy for me?"

"Shut the fuck up and leave him alone," I snapped as I put myself between him and Jace. "Better yet, get out of this house. Now."

Lorquin was probably harmless but the vicious way he talked about Jace had me more than concerned. He needed to get gone.

"This p-party sucks."

"Then you better leave," I insisted.

Lorquin finally took the hint and fucked off, leaving me and Jace alone. Or, as alone as we could get in a packed party room.

I turned around and met Jace's furious gaze head-on.

"What the hell was that?" Jace asked, pushing a hand to my chest.

"That was me saving you from that asshole."

"It was under control."

"You kept trying to back away." I stepped closer, and Jace didn't budge. "He was touching you and not taking the hint. And what he said about you and Preston—"

Jace's eyes darkened.

"Oh, so now you believe me?" Jace scoffed. "And I was dealing with it. I don't need you to rescue me."

"I didn't like it," I bit out.

"Him insulting me?" Jace asked. "Or coming on to me?"

"Him," I snapped. "Both."

Shit.

"I need another beer," I groused and made to move away.

Jace gripped my—his—t-shirt tightly in his fist and pulled me in closer.

"Oh no," Jace hissed. "You can't just say something like that and walk away."

I bit my lower lip in frustration. Jace was so close, his wicked lips right there, and there was nothing I could do about it. I wanted to kiss the fuck out of him, and I didn't want to stop.

"But you can. Right?" I scoffed, irritated and frustrated. "There's nothing going on here. Nothing at all."

"You're a liar," Jace declared, leaning in until his breath teased my ear. "And for once, I'd say we're two of a kind."

"What?"

"Back away, Ax, or swear to God, I'll kiss you right here, right now. And I know neither of us is ready for that. You, especially."

No. No, I wasn't. I think?

But instead of leaving, I reached up and grabbed his biceps, sparks of electricity racing over my skin.

"Ax."

I didn't notice—or care—that people nearby were staring at us. Not that anyone would remember much of anything given the amount of alcohol being consumed.

"Break it up, Hot n' Honey."

Fucking Ethan. How'd he get the sneak on us?

"There's nothing to break up," Jace replied, his voice hoarse.

"You gonna let go of him, Axel, or do I have to intervene?" Ethan asked with one raised eyebrow.

I dropped my hands and shoved them in my pockets.

"We were just having a conversation."

"Seemed pretty intense for a chat," Ethan remarked as he studied Jace and then me.

"Like Jace said—" I started.

"It's nothing?" Ethan interrupted with a laugh. "You're so full of shit."

"Ethan," Jace warned.

"Alright, I'll butt out. For now." Ethan shook his head. "Anyway, I came over here for a different reason. Hailey wants to get to know Axel."

"What?" Jace snapped.

"What's the problem?" Ethan smirked. "You're not dating her and Axel's obviously in desperate need of distraction. Maybe then he'll cool off."

I glanced at Jace, and the scowl I got in return? I wasn't the only one who needed cooling off.

"Uh, no thanks," I replied quickly. "Like I said in the locker room, I'm not interested."

"Come on, man, live a little," Ethan encouraged. "She's on the dance floor, join us."

Ethan wasn't going to let it go.

"One dance, but that's it," I offered to Ethan and then turned to Jace. "Are you coming with us?"

Jace crossed his arms and shook his head, his mouth pursed in a sulky pout. Fuck, I wanted to taste him so bad.

"Yes," Ethan encouraged. "Let's go, Jace. The rest of the team are already out there."

"I'm going to grab a drink first," Jace bit out. "I'll meet you shortly."

He stalked off and I followed Ethan through the maze of students. Dane and Jackson, as well as Finn, Colin, Silas, Kayden, and Maddox, were dancing in the center of the room, leading the crowd in singing Rush. I wasn't a great dancer by any means, but I had enough beer in my veins to let loose. And I freaking *needed* to let loose.

Until a pair of arms grabbed me from behind, sliding around my waist.

Arms that didn't belong to Jace.

I whirled around to find Hailey looking up at me with a wide smile and glassy green eyes. She wore tight black jeans that hugged her curvaceous hips, and a red v-neck sweater that revealed the swell of her tits.

"Nice moves," she teased and squeezed tighter.

I took a step back, untangling myself.

"I do okay," I shrugged.

"More than okay," she replied, giving me a heated once-over. "Don't be shy, dance with me."

"Sorry," I muttered, pointing over my shoulder. "I've gotta stick with my teammates."

It was a lame excuse, but I didn't care. I wasn't interested in her. It would be so much easier if I was.

"Come on," she urged and stepped closer. "You know you want to."

No, I really didn't.

"Sorry, I'm not feeling it. But I appreciate the interest."

Her smile vanished.

"Your loss," she snapped and took off into the crowd.

I was about to turn back to the guys when another set of hands reached for me, gripping my hips tightly. Only, I didn't need to turn around this time to know who was touching me.

And I didn't have any desire to move away from Jace.

Instead, I rocked my hips to the heavy beat of the music, and Jace did the same, until we were moving in perfect unison. His hot breath teased my neck, making me shiver, and I bit back a groan. He smelled like vanilla and musk and the scent drove me crazy. I felt every inch of his long, hard body as he rubbed against me, the pulse of primal energy flaring between us.

Why him? Why, of all people, did it have to be Jace?

Flashbacks of the night hit me; every kiss, every moan, until I wasn't just rocking to the music, I was rocking another hard-on. It was too good to stop.

"Look who's kissed and made up!" Ethan shouted.

I turned my head at the sound of Ethan's voice to find our teammates staring at us in amusement. Not that me and Jace dancing with each other was odd or anything. Everyone was packed into the space, crowded up against each other, it's not like we were the only ones. Although, most of the guys weren't grinding against each other. Only the couples, like Kayden and Maddox, and Dane and Jackson, were doing that.

Shit.

Instead of pulling away, Jace laughed and slapped my ass.

"Hey!" I glared over my shoulder.

"Told you he'd come around!" Jace called back to Ethan.

I elbowed Jace and stepped away from temptation. "Not quite."

"I think Hot's melted Honey," Ethan quipped. "Or, maybe it's the other way around."

"It's about fucking time!" Kayden yelled and crowded into us, slinging one arm around my neck and his other around Jace. "I'm so happy you guys are finally getting along."

Getting along? That was one way to put it.

CHAPTER 23

JACE

woke up the next morning—afternoon—in my bedroom, but on the covers instead of under them, and alone. Still, I could smell Axel, like he was right here beside me. I glanced down with bleary eyes and noticed the gray, stained t-shirt I was wearing. His shirt. Oh God.

Don't panic.

Maybe Axel and I hadn't done anything. Maybe last night was all a bizzarro dream.

I slowly got up, stretched, and headed for the bathroom to take a piss.

When I glanced at my reflection in the mirror, I spotted the huge hickey on my neck and stopped short. Not a dream. *Very fucking real.* I ran a finger over the mark, remembering how sexy it felt when Axel sucked my skin.

Oh God, this was bad. Like, next-level stupid.

And what was with all that ridiculously possessive behavior at the party? From him and from me. Axel wasn't happy about Lorquin coming on to me, but I wasn't happy watching Hailey flirt with him either. In fact, I was downright furious at the possibility they'd hook up. Why should I care?

Axel and I were, well, we were nothing to each other. Barely teammates, if that. Sort of friends?

Jesus Christ, I was totally out of my depth.

"What the fuck are you doing?" I said out loud to myself.

Fucking around with my teammate was bad enough, but Axel? Not that I had anything to worry about, it was done. He probably wanted to forget it ever happened. That was fine with me.

Or, not fine, if my morning wood was any indication.

After taking care of business—and ignoring my hard-on— I stripped out of my jeans and Axel's t-shirt, hopped in the shower, and scrubbed away any remaining traces of him. Bad enough I'd worn his shirt to the party. Thank God no one realized. And while our teammates teased us about dancing together, I played it off like we'd come to a stalemate, and it was all in good fun. Most of the guys would be too drunk to remember details anyway.

Fun. Right. That wasn't the word I'd use to describe the way I'd grinded against Axel. More like necessity, something primal, a need that I couldn't ignore.

A need that should've been sated.

But I knew that if it weren't for our teammates dragging us into a host of drinking games, Axel and I probably would've ended up having sex in one of the rooms of that frat house. Or, back here in my room. Which reeked of stale cum. Part of me wanted to revel in the musky scent, but the smarter part told me I had to get cleaning, now. Get rid of any traces that he'd ever been here or that sex had happened.

Forget about it. Move on.

A flickering memory hit me.

Axel and I stumbling home to the dorm with the rest of the guys, laughing and joking around, too drunk to be worried about anything but feeling good. But then, I was suddenly standing in the hallway, and Axel was inside the elevator, and we faced off once again. We stared at each other so intently that I was sure I was going to combust right there. I started to take a step towards him, but the doors closed shut in my face.

He was gone and I was alone.

The way it was supposed to be. Nothing good would've happened if I'd followed him.

Still, I couldn't remember the last time I wanted to chase after anyone. Try never. More warnings echoed in my head but with my hangover, I could barely hear them.

Self-recrimination, like cleaning, would have to come later.

After showering, I was hit with a wave of nausea, so I downed a bottle of electrolyte water and ate two protein bars. Feeling better, I headed for the gym, determined to flush out the remaining alcohol—and these crazy feelings for Axel— from my system.

The gym was quiet for a Saturday afternoon, but it suited me fine. I put my earbuds in, blasted Linkin Park, and did my weight routine.

An hour later, sweaty but feeling better, I took another shower and headed for the library to get some studying done. I finished a project outline for my biology class and was about to launch into a report for my practicum when my phone buzzed.

Dane: You awake yet?

Jace: LOL, for hours. Been to the gym and now the library. You?

Dane: Studying with Jackson.

Jace: So, not studying?

Dane: Not at all, LOL. but it's Saturday, and we only have one day a week to spend together.

Jace: Um, you guys share a room. And you were together last night.

Dane: Yeah, but with school, practice, and games, we're both busy. It's hard to find time just us two.

Jace: Then stop texting me and go back to your boyfriend.

Dane: I will. I just needed you to confirm that hell didn't freeze over first.

Jace: What??

Dane: You and Axel last night, dancing at the party. What the fuck was that?

Jace: Just what I said.

Dane: Why does that confirmation scare me?

Jace: Nothing to be scared about, we're fine.

Dane: Maybe it was the alcohol, but you were all over him, J, and he was pretty comfortable in your space. Call me crazy, but...

Jace: It was the alcohol. We were dancing and having fun. Nothing to worry about, Captain. At ease.

Dane: If anything changes...

Jace: You'll be the first to know.

Eventually I'd tell Dane what happened with me and Axel but not now. It didn't have any impact on me or the game, so why upset him? He was already stressed out with the pressure on our team as we headed into the semi-finals.

My phone buzzed again, and I shook my head. I loved my friend dearly, but he needed to relax. Only, when I stared at the message, it wasn't from Dane. It wasn't from any of my friends.

It was Preston.

Axel

'Back away, Ax, or swear to God, I'll kiss you right here, right now. And I know neither of us is ready for that. You, especially.'

I didn't care. I wanted him to kiss me.

Jace.

I reached out for him, but realized, too late, that there was nothing around me but cold bedsheets.

Idiot. You were dreaming.

Shit. I rubbed a hand over my face, trying to wake up, and then reached for my phone. Last night, after leaving the party, I'd come back to my room, alone. Jace was downstairs in his room. Safe and sound, and yeah, the farther he was away from me, the safer we'd both be.

I had a hangover, but it served me right. It hit me all at once; I was dizzy, nauseous, and my temples pulsed with a wicked headache. It was nothing that greasy food and a gallon of water wouldn't fix. Then again, it wasn't just the hangover that was making me feel out of sorts. It was the reality of what I'd done.

Not just fooling around with Jace but acting territorial about him. I could only hope that his hangover was worse than mine and that he'd remember none of what happened.

My phone began to ring and really, who the fuck was calling me on a Saturday morning (afternoon)?

When I saw the name on the screen, the nausea in my stomach had me swallowing down bile.

"Lo?" I answered, my voice hoarse with sleep.

"Axel, it's about goddamn time you finally answered your phone. I've been calling all morning."

I quelled at the sound of my mother's raspy voice.

"How can I help you?" I asked calmly even though I was anything but.

She didn't text or call me, ever, unless she needed something or wanted to remind me what a disappointment I was. Either way, it was never good. Never.

"I understand your team has a game in Albany in three weeks, against Grainger College," she continued.

"How—" I muttered as I rubbed my eyes. "How did you know that?"

"We live in a college town, Axel. I'm calling to tell you that your father and I will be there. After your game, we need to talk."

"Can't," I grumbled, reaching for my pill case and the bottle of water on my nightstand. I popped my meds and took a gulp of water. "Team dinner. No exceptions. Sorry."

"You'll make time after the game or we're coming to Vermont. Your choice."

I knew my mother and her singular determination. There was no point in arguing. I sighed and ran a hand over my scruff. "Fine. I can give you ten minutes after the game. We'll meet in the lobby."

"That works," she replied briskly. "Have you talked to Jonas lately?"

"You mean, did he call me asking for money? Yes, he did. And yeah, I gave it to him."

"Good. That's good," I heard a sigh of relief on the other end of the line. "Your father and I are a bit short of cash this month."

"This month?" I scoffed. "Try again."

"You really are an ungrateful little bitch, you know that?" she hissed.

I should've been surprised at the name calling, but unfortunately, I wasn't.

"I know a lot more than you realize," I warned her. "Is there anything else?"

"Your father—"

"Which one?" I snarked.

"Your father," she continued, ignoring my remark. "Has an important deal closing soon. With a family-owned company called Fullman. They're based in the midwest and very conservative. They believe in old-fashioned family values. It's important to them and to us."

"You're joking right?" I barked out a laugh. "Family values, my ass. Try again."

"I don't need your opinion, Axel. I'm calling to give you a heads-up. We need this deal to close. We need it. So, should you be approached by anyone, a journalist for example, you keep your mouth shut, understood? And for fuck's sake, don't create any college scandals."

"First off, journalists don't ever approach me. Our family isn't that important, it's just your ego talking. And I'm not the one who's in danger of causing a scandal, like being arrested for possession, or caught out for fucking someone's husband."

"I'm warning you to keep quiet," she replied sharply. "And Jonas is under control. He'll be fine. As long as he has the drugs that he needs, he'll be fine."

I couldn't take any more of this conversation.

"I have to go."

"Have you heard from Preston lately?" she asked.

The mention of his name made my stomach roil again.

"No, why?"

"Just curious."

She wouldn't have mentioned him for no reason. But I was too tired to care at this point. And if she wasn't going to offer any more details, I didn't give a fuck. I had to call him back anyway. I wanted to hear what Preston had to say and if he'd continue to lie to me, because yes, I was certain now that he'd been lying. That wasn't just my dick talking. The uneasy feeling I'd had recently about Preston only grew stronger as the distance between us grew wider.

"I have to go," I repeated and hung up.

I wanted to scream, loudly, after that conversation but settled for a cigarette instead. I wasn't supposed to smoke in my room, so I opened a window and figured it didn't count. When my anxiety calmed and my head started to clear, I stalked to the bathroom to rinse the tobacco from my breath, showered, and shaved.

An hour later, I headed for the cafeteria for breakfast and lunch, ate my weight in eggs, roasted chicken, and potatoes, and downed two iced coffees. Feeling better, but not great, I picked up my phone and texted Jace. Maybe he wanted to avoid me now, but we weren't going to go down that road again.

Axel: Are you busy?

Jace: I'm at the library.

Axel: Can I meet you there?

Jace: Sure. Third floor, I'm at a table near the front windows.

Axel: See you soon.

I thought about that guy at the party, Lorquin, and what he said about Preston. It confirmed what my gut was telling me.

I sent another text, this one to Preston.

Axel: I know the truth, but I want to hear it from you. Call me ASAP.

CHAPTER 24

JACE

looked around the third floor for the hundredth time, waiting for Axel to arrive. I was so nervous I kept tapping my stylus on the table, until another student gave me a warning glare.

"Sorry," I whispered.

This wasn't like me. It was that damn text from Preston. I'd refused to even look at it, blocking him as soon as I saw his name. Fucker.

"Hey."

I jumped, turning around to find Axel standing with his backpack in hand, a sullen look on his face. Or, was he sad? He looked as upset as I felt.

"What's wrong?" I asked.

He stared at me, silent for a beat. "Never mind me, what's up with you? You look like you've seen a ghost. Did something happen?"

"Preston texted me," I blurted out.

"What?" Axel shouted and students turned to stare at him. "Sorry."

He sat down beside me and pulled his chair in close. "What did he say?"

"I don't know. I didn't want to read it, so I just blocked him. I can't—" I whispered, my hands shaking. "I can't go there."

Axel took hold of my right hand, placing it on his thigh. He was so fucking warm, and the icy chill that had wracked my body finally calmed.

"When I saw his name, I freaked out," I admitted. "I ran for the bathroom but—"

"You didn't?"

I shook my head. "I'm okay. I talked myself out of it."

"I told him to call me," Axel muttered.

"Oh."

That made me feel nauseous again and I made to pull my hand away, but Axel gripped it tighter.

"I need to confront him about why he lied to me."

I nodded, too numb to say anything.

"I believe you, Jace."

The words were a relief and yet, I knew something was still holding him back.

"Do you?" I asked.

"Yes," Axel replied. "But, it'll take time for me to get over what Preston did. I thought he was my best friend. Even though we haven't talked much since high school, I thought that he was honest with me, and I really felt for him when he said that you hurt him. I can't believe I didn't see it. He was playing me all along and I should've known better."

"He's completely charming when he wants something. And very convincing."

"Like my parents," Axel hissed. "My mom called me today. She and my father are going to be at the game in Albany. They want to talk to me afterwards. I know it means nothing good."

"Oh fuck."

"Clusterfuck," Axel sighed and squeezed my hand. "Look, do you want to get out of here? I need to forget about that phone call. Let's go into town. We could play pool or something?"

"Yeah, I'd love that," I blurted out.

It sounded like we were going on a date.

No. No, no, no. Not a date. Don't even think of that word.

"I mean, sure, yeah, we can, uh, hang out," I replied, trying to stay cool but sounding anything but.

Axel nodded and stood up to his full height, but I was frozen to my chair, my face to his crotch. His jeans molded to that impressive bulge, and I remembered just how amazing he tasted. Fuck, my mouth watered.

Maybe Kayden was right. There was something about this library.

I quickly glanced up, but it was too late. Axel caught me.

"Pool?" he asked with a smirk.

"Huh?"

His chuckle was deep and sounded so dirty.

"My eyes are up here," he pointed to his face.

"They are. Dark as a midnight sky," I admitted as I stared up at him like a fool with his first crush.

Axel smiled slowly, and I'd never seen that look on him before. It had my heart kicking up triple time and my mouth aching to kiss him.

He rested one hand on the table and leaned forward. "That's sounds awfully poetic for a—"

"Hockey player?" I finished.

"Kinesiology student."

"I've got your poetry right here," I replied as I lifted my hand and kissed my middle finger.

He laughed, bending closer, brushing his mouth over my ear. "That's yet to be proven."

Ignoring his comment, and the hard-on it provoked, I gathered up my stuff and threw on my jacket.

"Let's see if you can finally beat me at something," I announced. "You play pool before?"

"All the time," he replied. "How about a friendly wager?"

"No cash, sorry."

Axel shook his head. "I didn't mean that. Let's make it more interesting. If I win, we go back to your room. If you win, we go back to my room."

I bit my lower lip, determined not to smile. *Don't do it. Don't do it.*

Fucking hell, I did it.

"So, we both win?"

"Exactly." Axel nodded. "We can work on the fundraiser, so we don't have to meet up on Monday."

All my sexy musings evaporated in a flash. Oh.

"Yeah, of course," I replied stiffly. "I mean, sure, that's fine."

Axel nudged me. "I'm meeting with my advisor Monday. I'm changing majors."

Oh.

"What did you decide on?" I asked, curious.

"Sports management. Seemed like the right fit. Finally. And, thankfully, some of my economic courses count as electives."

"That's awesome."

"I'm excited about it. When I'm too old to play, I'll become an agent and organize unruly hockey brats."

He looked right at me and gave a knowing smirk.

"You want to take on your first client? I know this incredibly talented, smoking hot player who's gonna make it big," I teased.

"Less talking, more walking," Axel replied as he motioned to the door. "And since I'll be playing in the professional league at the same time, sorry, I can't represent you. Maybe when you retire, though. I can get you ads for joint pain cream and shit like that."

I laughed at that idea. "Whatever pays the bills."

"Damn right."

We headed for the exit, but instead of catching the elevator, we took the stairs. Axel walked beside me, so close our hands brushed every time we took a step. I should've moved away but I didn't want to. Instead, I wanted to reach out and take his hand.

I want to hold his fucking hand. Jesus, I want to do that.

I stopped walking, too stunned by that realization.

Sex was one thing, holding hands meant…it meant… Oh God, no.

Axel paused on the next step down and turned around.

"Are you okay?" he said looking up at me.

No. I was far from okay.

"Yeah, just a bit lightheaded," I confessed, staring into his eyes. "Probably need to eat something."

"Is that all?"

I nodded, unable to say anything else.

We were alone in the dimly lit stairwell. The air between us grew heavier, thicker, until I was barely able to breathe. Axel slowly slid one hand up to my waist and then playfully tugged the belt loop on my jeans. Despite the layers of clothing, I swallowed hard when his fingers brushed my body.

"Gotta keep up your strength," he whispered. "Especially since we need to get a workout in later on."

A what?

"And I don't mean the gym."

He gave me a wicked grin and let go. When he started down the stairs again, he left me standing there with my mouth open and my dick hard.

Axel was flirting…with me?

"How come you're not freaked out?" I asked.

He stopped but didn't turn around, his broad back shifting as he shrugged. Axel ran a hand through his shaggy hair and then quickly glanced at me over his shoulder.

"About us?" he stated.

Why did I love the sound of that? *Us.* It was one tiny word and yet, it said everything. Everything and nothing. Because this wasn't a relationship. Even though a part of me now wished it kinda was.

"About what happened in my room," I corrected.

"Right," he replied and for a second, I swore I saw disappointment in his eyes. He blinked and his expression cleared. "Well, maybe it hasn't hit me yet. I don't know. If I'm bi, I'm bi. I'll figure it out."

I nodded, and I should've been relieved.

Only, I didn't want him to figure it out with anyone but me.

Axel

"Are you coming?" I asked Jace.

He stood in the stairwell staring at me like he was lost. Or confused. No, not that. He was probably just upset over Preston contacting him. Given what he'd told me, and their history, I wondered why Preston would try texting him at all. Why now? After two years? Something was off.

"Jace, are you alright?"

"Good, I'm good." He nodded and finally stepped down to meet me eye to eye. "Let's get out of here and find that pool hall."

"Got a thing for long sticks and hard balls?" I quipped.

"Fuck, yeah," Jace replied while giving me a lusty once-over. "I can chalk your cue with an expert hand."

"Cheesy, but cute," I chuckled as I stared into his eyes.

Cute? I don't think I've ever used that word in my life.

He stepped closer, our hips colliding, the tension that always simmered between us suddenly igniting.

Then he snuck his hand around to pat my ass. It wasn't nearly enough.

"If you're going to grab my ass, do it right," I insisted. "Don't tease."

"We're in public."

"We're in a stairwell, alone," I reminded him, feeling reckless, wanting more. "Touch me like you mean it."

I called his bluff because Jace gripped my ass cheeks in both hands and squeezed tight. Oh fuck, I loved that. A dirty moan rumbled out of my chest and the sound echoed in the silence. Then he pushed me against the wall, and I grunted when my back hit cement. Not because it hurt but because the manhandling caught me off guard. In the very best way. It was unexpected but incredibly hot. I'd never been wanted like this before. And having Jace take control was something I didn't know I needed. Until I did.

His wicked slapshot stunned goalies without warning.

And suddenly *I* was the one standing in the net.

It turned out, my feelings weren't complicated or confusing. And it wasn't just that I was bisexual.

It was simple. I needed *him*.

Reaching up, I cupped his face, sinking into pleasure as he kissed me languidly, deeply, so deep that we both groaned when his tongue tangled with mine. He tasted so good, sexy and sweet.

I didn't want to stop. *Please, fuck, never stop.*

"What are you doing to me?" I whispered.

"Me? It's you."

"It's us."

Jace shuddered, closing his eyes.

"Look at me," I demanded, and he blinked, meeting my gaze. "You like that. You want me. Only me."

"Stop talking," he growled, but I shook my head.

I couldn't help but smile at his put-out tone. I was right. My instincts were spot-on. He wanted me as badly as I wanted him. One night wasn't a fluke.

And when he took my lips again, hard, possessive, I knew it. But I needed to hear it.

"Jace."

A sudden bang interrupted the moment and had us jumping apart.

It was probably a door slamming shut on another floor, but still. Getting caught like this wasn't a smart idea. Not until we figured out what the fuck we were doing.

"Let's get out of here," Jace whispered as he licked his lips. "I think we need a cool down."

It took every ounce of control I had to stay calm and not reach for him. But he was right.

"You still want to play pool?" I asked, and he nodded. "Loser buys dinner?"

"I'm not a cheap date," he quipped.

I swatted his ass in retaliation and took off running down the rest of the stairs.

CHAPTER 25

AXEL

"Is this your first time here?"

Someone was talking to me. I think?

I was busy watching Jace as he bent over the pool table, setting up the break shot. The sight of his sexy ass in those worn jeans was painfully distracting, so distracting that I didn't even notice the guy talking to me. Shit.

"You're Axel, right? Axel Lund. You play for the Cougars."

At the sound of my name, I turned around to find a tall, lanky guy with big green eyes, dark hair, and a shy smile greeting me. He looked familiar but I didn't know where from. One of my classes, maybe? He was leaning against the wall, a bottle of Dr. Pepper in hand, surveying the room.

Free Bull—yep, that was the name of the pool hall—was packed. With twelve tables on the first floor, and video arcade games on the second, the place was crawling with students and locals alike. There wasn't much nightlife in a small town like Sutton so I could see why a venue like this was popular. I hadn't explored the town much since I arrived, preferring to keep myself to myself. Growing up in a college town where everybody knew your business didn't exactly endear me to this one. Not at first. But, like the cockiest forward on my hockey team, Vermont was growing on me.

"That's right, and yeah, first time here," I replied. "Have we met before?"

"Not formally. I'm Archie Dunn," he offered his free hand. "I'm friends with Jackson. We row crew together."

"I thought you looked familiar," I said as we shook hands. "Were you in the crowd last night?"

He nodded and raised his bottle. "Hell of a game. You did Sutton proud."

"Thanks. It was a tough one. I used to play for Langston."

"Ouch. Well, you did good. Better than that. Your assist in that last period was phenomenal," Archie commented and glanced at Jace. "So, you're here with Jace."

"Yeah, we needed a break between hockey games," I explained, hoping like hell I didn't start blushing. "You know him?"

"Oh yeah," Archie replied, his face turning bright red.

Wait, was this one of Jace's hookups? My blood pressure went from normal to dangerously high in the blink of an eye.

"I mean, I'm friends with Hailey and Tyson," Archie added quickly. "They know him better than I do."

Hailey certainly did. And Tyson? Fuck me. It was another reminder that Jace could have, and did have, anyone he wanted. What was he doing here with me?

"Awesome," I bit out, not knowing what else to say but forcing my mouth to move. "Are you here alone?"

"My friends are upstairs in the game room. I came down to use the bathroom and grabbed another drink."

"You want to play with us?" I asked, trying to break the awkward tension.

"Thanks, I'd love to," Archie grinned and placed his drink aside.

I turned back to the table only to find Jace giving me the side- eye.

"What?" I mouthed.

He shook his head but stood up and offered his hand to Archie.

"Hey, Dunn, how are you?" Jace asked with a tense smile.

"I'm great. Finally got to meet Axel." Archie smiled at me. "Jackson's talked about your game, but watching you play on Friday was something else."

I wasn't comfortable with accolades and waved him off.

"I mean it." Archie leaned in. "But a guy like you, who can push it hard every period, you should be rowing, not skating. Ever think about it?"

I laughed out loud at that idea. No way.

"Me, sitting in that tiny boat? Pfft. I'd sink like a stone. Plus, pro hockey, dude. Come on."

"Why don't you stop by the club sometime and try it out?" Archie offered, running one hand through his thick hair. "I'd be happy to take you out. I mean, obviously in the spring, when the lake isn't frozen. And, after hockey's done, of course."

It sounded like fun and probably a good way to stay in shape in the offseason. I was about to reply when Jace slid up beside me, offering me a cue and a warning look.

"We'd love to," he replied.

"We?" I turned to him.

"I'm sure the rest of the team would love to try it out," Jace added with a polite smile. "We could make a day of it. Or, a weekend."

"Sure, why not?" Archie replied. "Jackson's been talking about getting the teams together for a while for a competition. That's a great idea."

"Super," Jace muttered and tapped my ass with the end of the pool cue. "You're up, Hot Shot."

"Okay, Honey," I teased him.

"Honey?" Archie's eyes widened.

"It's our team nicknames," I explained. "Thanks to Ethan Walker. I'm Hot and Jace is Honey."

Archie nodded in understanding and stared at me. "I can see it."

"Are we going to stand around or are we going to play?" Jace asked as he put a hand on my lower back.

Was he even aware of what he was doing?

I leaned into him, closer than I probably should've, closer than I did with any other teammate, and Jace finally met my gaze head- on. I should've stepped away, but I didn't. Was Archie staring at us? Did he know? I didn't care, or rather, all I could focus on was Jace. And his proprietary gesture was hot as hell. So hot that I couldn't move.

Not for anything.

————

An hour later, and the pool game was a wipeout. Archie won. I offered to buy him dinner too, but he declined and excused himself to meet up with his friends again.

While Archie headed back upstairs, Jace and I gathered our stuff to head out.

"Where do you want to eat?" I asked Jace.

"You still want to take me out?" he replied, his voice clipped.

He'd been tense the entire time we were playing pool. Which wasn't like him.

"Of course. Or, we can go back to the dorm and order in."

"Dorm," he replied curtly as we stepped outside.

"Everything okay?"

"Fine. Great. Just, you know, I'm hangry."

Snow crunched under our boots as we made our way down Main Street.

"Is that all?" I teased him, but I got no response.

"Don't push me, Ax. I'm like dry tinder at this point."

"I can handle it."

"I don't think you can. Or that I can." Jace stopped and stared at me. "I don't know what I'm…what we're doing. Or why you're…I mean, what even is this?"

"Not here," I replied and motioned for him to keep walking.

"In case someone overhears us?"

"That's not my concern."

"It should be. We're flirting in public, for fuck's sake," he hissed.

"I know," I admitted. "I can't help it."

"You?" he looked at me with incredulous eyes. "I'm the flirty one."

"Yeah, you are. You're also possessive. You didn't like Archie talking to me or asking me to join him at the rowing club."

"Oh really?"

I nodded, grinning at him, finally gaining the upper hand.

"You could've just grabbed that cue chalk and marked your initials on my ass," I quipped. "And for some reason, I more than like that idea. It's so fucking hot."

"Argh!" Jace held up both hands and then stormed off.

I caught up to him, reaching for his arm.

"What's wrong?" I asked.

"Don't make things worse."

"Fine," I replied. "Let's go back to your room and make it better."

He shook his head.

"I just…I can't handle this right now."

"Can't handle the fact that you want me?" I asked him. "Or that this is more than fucking?"

"Both."

His admission left me reeling.

"Alright," I replied calmly. "Can I at least walk you back to the dorm?"

He shook his head.

"If you so much as take one step closer, Ax," Jace licked his lips. "Just one step."

I wanted to, fuck, did I want to. But my instincts told me not to push him. Instead, I motioned to the campus.

"Go on. Go. I'll see you at practice," I muttered in resignation.

Jace hesitated for a second and then nodded. "See you then."

I shoved my hands in my pockets and watched Jace as he walked off. Every step grew fainter and yet the silence when he was finally out of sight, when I was alone, was really loud.

"Fuck."

Instead of feeling sorry for myself, I pulled out a smoke. Okay, smoking was feeling sorry for myself. And not what Coach would've wanted. Still, it was better than losing my temper.

After I'd sucked the cigarette down to the filter, I crushed it under my boot and wandered back to the dorm. I checked my phone and decided that now was as good a time as any. Preston still hadn't responded to my text, so I called him.

When he didn't answer, I left a simple message.

"Call me when you get this. We need to talk about Jace."

———

Jace

You did the right thing. You can't be losing your head over some guy.

Not just any guy. Axel.

I hardly slept Saturday night. Or, Sunday either. I could barely eat, never mind study. When I did eat, my anxiety reared up and so did my urges. Instead of wallowing in guilt because I wanted to binge and purge, I reached out to my therapist. We had an online session Sunday night. Afterwards, I felt better, but I was still unsettled.

All I could think about was Axel.

I hadn't heard or seen him since I'd walked away Saturday.

By Monday night, I found myself pacing my room and since I was about to lose it, I gave in.

Jace: How was your meeting with the advisor?

He surprised me by responding right away.

Axel: It's all set. I'm pumped.

Jace: That's great.

Ugh. I'm so lame.

Axel: Can I come down to your room?

My dick grew heavy in my jeans, but I ignored it.

Jace: Probably best that you don't.

Axel: Best for who? I need to see you. It's been two long fucking days.

Jace: I know.

Axel: I can't think about anything but wanting to touch you. I'm going crazy here. Don't tell me you don't feel the same.

Jace: Jesus, you're relentless.

Axel: You bet your sweet ass. And speaking of ass, I want to eat yours.

That sexy image had me shoving my free hand down my jeans so I could grab ahold of my hard cock.

With only one hand left to type, it took me forever to write out a message.

> Jace: You not freaking out is still freaking me out. You've never been with a guy before. Why are you all in?

There was a knock on my door.

> Jace: Hold on…

I placed my phone on the nightstand, took a few deep breaths to calm myself down, and stalked over to the door.

Without actually knowing who was on the other side of it, I knew. I just fucking knew.

When I opened the door, I wasn't in the least bit surprised, but I sure as shit was excited. Excited, and a bit scared. Okay, a lot scared. I couldn't get a handle on my emotions when it came to Axel, and for the first time in so long, I didn't want to.

He leaned against the doorjamb, in threadbare jeans and a Cougars t-shirt, his phone in one hand and a white paper bag in the other. His smile was indecent, and so was his sexy scruff. The playoff beard was here to stay, and it was a total turn on. But it was those fucking eyes of his that did me in. I couldn't resist them, or him. I was so fucked.

"Can I come in now?" he asked, his voice a husky murmur.

"What's that?" I pointed to the bag in his hand.

"It's a gift."

"For me?" I asked incredulously.

"Yes, for you. Is there anyone else here?" he replied, his lips curling in a wide smile. "Now let me in."

Axel was here. And he'd bought me something? A gift? What was he doing? And how was I going to resist?

"If you want me to beg, Jace, I'll do it. In fact, it's all I've thought about for the past two days. Getting down on my knees for you. I have no idea how to suck cock but—"

"Get in my room," I hissed and reached for his arm, pulling him inside.

His filthy chuckle was loud, and I shushed him, hoping my neighbors wouldn't hear. Not because I was embarrassed, but because I was protective.

Of him, and us. Whatever 'us' was.

"No one's in the hallway," he reassured me as he stepped into my room, placing his phone and the bag on the side table. "And even if they were, fuck 'em."

"You're pretty sure of yourself."

Axel came at me, walking me backwards with the same intensity he displayed on the ice, until my ass hit the wall, and I was surrounded by him.

"I'm sure." He cupped my face in his rough palm. "Are you?"

CHAPTER 26

JACE

"Yes," I admitted just before our lips met. "Want this. Fuck, I want you so badly."

"Then stop holding back," Axel whispered. "That's not you."

"But why—"

He gripped my hand and placed it over his crotch, and I moaned at the heat and hardness of his dick.

"You do this to me. You," Axel confessed. "No one's gotten me this excited before. Ever. Sex was fun, and I got off, but it wasn't like this. I didn't need it. But I need you."

"Axel," I moaned, and the words I'd been fighting suddenly poured out of me. "Fuck, I need you, too."

"Tell me."

"I need your dick in my ass. Your cum."

"Fuck, yes," he growled. "Jace."

One moment, Axel was staring down at me, the next, we were kissing like we'd never get the chance again. His lips were as hungry as mine, his tongue hot, desperate, his taste, God, I was addicted to his taste. I couldn't get enough, kissing him deeper, needing more. He pulled back for a second, only to reach behind his head so he could yank off his t-shirt. Then he reached for mine and we grappled, stumbling, frantically throwing off clothes until we staggered naked to my bed.

Thank fuck for small dorm rooms and beds within close reach.

"Making me wait two fucking days," Axel grumbled, and his grumpy tone made me smile.

Then he reached for me, grabbing my ass and hauling me up in his arms. Not many guys could carry me like that, and the move was sexy as fuck. I wrapped my legs around his waist, holding on for the ride. He kissed my neck, lower, near my collarbone, his rough beard teasing my skin as he sucked hard on the spot that drove me wild.

"Don't do it again."

His heated reprimand made my balls draw up tight.

"Jace?"

"What?" I asked him, painfully distracted by his touch.

"Did you hear me?"

Instead of replying, I attacked his lips, nipping them, plunging my tongue deep in his mouth.

"Promise me," he urged.

"Yes."

He sat down on my bed, and I straddled his lap, loving the feel of his hard, hairy body against mine.

"I know it's the last thing either of us expected," Axel continued and kissed me. "But it feels right. I can't explain it any other way."

"I know." I closed my eyes, fighting back my emotions.

"And don't second-guess me. I wouldn't be here if I didn't want to be."

My eyes flew open. "Stop saying all the right things."

"It's only right because it's you. You and me," he whispered. "And it's only you and me, right? I don't want to be with anyone else. And I sure as fuck won't share."

I nodded, swallowing past the lump in my throat. This

wasn't playing around or hooking up. And that made me nervous.

Winning and losing, that's what I knew.

But I didn't know the rules to this game. Or maybe, there were none.

If the ache in my chest was any indication, maybe I'd already lost. Then again, losing never felt this good.

I pushed at Axel's shoulders until he fell back against the mattress, looking up at me with heated possession in his eyes.

"No one else," he whispered. "I mean it, Jace."

I felt the same way about him. The pool game with Archie proved that.

"Do you see anyone else here?" I gave his words back to him.

I got a well-deserved swat on the ass for that comment.

"No Hailey," Axel started. "No Tyson, or—"

"No Archie," I insisted.

Axel's knowing grin was too much for me to resist.

I kissed my way down his chest, pausing at his dark pink nipples, laving, sucking, and licking, as Axel writhed and pleaded for more, gripping my hair and urging me on. I trailed teasing bites down his abs, and then over to those incredible v-lines, tracing one, then the other, getting closer and closer to his cock.

"Please," he whispered. "More."

"Reach into the nightstand and grab the lube," I whispered as I sucked on his skin and left a hickey on his hip.

There was a lot more swearing from Axel as I took the tip of his cock in my mouth and sucked hard. He let out a loud grunt and then I heard the drawer opening with a snap. Not long after, the bottle of lube was thrown onto the mattress, just within reach.

I gave his cock one last, teasing lick and then sat up, reaching for the lube and pouring a generous amount in my palm to warm it up. His hands slid over my ass cheeks, massaging them, then spreading me wide open.

When I made to reach behind me, he shook his head.

"No," Axel panted, and I stopped. "I mean, I want to… let me—"

I reached for one of his hands, slicking his fingers, then guided him to my ass.

"Take it slow and easy," I urged him.

"I want to make it good. " He licked his lips. "Show me."

His body tensed up, rigid, a tremor wracking his body. I spread my knees wider as I looked down into his eyes.

"Relax," I whispered. "It's already amazing because you're touching me."

He groaned and I pushed his fingers over my crease, down between my cheeks, until his callused fingertip caught on the rim of my hole.

"Yes, tease me just like that," I moaned as he continued to rub my hole, the pressure getting harder, firmer, until he pushed the tip of his finger inside of me.

"Fuck, fuck," Axel grunted, sweat dotting his face, a flush creeping up over his chest and neck.

"More, deeper," I encouraged him, my thighs beginning to quake.

God, he hadn't even started fucking me yet and already I was a mess. His dark blues were so intent, watching me with an incredulous expression. I looked down his body and his cock was red and hard, precum leaking all over his abs.

He pushed his finger inside me, slowly, nearly all the way in, and the burn was so good. I loved that bite of pain that prefaced all the pleasure.

"That's it, baby, fuck me like that. Don't stop," I grunted.

He sat up, reaching for me, mauling my lips while his finger screwed in and out of my hole.

"So fucking sexy," he moaned. "You're so hot and tight and fuck, Jace."

"That's right," I whispered. "Fuck me."

His finger drilled deeper, and I shuddered, holding on to his shoulders.

"More," I urged him. "Add another finger and fuck me."

Axel did just that and suddenly, I couldn't speak.

"Okay?" he asked.

I nodded quickly. Holy fucking hell. His fingers, like the rest of him, were thick, and two of them was…a lot. Then again, he had a monster cock, and I needed a good amount of prep for the pounding I craved.

"And another." I pushed back while he pushed in, stretching me wide with three fingers. "That's it."

He spat in his other hand and slipped it around the base of my cock. I groaned when he started stroking me off like a man possessed. Our movements were rough and desperate as I rocked my hips back and forth, chasing the fingers in my ass and on my cock, our lips smashing together, tongues dueling, straining closer and closer. I couldn't get close enough.

"I need your cock," I finally demanded when we came up for air. "I need it now."

"I don't want to use a condom," he admitted.

"I'm good if you are."

"I want to come in your ass. I want to mark what's mine."

"Oh God, Axel."

I nearly screamed when his fingers left my ass, because I was so damn empty. But not for long. Axel fumbled with the lube and while he slicked up his cock, I reached for him again, taking his lips, needing his kiss like I needed air.

"Ready?" he asked me.

I nodded, and he notched his dick to my hole.

I leaned back, taking him in, inch by inch, the pleasure-pain so intense I cried out his name. His fingers dug into my hips, hard, unrelenting. Just like his cock. My thighs trembled as I slowly sat down, until he was all the way inside me, and I was seated on his lap.

Nothing between us, and nowhere to hide.

"Oh God, yes," his strangled moan had me shivering. "I need…I need this. I need…you."

Face to face, this kind of fucking was intimate. Axel stared into my eyes with a look I couldn't quite believe. There was shock and pleasure and want all at once. I'm sure I wore the same expression because I felt all those things; like lightning striking me over and over, with every breath, every moan, and every movement.

I levered up and down, slowly at first, fucking myself on him. When his cock hit my prostate, I shuddered in his arms. He slid one big hand up my back, taking hold of my neck and pulling me in for a frantic kiss as we rutted against each other.

"Give it to me. Just like that," I moaned. "Axel."

"You want my cum?" he growled.

"Yes. Fuck, yes."

"Then take what's yours."

Axel

Jace rode me, hard, and I met him stroke for stroke, fucking into him in a frenzy, the mattress squeaking, the bed frame banging against the wall. My bare cock in his hot, tight ass was…I couldn't even think, let alone speak.

Unless it was dirty words and then they all came tumbling out of me.

"More, I need more," I whispered as I dug my fingers into his ass cheeks. "Gonna fill up this sweet ass with my cum. I'm the one inside you. Me. Only me."

"Yes, Ax. Fuck."

Jace's knees dug into the mattress as he rocked his hips, riding me like a man possessed.

If he was, so was I.

"That's right," I moaned. "Taking my cock so good,

Honey. So good."

"Ax." He threw his head back. "Baby."

Jace calling me 'baby' had my balls drawing up tight. I licked a path along his neck, loving the musky taste of his sweat, feeling his Adam's apple bob up and down as he swallowed, remembering how amazing it felt when he deep throated my cock. My lips tingled as I moved up to his jaw, the rough scruff teasing my skin. And then his lips. Those wicked fucking lips. Everything about sex with Jace was different. Intense. Primal. Passionate.

It was everything I wanted, even though I didn't know I could ever want this much.

The two of us were racing, but this time, towards each other. There was no competition.

Both of us were going to win and win big.

I slammed one hand on the mattress for greater leverage and pumped my hips hard, matching Jace's frantic rhythm as we grinded together, so close and yet, not close enough. My other hand snuck around his hip, reaching for his dick. I spat in my shaky hand and started stroking him the way I liked to get off. I had no idea if I was making it good for him, I just let my instincts guide me.

When he cried out my name and murmured encouraging words, I figured my rookie moves were enough. And then he leaned back and suddenly, my cock was even deeper inside of him. Fucking hell.

"I'm gonna come," he whispered in a raspy voice. "Come with me. Come inside me."

It was probably the worst hand job Jace ever received because with those words I completely lost control. My hand moved roughly, jerking hard, as my desperation to watch him come undone blew everything else away.

"Yes! Ax, yes!" he roared, and his cock jerked, hot cum lashing my hand.

His hole clenched around my dick so tight, so good, and

the climax that spiraled higher and higher inside of me, unleashed. I grabbed his ass with both hands, canting my hips, trying to get as deep inside him as I could get, feeling my balls draw up painfully tight and then...

Total pleasure. Complete annihilation.

"Jace!"

I screamed his name as I came long and hard, one relentless pulse after another, until I felt the heat of my cum surrounding my dick. The knowledge that I'd come in his ass made me shudder even harder. I'd never fucked bareback before. Never had anal sex either, but damn, had I been missing out. Still, it wasn't just that, it was Jace. When he and I came together, fucking hell, talk about explosive. And knowing that my cum was inside of Jace?

"Oh God," Jace panted, his hips finally slowing down. "That was...I need a minute. Or, like, a couple of days."

I chuckled, wrapping him up tight in my arms, burying my face in his neck and smiling against his skin when he let out a throaty murmur of pleasure. I rolled him over, our legs tangled up, until his back hit the mattress, and I could stare down at his face. His high cheekbones flushed a gorgeous shade of pink, his lips swollen from my kisses. I couldn't resist and kissed him again, gently nipping his lips until he retaliated, and we ate at each other's mouths like we hadn't just fucked our brains out.

Slowly, I eased my softening cock out of him and saw the proof that he was mine. But none of my previous experience with sex prepared me for the sight of my cum leaking out of his hole. It was dirty and sexy, and I reached down, touching him, rubbing the cum into his skin. He smelled like me, and I fucking loved it.

"So hot," I admitted when I met his eyes. "You taking my cock like that and now my cum's inside you? Fuck, Jace."

My cock stirred, ready for the second round. No time-out required.

"Ax," Jace whispered as he stared at me.

I took his mouth in a hard kiss, not giving him any room to pause. I didn't want to let go of him or these wild feelings rattling inside of me. I wanted to stay locked up in him, head to toe, smelling of our sweat and cum.

"What did you get me?" he finally asked after I let him come up for air.

"Go find out."

"I will. If you let me go," he quipped and playfully bit my shoulder.

I swatted his ass and reluctantly did just that. Jace padded over to the table, and I all but swallowed my tongue at the vision of his tight ass, reddened from my hands, with streaks of cum dripping down his thighs. My cum. Jesus.

Jace opened the bag and gave a husky laugh.

"Wild honey," he chuckled as he pulled the jar out of the bag.

"That's right."

He gave me a knowing smirk and stalked back over to the bed with said jar in hand. I spread my legs to welcome him and when he slid between them, fuck, I didn't think I could get that hard again, but it was happening. Jace opened the lid, slowly tilting the jar, and a stream of golden liquid dripped over my abs. Abs that were covered in his cum, and now, even stickier.

Jace put the jar aside, leaned down, and made a provocative show of sticking his tongue out. He licked the honey—and his cum—off my body, one teasing stroke at a time, and slicked that wicked tongue over his lips, humming softly.

I'd never felt so dirty and so good.

"Mmm, you are fucking delicious," he moaned.

"Kiss me."

Jace bent his head and kissed my stomach, lower…

"Not what I…I—" I moaned as my voice trailed off, too distracted by his mouth to remember what I was saying.

"Yes?" he asked me.

Slowly, he crawled up my body, dropping kisses along the way, every touch making me groan, until he reached my mouth.

"Jace, please. Please kiss me."

I didn't recognize the neediness in my voice, but I didn't care how I sounded. I was that desperate for him. He leaned in and brushed his lips over mine, but it was just a tease, not nearly enough.

"Thank you," he whispered.

"For what?"

"For tonight. For the gift."

"I'm the one who should be thanking you," I admitted and reached for the jar. "Now let me do just that."

CHAPTER 27
AXEL

The bus ride from Sutton to Albany took three and a half hours and I slept through all of it.

Which wasn't my norm, but then again, nothing about my life lately was the usual.

The past several weeks were frenetic and I'm not talking about classes and hockey practice. Jace and I stole away together every spare moment we could. Frotting was my new favorite activity. His room, my room, it didn't matter. Our coming together was always heady and desperate, like if we didn't get our hands on each other, we'd both spontaneously combust. And we did. Every. Fucking. Time.

And when we weren't together, I was thinking about him.

Replaying every kiss, and every conversation.

Except for yesterday and today. We needed to rest up for the game and that meant no sex. Not even jerking off. To avoid temptation, we agreed that there would be no texting, no talking, no seeing each other, period.

But, by the time Friday rolled around, I was out of my

mind, so excited to see Jace that I was like an eager kid meeting his hockey idol for the first time.

Okay, I caved and texted him.

> Axel: Can't wait until after our game tonight. Your cock is mine.

Then I realized I'd sent the text, by accident, to my brother Jonas. So much for being careful. I quickly changed Jace's contact name to Honey so I wouldn't make that mistake again.

> Jonas: Didn't know you were into fucking guys. Send me two grand or I talk.

> Axel: You'll talk? What is this, a bad movie? Fuck off.

Even if Jonas told my parents, I wasn't worried. They lived in denial about everything. And what could they do? Threaten me? With what? I guess I'd find out tonight since they were supposed to be attending this game. I still wasn't convinced they'd show up.

I pushed thoughts of my family out of my mind, where they belonged.

And I also ignored my urge to text Jace, shoving my phone back into my pocket.

Jace and I didn't put a formal name to what we were doing, but we weren't doing it with anyone else. I hadn't just spoken in the heat of the moment; I wasn't sharing him. And he felt the same. But we were keeping our boyfriend status quiet for now. *Boyfriend.* The word made me shiver, in the very best way. *Lover* made me roll my eyes, and *hookup* or *fuck buddy* wasn't enough. When the urge for endearments struck —and when they did, hell, I didn't even recognize myself—I settled for *Honey.* It suited him, and the guys on the team wouldn't question me if I blurted it out. The bigger part of me worried that if I told Jace that I wanted to be boyfriend official in front of the rest of the team, I'd scare him off. And probably myself as well. Both of us were tentative in this, uncertain like we never were on the ice.

And thinking about coming out to our teammates had me sweating up a storm. When it was just the two of us, it was easy to envision, it was all good. But when I stepped out of his room, the 'what- if's bombarded me. I didn't like the feeling. Then I reminded myself that there was time for me to figure stuff out. And, until we both felt secure in where this relationship was headed, it was better to let things go unsaid. There was a lot of pressure on both of us, in hockey and in school, and distractions had consequences. Secrets had a way of rising to the surface too, if we weren't careful.

With that in mind, I boarded the bus, determined to be cool and not let my emotions get the better of me.

Head in the game.

Jace was already on board, sitting at the back of the bus, next to Dane. He was wearing his baseball cap, backwards of course, his dark curls peeking out from under the band, and I noticed that his beard was growing in thick. I loved the way that scruff felt as he rubbed it over my skin. Fuck, he was gorgeous, and I let myself steal a glance. My feet wanted to carry me straight to him, but I resisted. It felt like months, never mind days, had separated us. I gripped my bag so tight I was in danger of hurting my hand. Not smart.

Instead of doing something stupid, like reaching for him, I headed down the aisle until I spotted an empty seat in the middle. It was the one beside Ethan, the one no one wanted. Ethan had his headphones on and was singing out loud. Badly. I hoped hockey worked out for him, because he sure as fuck couldn't make a career out of singing.

I nodded to my teammates, passing Silas and Finn, and then Kayden and Maddox.

"Why're you smiling so hard?" Silas asked me. "Or at all."

I gave him my favorite finger in response.

"You finally got laid," Finn blurted out.

"Who got laid?!" Ethan yelled and looked around.

He was really, really loud. And how the fuck had Ethan heard that comment with his headphones on? I could feel the eyes of everyone on the bus staring at me.

"Axel," Silas announced and smirked at me. "Don't bother to deny it. You've lost that resting asshole face."

"You mean the one I borrowed from you?"

This time, it was Silas's turn to give me the middle finger.

"Deets! Deets!" Ethan urged as he pulled off his headphones.

I shook my head. "Fuck off."

"Was it Hailey?" Ethan asked.

"Nope," I replied and shoved my bag into the overhead bin. "Now shut it, I need to rest."

Once my ass hit the seat, my nerves crashed, and I passed out. But even in sleep, Jace wasn't far from my mind. I dreamed about him, about the two of us, and that was as startling as the feelings he'd sparked. And from someone who used to take or leave sex, and who also avoided relationships, I was now officially obsessed.

It wasn't just sex, though, and that's what had me hung up. We talked about our hockey dreams and living in a big city one day, and all the places we'd travel to. We talked late into the night, and then I'd sneak out of his room—or him from mine. And when I thought about the way we kissed, and how I couldn't ever get close enough to him, it almost didn't seem real.

For the first time in forever, I was close to someone. Someone who didn't care that I was a Lund. It appeared that Jace wanted me for me. Why? What did he see in me? Or was this just sex for him? Sex and maybe friendship too. I didn't know, and though it was tough to admit, I was too scared to ask. Our relationship—if it was a relationship—was exhilarating and unnerving in equal measure.

"Axel! Wake up! Come on, we have a game to play."

What? Didn't we just leave Sutton?

I blinked and there was our captain, standing beside my seat, staring down at me with concern. Glancing around, I realized the bus was empty and we were the only two on board. I swiped a hand over my face.

"Already?" I murmured.

"Already? Dude, we had to listen to you snore for over three hours."

"Haha," I replied and stood up, stretching.

"I'm not joking. Thank God I don't have to room with you," Dane quipped and patted my shoulder. "You ready for tonight?"

"Fuck, yes," I insisted. "I'm so ready to do this."

Dane chuckled. "That's what I want to hear."

"Why isn't Jace...I mean—" I coughed and cleared my throat. "Jace didn't wait for you?"

"He was too fired up. He was halfway to the door before the bus even came to a stop, so I let him go. We'll catch up in the locker room."

I nodded and reached for my bag, following Dane off the bus. Snow was coming down fast and heavy, and the temperature in Albany was even chillier than Vermont. Or maybe that was just me. I had the cold sweats thinking about my parents showing up to the game tonight.

"I'm happy to see Jace like that. He's always got the drive, the fire, but lately I've been worried. And I've barely talked to him the past few weeks. He's been quieter than usual. Any issues that I should know about?" Dane asked me with a pointed look.

"Nope," I replied, not meeting his gaze. Would he see the truth there? I didn't want to take that chance. "Did you see any problems at practice?"

"No, I didn't," he replied. "Just the opposite. Which is great but also, surprising. I guess you two finally figured your shit out and made up?"

I slipped on an icy patch of sidewalk, but thankfully, managed to stay upright and uninjured.

"In a manner of speaking," I muttered, shaking off my clumsiness, and keeping my head down.

I could feel Dane's gaze on me, but I ignored it. Our captain was a smart guy. Smart and perceptive. He knew his friend. But Jace obviously hadn't told him anything about us. Which should've been a relief. No one knew, so there was no problem. So, why did I suddenly feel like crap?

"Awesome," Dane continued. "Because I think that you two, as partners, are unstoppable."

Partners? My gaze flew to Dane.

"What?"

"You know what I mean. Playing off each other, instead of against one another. Your body language. The unspoken connection between you. The power, the passion. It's all there."

It certainly was.

Jace

I sat on one of the wooden benches in the visitor locker room, staring at the skates in my hands like I didn't know what they were or how to put them on. It was game-day nerves times a thousand. But now wasn't the time for a crisis.

Still, that bus trip from Sutton felt like *the* longest ride of my life. I was hyped for the game but more than that, hyped to see Axel. Even though we'd agreed to no contact until the game, it was hard to stay away.

Was he feeling the same? Or was I the only one with my dick hanging out and my heart not far behind? Not that my dick was *actually* hanging out, it was safely hidden by my cup.

But my heart? That poor sucker had no protection.

So, when Axel boarded the bus, I didn't get up or go near him. But then he ignored me, sat down, and passed out cold, and I thought what the fuck? Wasn't he affected by what had happened between us? Or was he done? No, not if his recent texts were any indication. But was I the only one here who was far gone? I was fixated and frustrated with myself. It was one guy. It was sex. Really hot, intense, incredible sex. And laughter. Teasing. Talking. Bickering too, of course. Shit. I'd never been so wound up over anyone, not even Preston.

Looking back, I realized that my relationship in high school was all about infatuation. I wanted to feel like I mattered, and not just as a friend. And if someone as charismatic as Preston wanted me, it was about my ego too. It certainly wasn't love.

But Axel? He was different. Or, I was different with him.

For some crazy reason, I needed him, and I didn't need anyone. Not outside of my aunt and my friends, that is. And the strange thing was, it seemed like he needed me too. There were a lot of layers to Axel Lund and more than met the eye. He was just as obsessed with hockey and winning as I was. He was confident, for the most part, but also, quietly self-conscious. Like when he talked about his grades or his family, I could hear his self-doubt. Physically, Axel was strong and ready to take his playing to the next level, but mentally, he struggled. All players do, but as to how much it affects their game, well, I was reasonably certain that *that* was the reason why Coach picked me for center line.

Axel was also stubborn, quick to return my sass, and surprisingly sweet.

Sweet and insatiable. Hot n' Honey all the way.

Still, being in a situationship with my teammate reminded me of that moment just before a bench-clearing brawl, when the tension ignites, and the players lose their cool. Chaos was about to erupt, and I had a feeling that my heart would be the first one hit. Not that I ever let fear stop me. Not when it came to hockey or anything else. I'd rather feel everything, even if it meant pain, than nothing.

And this week, I wasn't so much in my head as I was in those feels. And when Axel and I synced up on the ice? Now that he wasn't glaring daggers at me, or me at him, things clicked. The intensity was still there, and our fierce desire to win, but instead of working against us, we made it work in our favor. It was intoxicating. Just like in bed. Every time we discovered something new about each other, it just got better.

"Penny for them."

The comment snapped me out of my daze.

"Huh?" I looked up to find Kayden smiling down at me.

"Your thoughts. You look like you're about to have a deep conversation with someone. Like, talking about feelings and shit."

I waved him off. "Just got a lot on my mind. Don't worry."

"We're ready for this game."

"We are," I paused and shook my head. "Anyway, it's not about hockey."

I couldn't say anything. I hadn't even told Dane about what had happened between me and Axel.

"Oh sure. You're in love."

I dropped the skates I was holding and thank God the guards were still on. They clattered to the floor between my feet and my teammates turned to look at me.

"Have you been popping Maddox's edibles?" I hissed.

"Not before a game," Kayden laughed and sat down beside me. "And it wasn't a huge jump in logic. You have that dopey look on your face. It's like looking in a mirror."

"I'm not—" It was way too soon for the L word. I'd just gotten used to calling him my boyfriend and that was a shock in itself. "I'm just sort of...hung up on someone."

"Anyone I know?"

"Can't say."

"Ooh, why not?"

"Kay—"

"Alright. I won't push," he replied and nudged me with his elbow. "Guy or girl?"

"What does it matter?"

"It doesn't. I'm just nosy as fuck. You know that."

"He's not—" I swiped a hand over my face. "Shit, he's not out, okay?"

"Got it. Say no more."

"Thanks."

Kayden leaned in. "He must be special if you're worked up over him."

"He is," I confessed. "But I don't know if he feels the same. I think he does. Or maybe he's just experimenting."

Stating my anxiety out loud left me colder than this drafty locker room.

CHAPTER 28

AXEL

It was never easy to step onto the opposing team's home ice, and hearing the thunderous roar of the crowd chanting Grainger College's name only ratcheted up my adrenaline.

Suddenly the reality of this game, do or die, hit me. We were playing for a spot in the finals and that was huge. It was funny, because in all the games I played with Langston, I never felt pressure. Maybe because I knew that I wasn't staying with the team, or because my instinct told me that bigger things were on the horizon.

Speaking of bigger things, there was a rumor that several professional scouts were here at this game. I'd heard Finn and Colin talking about it with Sean when we headed out of the locker room. I forcefully pushed that thought out of my head. Nothing was going to threaten my concentration.

Well, except for my parents. No. I couldn't let that happen either. Fuck them.

Instead, I focused on my usual pregame routine and replayed the drills from our recent practice. One thing for sure was different from the last game. The only opponent I was playing against now was the other team.

And maybe, sometimes, myself.

Jace skated by me, and my pulse spiked higher, our eyes holding for a long moment. If anything was going to screw with my head tonight, it was him. Playing with someone I was sleeping with was new. New and unnerving. How was I going to stay calm when the other team would be gunning for him? The guy I once hated was now the one I was possessive of. And the thought of anyone touching what was mine made me ragey as fuck. The only way to cope was to channel my fire, and make it work for me. Listen to my teammates and focus on our strategy. Coach wanted communication on the ice, and he was going to get it.

So much went unsaid in one look, and despite the space between Jace and I, I'd never felt closer to anyone. Or more certain that this was where we were meant to be. Instead of angsting about my past or worrying about the future, there was only here, now.

Me and Jace? We could do this.

"We got this," he whispered, as if reading my mind, and I nodded.

"We do."

Ethan and Sean started chanting 'cougars roar' and the rest of us joined in, gathering in a circle, feeding off each other's energy, the excitement outpacing our nerves.

"We're gonna kick ass!" someone yelled out.

Holy fuck, it was me.

My teammates shouted "hell, yes" in return and we bumped fists, patted helmets, and headed into our warm-up, psyched and ready to play.

And when Coach put me on the first line, along with Jace, Dane, Kayden, and Finn, I was beyond happy. Even with the weight of expectations sitting heavier than my pads, I was ready.

I glanced down at my red laces and took a deep breath.

Get that fucking win.

By the time the ref blew the first whistle, I was centered, calm. Calmer than I'd ever been during any game in my life. The puck dropped and Jace stole it in a dizzying flash of movement. Warrington, one of Grainger's best forwards, couldn't compete. We were off, breaking away in a rush, as I raced after Jace, with our captain joining in the fray.

The first period of play felt like forever, but despite our best efforts, we couldn't break through Grainger's defensive wall. Everywhere we moved they were there, stealing passes and blocking shots. Hell, they probably didn't need a goalie at this point, they were that good.

Second period, and we finally got our mojo back.

Dane scored halfway through with an assist courtesy of yours truly. Instead of being hung up on the fact that I wasn't the one to sink the puck, I counted my win and kept my eyes out for another opportunity, another play. Doing what I did best. And the rush of being a part of any winning play was everything.

By intermission, we were still ahead by that one goal, but I could tell from my teammates' faces that they were as frustrated as I was. One goal was good, but the tide could turn against us just as quick.

It left no room for error.

By the last period, we weren't just fighting for the puck, it was all-out war. Maddox's blocking skills were put to the test, three, no, four times.

Warrington scored and suddenly the game was tied.

After a time-out and a 'push harder' talk from Coach, we hit the ice with all the energy we had. The momentum came to a head, with Jace taking control of the puck and deke'ing around so many players, it was hard for me, let alone our opponents, to keep track of him. Then Delaney, Grainger's captain, got the drop on Ethan, cross-checking him into the boards, the loud crunch of contact making everyone wince. We skated over to check on our teammate, and a fight almost broke out between Colin and Delaney. Thankfully Ethan was just rattled, and not seriously injured. He and Dane managed to calm Colin down, before things got ugly.

No penalty was called, though, and while we were trying to stay in the cool zone, Coach went ballistic. No power play.

With five minutes remaining, Delaney aimed his sights on Jace.

I was too far away and couldn't get in between them. My heart leapt to my throat as I watched Delaney gunning for him. Thankfully, Jace moved like a slippery eel and narrowly avoided getting crushed into the boards. But me? I broke out in a cold sweat, brimming with fear and fury.

As if sensing that I was about to go full throttle on Delaney, Jace skated past me and patted my ass. Just one reassuring touch and I was good.

Three minutes later, Jace, with an assist from Ethan, scored a hell of an amazing goal. We celebrated as the crowd around us grew silent.

Next thing I knew, the final buzzer sounded off.

2-1 isn't the best game we've ever played, but it's enough to win this one and secured our place in the finals. We flew at each other, hugs and shouts and bouts of swearing mixed in with the celebratory cheers. I was riding a high that couldn't be contained as we skated off the ice and headed back to the locker room. The feeling stayed with me until I got dressed and my phone buzzed.

I had to get this meeting with my parents over with as quick as possible.

Jace walked over to me as I made my way to the exit.

"You okay?" he asked.

I wanted to reach for him, but I steeled myself.

"I'm fine. Just want to get this visit over with."

"I'll meet you out front in fifteen."

I nodded, relieved, and pushed open the door, then headed

out into the hallway, trying to ignore the icy shivers that didn't want to leave my body. And when I spotted my parents, standing by the front door, all dressed up like they were at a cocktail reception rather than a hockey game, that dread turned to full-on panic. My mother had her blond hair tied up, wearing a scarlet coat trimmed with fur. My father was busy on his phone, per usual. They were standing so far apart you wouldn't've assumed they were together. Nothing had changed.

Until they noticed me, and suddenly, stalked in my direction, a wall of perfume, pearls, and power suits.

"Venetia. Bradford," I announced, using their first names, knowing they hated it.

Immediate scowls greeted me. The battle on the ice was done but there was plenty of game left to be played.

"Stop doing that Axel, it's so unseemly," my mother sneered and stepped closer, reaching for my arm.

I didn't want to make a scene, but I pushed her hand away. A wave of Opium, her signature scent, choked me, and I bit back a cough.

"Why are you here?" I asked.

"I told you, we wanted to see your game," my mother insisted, her face an emotionless mask. "You seem to be playing better than you did at Langston. Maybe this hockey thing isn't such a stupid idea after all."

"Well, gee, thanks," I snarked as I stared at her, my gut churning. "I work hard and I'm getting better with every game. But I know that's not the reason why you're here. You couldn't give a shit about me or my hockey career. What's going on?"

"We'll need next year's tuition money back," my father stated.

"What are you talking about?"

"If you push yourself and get drafted as a professional hockey player, you'll make a lot of money. Why bother finishing college?" my mother added. "And we need the money. I want it transferred back to our account this week."

I stood there in shock. I knew they had cash flow problems, but I didn't think they'd stoop to this.

"You can't be serious?" I hissed.

"Does it look like your mother's joking?" my father asked, his eyes boring into me. "She told you about the deal. Until I get this closed, I need all the cash I can find."

"Get a loan," I snapped.

"Same goes. And don't be so fucking naïve, Axel," he hissed. "You don't think we've gone down that route? Just transfer the money and be quiet about it."

"And if I refuse?"

My father shook his head. "You don't want to do that."

I swallowed hard, glancing at the determined expressions on their faces. They wouldn't access my trust fund, would they? No, they couldn't. Still, I should probably find a lawyer to confirm. Not that I'd be able to afford one at this point.

"And you don't want me revealing family secrets," I lobbed back.

My father stepped closer, and the warning glare had me preparing for the worst.

"You're not experienced at this kind of game, Axel. Stick to hockey."

"Fine," I replied, tired of their bullshit and too wrung out to care anymore. "But I'm finishing my degree. I just switched majors and I'm not quitting."

"That's your choice."

"Yes, it is," I replied confidently even though I was anything but. I'd have to find a part-time job, stat, and then maybe two in the summer. But I could do it. "I'll transfer the money this week. If there's nothing else, I've got to meet up with my team."

I didn't see Jace so much as sense him nearby.

When I glanced around, sure enough, he was waiting by

the locker room doors with Kayden, Maddox, and Dane. He stared at me with a questioning look, like he was about to walk over to me. I shook my head. I wanted him by my side, but no way was I going to expose him to my parents.

"Have you spoken to Preston?" my father asked.

"We don't talk anymore. I found out that, just like you, he's a liar. Why?" I asked. "What's going on?"

My mother gave a sharp inhale and my father's face turned ruddy.

"He got arrested."

"Arrested? For what?"

"It doesn't matter," my father insisted. "Just don't talk to him, alright? If he tries to contact you, ignore him. The last thing we need is to be associated with someone like that."

He was joking right? Preston, arrested?

"I've got to go," I stated.

"The money. Tomorrow."

I nodded at my mother's clipped voice.

"You'll get it within a week," I returned and shoved my hands in my pockets. "And FYI, I'm not coming home for break or ever again. I'm done."

"Don't be dramatic."

"I've got my own life now. I'm feeling good about myself for the first time in, well, forever. I don't want anything from you. Nothing. And don't even think of going near my trust fund. That's protected."

With that warning, I stomped off. Never mind dinner, I needed a drink. And a smoke.

The scowl on my face probably scared away half the people in the lobby, but not Jace. He just kept stalking towards me, never losing eye contact, until we met halfway. Without thinking, I reached for his hip, the touch grounding me, settling one storm inside me and unleashing another. Jace's body stiffened in reaction.

"Shit. Sorry."

What was I doing, touching him like that out here? I dropped my hand.

"It's fine. Just, unexpected."

I looked around but no one was paying us any attention.

"Hey," Jace whispered, and I met his gaze. "Are you okay? That looked intense."

"I'll explain on the way to dinner."

The rest of the guys wandered over to join us and we headed for the bus. Even the gust of frigid air as we left the rink was a relief, and I took a few deep breaths, the calm washing over me.

This time, I headed for the last seat at the back of the bus and Jace took the one beside me.

"To start, I'm going to have to find a job," I announced.

"What?"

"I won't have money for next year's tuition. They've cut me off. Well, I have the money, but they want it back."

"No fucking way."

"It's true. But I'll be alright. I'll find a way. And there's more," I paused. "Preston's been arrested."

Jace sat silent, staring at me with an open mouth and wide eyes.

"For what?"

"I don't know. They wouldn't tell me. Just that I shouldn't contact him and with a warning to keep my mouth shut."

"Holy shit."

We pulled out our phones and began typing.

"I can't find anything on his socials," I whispered.

"Me neither."

"What about his parents?" Jace asked.

I thought about that. "Yeah, let me call them."

I searched my contacts and found their info. My hand was shaking when I tapped on their number. It went right to voicemail.

"Hey, Mr. Pearson, this is Axel Lund calling. I'm trying to

reach Preston but he's not responding. Can you please call me back? Thanks."

I hung up and glanced at Jace. "I could also reach out to some of our high school classmates."

"It's a start."

"Okay," I paused and nudged him. "Aside from that, there's something important we need to talk about."

"What's that?"

"When can we meet up?" I asked. "Your room?"

"What about Finn?"

"Let's get him to swap," I suggested. "It's only one night."

"You know Coach and the rules. There's got to be another way."

Jace worried his lower lip as he worked on a solution. I so wanted to lean in and taste him. Fuck, it had been too long since we'd kissed, and I needed my fix.

"Don't do that," he hissed.

"Do what?"

"Look at me like that," Jace reached down and adjusted himself. "Everyone's gonna know what you're thinking."

"And what am I thinking?" I asked him, leaning closer, until we shared the same breath.

I should've been concerned about our teammates watching us, but suddenly I didn't care.

Between Jace and the game tonight, I was riding a high that couldn't be stopped.

"You want to do dirty, filthy things to my body," he suggested.

"And the problem is?" I teased.

"Stop it, Ax. The last thing I need is a boner right before we head in for dinner."

I glanced down at the bulge in his jeans and licked my lips.

"I know what I'm in the mood to devour."

"Oh God," Jace groaned, and it made me laugh.

Despite the bombshell my parents dropped on me tonight, being around Jace had me feeling right again.

"We need to be alone," I confessed. "There's got to be someplace, other than our room, where we can meet up."

Jace tapped his lips, his shoulder bumping mine, a playful light in his eyes.

"I think I have an idea."

CHAPTER 29

JACE

My idea—meeting up with Axel in the hotel gym, the bathroom to be exact—wasn't going to happen.

The damn place was under renovation. With that gone, I saw only one solution.

"Do you mind switching rooms with Axel tonight and rooming with Colin?" I asked Finn quietly while we were seated at dinner.

No one could hear me above the din. Team dinners were always loud, but after tonight's game, spirits were higher and more raucous than usual. Thankfully, Axel took a spot on the other end of the table, far, far away from me. I couldn't take any more of his teasing, it was addictive and had me so turned on I wouldn't have been able to make conversation, never mind eat.

"Uh, why?" Finn glanced at me.

"Because…because Axel and I need to work on the fundraiser," I replied and took a sip of water. "We're going to be up late trying to get all that admin shit done. It's just easier if we share a room."

"I can help with that."

I choked on my drink and coughed.

Finn continued, oblivious to my discomfort. "I mean, you could come to our room, and we can work for a few hours and get it all done."

"Uh, thanks, but we have to…um—" I cleared my throat. "There's stuff that only Axel and I can work on for now."

Finn gave me a questioning look.

"Please."

I was not above begging at this point.

"If Coach finds out, I'm done for," Finn whispered.

"He's not going to find out. It's one night."

"Then again," Finn mused. "Axel's snoring could wake the dead. Fuck knows I hardly sleep when we're on the road."

"It doesn't bother me at all. Quite the opposite."

Because Axel would fuck my brains out and we'd both pass out. Problem solved.

"Really?" Finn mused and nodded. "Okay, but if Coach discovers the truth, you take the blame."

"Absolutely."

Finn tapped my arm.

"What's changed with you and Axel? Suddenly, you're buddies?"

'*Yeah, fuck buddies*' I nearly blurted out. No, we were more than that. I wouldn't break one of Coach's steadfast rules for a hookup.

"We've come to an understanding," I replied. "It's not perfect but it works for us."

I picked up my phone and texted Axel.

> Jace: Finn's agreed to swap rooms. I told him we've gotta work on the fundraiser.

I casually looked around the room. Axel laughed at something Ethan was saying, probably a joke, and Colin and Sean, who were seated next to him, joined in. I was honestly surprised that Axel didn't beg off tonight after what happened with his parents and the news about Preston. Then again, he needed distraction more than anything. And I was going to make sure he got it.

Axel casually pulled out his phone and my heart began to race when I saw the smirk on his face.

> Axel: If by fundraiser you mean we're going to fuck all night, yes, we will work on that for sure, boyfriend.

I bit my lip, trying not to smile or, worse, laugh out loud.

> Jace: Can you tell Colin? Then give him your key card.

> Axel: On it

Axel leaned over and bent his head to talk to Colin. I checked and responded to some of my messages while I waited for his response.

> Axel: Done

I leaned into Finn.

"Colin's agreed. You okay rooming with him?" I asked, suddenly feeling guilty for deceiving my friends.

"It's good. But only this one time."

I nodded, relieved, offering my hand under the table. "Pass me your key card. Colin will have yours and you can grab it after dinner."

Finn passed it over and I quickly shoved it in my pocket.

> Jace: What did you tell Colin?

> Axel: The truth.

> Jace: ???

Axel: Finn can't take my snoring, and you sleep like the dead.

Jace: LOL, he didn't question it?

Axel: I didn't say that. He gave me a look. It's only a matter of time. You know that?

Jace: I know.

Axel: Are you worried?

Jace: Are you?

I held my breath.

Axel: No.

Thank Christ I wasn't the only one.

Jace: So, it's not a matter of if the team finds out, but when?

Axel: Yes.

Jace: Just like that?

Axel: Just like that. Now get your sweet ass up to our room, Honey.

I shot up out of my chair like a spring.

"You're leaving already? We haven't even had dessert yet," Finn announced.

"Like I said before, I've got a lot of work to do," I croaked. "A lot of it."

I said my goodbyes to the team and headed for the elevator, my heart knocking hard against my ribs, so loud I was sure anyone standing nearby could hear it.

Reaching into my pocket, I fumbled for my key card as I stepped into the elevator.

"Hold the door!" a familiar voice called out.

It was Dane.

"Oh, hey, sorry," I said as I put my hand on the door to keep it open.

"No worries," he replied and stepped in beside me. "You took off so fast there, I got worried. Are you feeling sick?"

Dane was always looking out for others, and the pang of guilt that hit me earlier came roaring back. I wanted to tell him about me and Axel, I had to, but...

"I'm fine," I replied as I hit the button for the eighth floor. "I want to finish work on the fundraiser, get it over with. You know, so I'm free to party tomorrow night, and sleep all day Sunday."

"Sure," Dane chuckled as the elevator began to rise. "Tough game today. Been thinking about it all through dinner. I didn't expect Grainger to play like that."

"Me neither. I don't think any of us did," I returned.

"It's only going to get more intense from here."

"I know," I admitted. "You didn't leave dinner early just to check up on me, did you? I really am okay."

Dane swiped a hand through his hair.

"I'm wiped. My sleep's been hit and miss this week. And, I want to call Jackson," Dane replied with a big smile. "It's funny, even just a day away and I miss him like crazy."

"You're so in love it's sickening," I teased him.

He laughed and when I looked up, I caught our reflections in the mirrored doors.

Dane's expression was the same as mine.

You're so in love...

Holy fuck, was I in love with Axel? My stomach dropped out, but it had nothing to do with this elevator ride.

"You know it." Dane nudged me with his shoulder. "What

about you? I haven't seen you doing the stride of pride lately."

Oh, I was doing it. Just not so anyone would notice.

"Busy with class, you know."

"That's not it. You've been acting quiet. What's really going on?"

"I—"

The elevator pinged when it hit the eighth floor and Dane got out first.

"Aren't you coming? You're on this floor too, right?"

"Uh, yeah," I replied, shaking off my unease and stepping out into the hallway.

How could I forget that Dane was on the same floor? Hopefully Axel was stealthy enough to avoid detection from our captain.

"Jace, seriously, what's up?" Dane asked me again as we stood alone. "I'm worried."

First Kayden, now Dane.

"It's nothing about my health, mental or otherwise, I promise. It's...it's a guy."

Fuck, that was a relief to say, and yet, frightening as fuck.

"Whoa, you mean, more than fucking?"

I nodded. "And the fucking is off the charts."

"Oh my God, is that why you've had that spaced out look on your face for weeks?"

I shoved his shoulder. "Stop."

"Who is it?"

"I can't say," I replied, and Dane's face fell. "He's not out, D. You know how it is."

"Shit, now I'm really worried."

"It's okay, *Dad*, I'm a big boy," I reassured my friend. "I know what I'm doing."

"You swore off relationships."

"I did, but—"

"This guy's special?"

I was suddenly too choked up to speak, so I nodded instead.

"You've always moved too fast to be caught," he mused. "But it sounds like you've met your match. That's heady stuff."

"It is," I admitted. "Only, he's never been with a guy before. Maybe it's just new and exciting for him now. But fucking around isn't the same thing as being out. I'm waiting for him to wake up and realize this isn't what he wants. Or, maybe the fucking is all he wants."

"And you want more?"

"I want him. Only him."

Dane whistled.

"Never thought I'd see this day."

"You and me both."

"Have you told him how you feel?"

I shrugged. "Sort of? We're not seeing anyone else. But it's complicated."

"Because he's not out? Or for another reason?"

I'd already said too much.

Dane's eyes narrowed. "It's someone I know, isn't it?"

There was nothing I could do to stop the blush from creeping up my cheeks.

Ping.

The elevator doors suddenly opened and there was Axel. We locked eyes, only for a moment, but it was enough. Axel gave me a filthy, possessive once-over until he noticed Dane standing nearby.

Shit.

"Lund," Dane offered. "I thought your room was on the sixth floor."

"Uh, yes," Axel muttered as he joined us in the hallway. He ran a hand through his blond shag and then pointed at me. "But I have to speak to Jace about something first."

"Really?" Dane glanced between the two of us and rolled his eyes. "You guys suck at this."

"Dane," I warned.

"It's none of my business, but as captain of the team, and as your friend, I'm always here if you need to talk."

"We're fucking," Axel blurted out. "Shit. Sorry. I mean, we're seeing each other. We're boyfriends."

"You don't have to—" I started, reaching for Axel but stopping myself.

"It's alright, I want to tell him," Axel replied quietly as he reached for my hand. He was holding my hand, in front of Dane, and I felt like I was flying. "If it's okay with you."

"Yeah," I nodded. "It's more than okay."

"Damn, I owe Ethan twenty bucks," Dane muttered.

"Are you kidding me?" I turned to my friend. "Who else knows?"

Dane shrugged. "Who doesn't? You were grinding all over each other at that frat crawl. No one dances that close, even teammates. But I think Ethan and I were the only ones who noticed. Or remembered, because hello, hangovers. Anyway, having sex isn't exactly what I meant when I said 'work it out' between you."

I gave my friend my best finger.

Axel pulled me into his side, placing a protective arm around my waist. The move was as unexpected as the hand holding and had me flushing hot.

"So, that party wasn't a one-off," Dane admitted as he stared at us with wide eyes. "But I have questions for Axel. A lot of them."

"Dane—" I started.

"Given how badly you reacted to Kayden and Maddox being together, I think I have a right to be worried about my friend," Dane continued, staring at Axel. "Not to mention the fact that your so-called best friend treated Jace like shit. If you're playing some kind of twisted game—"

"No. This is real. I know that Jace was telling the truth," Axel insisted. "And I know I'll never be able to make up for what I did to Kayden and Maddox, but I regret it every day. Trust me."

"And now you're in the same scenario, but on the other side of it."

Axel nodded and bit his lower lip.

"When Jace is ready, if he's ready, we'll tell the team," Axel stated.

"You don't have to come out," I reassured him.

"I'm going to. I'm not hiding us," Axel's gaze perused my face. "I can't."

He cupped my face and before I knew it, he was kissing me.

"Holy shit."

Dane took the words right out of my mouth.

CHAPTER 30

AXEL

"Go back to your rooms," Dane ordered. "Separately."

I didn't let go of Jace and I had no intention of listening to my captain.

"Or don't," Dane muttered as he walked off.

Thankfully, in the opposite direction of Jace's room.

"What did you do?" Jace whispered as he smiled at me.

"Me?"

"Yes, you. Kissing me like that in front of Dane."

"Are you telling me you didn't like it?"

Jace's flushed cheeks said it all.

"Dane needs to know that I'm all in when it comes to you. I don't want there to be any doubt. Not for him, but most importantly, not for you," I admitted, staring deep into Jace's eyes. "And we're wasting time."

I steered Jace down the hallway, his body tight to mine, my hand on his hip, his scent teasing me. There was no way I was letting go of Jace.

Not now, not tomorrow, maybe not ever.

"I can walk just fine on my own," Jace replied. "Someone might see."

"They might," I replied and slid my hand over his ass, squeezing tight. "But no, I'm not letting go."

Jace shivered. I saw it, and I felt it.

"Throw me over your shoulder and carry me off to your cave," he quipped.

"If we didn't have an upcoming hockey championship to claim, I would." I swatted his ass. "Give me the key card."

Jace pulled it out of his front pocket and handed it over.

"Any more demands?" he asked when we stopped in front of his room.

I chuckled and swiped the key.

"Lots of them."

I opened the door and ushered him inside. The room was your standard hotel; two queen beds covered in white linens, brown and black patterned carpeting, with a lounge chair, desk, and a lamp in the corner. The olive-colored curtains were open, with floor-to-ceiling windows that looked out over the snowy rooftops of the city.

"Completely stunning," I admitted.

"Albany in the winter?" Jace quipped as he walked ahead of me.

"I'm not talking about the view of the city," I replied as I stared at him, watching his confident strut and the way those snug jeans clung to his ass and thighs.

But Jace didn't look back at me. He walked to stand in front of the window instead, placing one hand on the glass.

"Did I say something wrong?" I asked, dropping the card on the nightstand between the two beds.

He dropped his forehead on the window.

"Jace?" I repeated as I walked to stand behind him, reaching for his shoulders.

They were tense under my fingertips.

"Why do you have to do that?" he whispered.

"Do what?" I asked him, bracketing his body with mine

until there wasn't any space between us, watching our mutual reflection in the glass.

Fuck, we looked amazing together. Sliding my arms around his waist, I felt him relax against me and everything was right again.

"You know," he paused, still staring out at the city. "The way you talk about me. Where's this coming from?"

"I can't help it. Don't you like it?"

He trembled and I tightened my hold on him, notching my head into the curve of his shoulder, teasing the skin of his neck with my mouth, relishing in his warmth and his unforgettable scent.

"You know I like it too damn much," he confessed.

I chuckled as I kissed my way up his neck.

"So, you won't mind then if I tell you that I can't stop thinking about you. That the past two days of no contact has made me fucking desperate to be inside you," I whispered gruffly, reveling in his sharp inhale. "How I can't get close enough or kiss enough, and I'm not sure I'll ever get enough."

"Ax."

I shivered and nipped his neck, licking and sucking, confirming my words on his skin. Jace writhed in my arms, letting out a deep moan, reaching for my hand, pulling it down to cup his cock. Mine was painfully hard as I rocked against his ass, needing to be as close as possible, closer.

"Strip," I demanded. "I need to see you naked. Now."

"I can't undress if you don't let me go," he teased.

I let him go long enough for him to reach for his shirt but once that came off, I plastered myself to him, pushing his hands back against the window.

"Stay like this," I murmured and reached for the button on his jeans. "Stay just like this."

When I lowered his zipper, and delved my hand inside, my palm met bare skin.

"You went commando to our team dinner?" I hissed.

"I wanted to be ready for you."

"Fucking hell, Jace."

Shoving his jeans down his legs, I stared at his naked reflection in the glass and nearly swallowed my tongue. He was long and gorgeous, his cock hard against his abs, his forearms rigid.

I dropped to my knees and cupped his taut ass, spreading his cheeks so I could shove my face between them. When I flicked my tongue over his tight hole, he let out a strangled groan that hit me right in the balls. Rimming brought a whole new level of intimacy to fucking, one I'd never experienced before. One I was now addicted to.

I licked and sucked on his skin, then pushed my tongue in his hole and rubbed my scruff against his cheeks. Jace pushed back, keening so loud I'm sure everyone on this floor, and the next, could hear him.

"I want you to come just like this," I whispered against his skin.

"No."

"No?" I repeated and rose up, kissing the dimples above his ass and higher, higher, marking each knob of his spine until I reached his neck.

"Not until you fuck me," he moaned. "Right here. Grab the lube. It's in my bag, by the bed."

"Don't move," I demanded and raced over to rummage through his bag, yanking out the lube.

I turned around and stopped short when I spotted Jace kicking away his jeans. Placing his hands back on the glass, he spread his legs and offered me his ass. The sight was so sexy I had to grab the base of my dick with my free hand to stop myself from climaxing.

Two days away from him and I was ready to blow my load all over this ugly carpet.

"Your cum is mine," Jace announced, looking over his shoulder to lock eyes with mine. "Give it to me."

"So possessive," I whispered, slowly making my way back to him.

"That's right."

He faced the window again. I opened the lube and quickly slicked up my cock.

Every step closer to Jace had my adrenaline pumping wild, sweat trickling down my face and neck, the rush of blood pounding through my body, centering in my cock. It didn't matter how many times we'd kissed or fucked, every time was better than the last. I never imagined sex with one person could be like this, but as usual, Jace proved me wrong. Only, it wasn't just the promise of fucking him that had my heart squeezing hard in my chest.

"Is that all you want?" I asked, the question slipping out before I could stop it.

"You, Ax, I want you."

"Jace."

"I fight for what I want. Always have, always will," he confessed. "You need to know that I'm fighting for you too. I'm falling hard for you."

His admission had me trembling as I took hold of him, bringing him into my chest, sliding my cock between his ass cheeks, both of us shaking hard.

"I'm falling for you, too," I confessed, kissing his shoulders, his neck. "I'm so far gone, I can't think about anything else."

Jace turned his head, and I slammed my lips over his, hard and hungry. He sucked on my tongue, and I released a groan I'd been holding onto for days. I slid one hand over his chest, tracing his tattoo, then teasing his nipples, tugging, then lower, over his abs, until I reached his cock.

"Get inside me," he whispered between kisses.

I pushed one finger in his hole, and he pushed his ass back.

"Deeper," he groaned. "More."

I added a second finger, then drilled them deeper, touching his prostate. Jace cried out and I tasted his moans.

"More."

I finger fucked him, pushing in and out, getting him ready for my cock. Being inside Jace like this was so hot, and watching my fingers in his ass had my dick begging for release.

"I'm ready."

"Not yet," I bit out, adding a third finger to ensure he was good and stretched. "Patience, Honey."

"Ax, so help me, if you don't fuck me with your dick in the next five seconds—"

Jace's exasperated voice had me biting back laughter.

"What?" I goaded and pushed my fingers in deeper, my lips nipping his jaw. "What are you gonna do?"

"I'm gonna…I'm…you," Jace panted. "I'll think of something."

I let out a dirty chuckle. "I look forward to your payback."

"Not if I edge you for hours."

"I'm willing to take that risk," I countered.

"Like taking one for the team?"

"Only if the team's you."

I withdrew my fingers, notching the head of my dick to his hole.

"Keep your hands on the glass," I demanded as I pushed inside him.

I didn't think our coming together could get any hotter until I realized I was watching Jace, watching me, as I fucked him. Against the night sky, the glass was a perfect mirror, and I could read every expression on his beautiful face. And Jesus, I was going to come hard and embarrassingly fast if my aching balls were any indication. I pumped my hips, pushing in all the way as Jace pushed back, greedy for more.

"Jace, holy shit. Slow down."

"No," he moaned. "I need my boyfriend to fuck me like he means it. Harder. Deeper."

Boyfriend.

That word snapped my control, and I punched my hips, driving as deep into him as I could get, until my balls slapped his ass. I hoped like hell that the window was solid because we were about to test the safety standard.

I rutted into him, setting a punishing pace, fucking Jace like my life depended on it. I couldn't get close enough, thrusting as hard as I could, and knowing that Jace was as far gone for me as I was for him had me edging the line between pleasure and pain. I reached for his cock, stroking him off, desperate to please him, to feel him come undone.

And I wasn't watching our reflection anymore because I was mesmerized by the sight of my bare cock sliding in and out of his hole.

Nothing between us. Not a damn thing.

"Come for me, Jace," I urged him. "Come for me, please."

Jace's hole squeezed tight around my dick and his body locked up as I continued to pound into him, not losing rhythm.

"Right there, Ax. Don't stop!"

I fucked into him again, over and over, until Jace let out a long, dirty moan, so loud that passersby on the street, never mind the hotel hallway, could probably hear him. The heat of his cum lashed my hand and I glanced up to watch him paint the window with it. The filthy scene was burned into my brain and knowing that I was the reason he'd come so hard had my climax unleashing.

"Jace, I can't...I can't hold on," I gasped.

The orgasm slammed into me, as I shouted his name and shot my load in his ass.

Aftershocks rolled through my body. I rested my head between Jace's shoulder blades, trying desperately to get air in my lungs. My legs wobbled, and I slid my hands from his to grip his waist.

"We're going to get charged for extra housekeeping," he panted.

I chuckled at his comment, marveling at how Jace could make me laugh one moment and want so intently the next. Slowly, I pulled my cock out, and reached for his hole, rubbing my cum into his skin.

"We need to continue this in bed," I admitted.

I dropped to my knees on the carpet, staring up at him, until he turned around and did the same, meeting me eye to eye. Before I could utter a word, his mouth was on mine, kissing me hungrily, taking my remaining breath and leaving me completely wrecked.

"I want you inside me," I confessed between kisses. "Now. Tonight."

Jace insisted that he was fine with the way things had been so far, me fucking him, but I wanted him in my ass. And I knew he wanted to fuck me. But he wasn't pushing.

I was ready. Ready, but also really nervous. I wanted to experience everything with him. I wanted to please him.

"You don't have to."

"I know that," I whispered. "But I want to. I want it more than anything."

CHAPTER 31
AXEL

" know what I want," I repeated.

Jace looked into my eyes and cupped my face.

"Then get up on the bed. On your hands and knees."

My cock was half hard and getting harder.

I scrambled to stand up and thankfully, I only had to take two steps until I hit the bed. One of them. I tumbled onto the mattress, and leaned on my forearms, my head hanging low, my body vibrating with anticipation and nerves. But when Jace got on the bed behind me, his skin touching mine, I began to shake.

"You tell me if you need me to stop."

"Jace," I bit out, sweat trickling down my face. "I swear to God, if you make me wait any longer—"

He suddenly swatted my ass, and the bite of pain had me groaning out loud.

"You were saying?" he quipped and squeezed my cheeks.

"That's more like it."

I heard the click of the lube cap, and then Jace's warm fingers were on me, one holding my ass cheek and the other teasing my crease, rubbing up and down and over my hole, then my taint. It was so good and yet, not nearly enough.

"More," I urged him, spreading my knees wider, offering him my hole.

One orgasm with Jace was never enough and my cock leaked furiously, my balls so damn tight. I noticed Jace's sharply indrawn breath and glanced over my shoulder. He was staring at me intently, his chest moving in and out like he was running at full speed, not kneeling behind me.

Our eyes met and he gave me a wicked grin before lowering his head.

I turned back to the headboard and reached for a pillow, knowing that what was about to happen next was going to leave me screaming.

Loudly.

Sure enough, the moment Jace's skillful tongue speared my sensitive hole, I was done for.

But he didn't just lick my hole, he tongue fucked me until I was an incoherent mess. I shoved my face into the pillow and released a strangled groan. The sound was muffled, thank God, otherwise it would've had everyone in this hotel banging on our door in no short order.

"Mmm," he whispered and flicked his hot tongue over my rim. "How badly do you want me inside you?"

"More than anything. Please."

"Since you beg so nicely," Jace teased and slid one slick finger over my hole.

"Only for you."

"That's right. Only for me," he replied and pushed the tip of his finger inside me. "Mine."

"Yes."

I pushed my ass back, trying to take more of him. The burn was intense, but I was relaxed from the rimming, and ready for more. Ready for all of it.

He pushed his finger in deeper, slowly, taking his time. Driving me insane.

"More, Jace. Please," I demanded, clutching the pillow so tight I'd probably rip the damn thing into a dozen pieces.

Jace pushed his finger in and out, and where there was pain at first, now there was intense pleasure. He added another finger, going slow and steady, deeper this time. And when he touched my prostate, everything in my body lit up like fireworks. I nearly came off the bed.

"Motherfucker!" I shouted, overcome with intense bliss.

"Is that good or bad?" he asked me, pausing.

"Good, so damn good. Fuck, I feel like a hockey god," I admitted, having no idea if I was making sense or not.

Hockey god? Definitely not.

"Your ass is my temple," Jace teased, pushing his fingers in and out. He grazed my prostate again and my climax threatened to let loose.

"Get your cock inside me before I come," I moaned.

Jace withdrew his fingers, and I hated the feeling.

I was so empty. I'd had enough of that feeling throughout my life. No more.

"If it's too much, tell me," he insisted as he notched his dick to my hole.

"Jace."

He pushed inside me, just the head of his cock, and I bit the edge of the pillow.

The pain was even more intense than I'd imagined.

"Okay?" he asked, rubbing a hand along my ass, then around my hip to take my now-flagging erection in his hand.

"I need…a minute," I admitted, and tried to focus on my breathing as Jace stroked my cock and leaned over my back, tracing the skin of my shoulders with his tongue. I shuddered from the exquisite pleasure-pain in my ass, letting go, letting him take control of my body. With every touch, I began to relax, and Jace pushed inside me again, deeper this time. God, I was so full. His cock was hot and hard, and it was so much, too much.

Emotions I couldn't contain rose to the surface and I reached for his hand, guiding him as he stroked my dick, wanting him all over me, everywhere.

"More."

My voice was hoarse with need, and I shivered when he thrust his hips. Then, he was all the way inside me, his balls to my ass, his chest to my back, both of us slick with sweat, all heat and power as he moved inside me, giving me everything I never knew I needed.

"Just like that," I groaned as I swiveled my hips, needing more. More cock in my ass, more friction on my dick. "Oh God, don't stop."

"Axel, you're killing me," Jace whispered in my ear. "I'm trying to go slow."

"Fuck that," I panted. "I'm good. More than ready. For *all* the fucking."

"Baby," he moaned, and the word made me shiver.

"Give me your cum," I urged. "Paint me like you painted the window."

"I'm gonna come too soon if you keep talking like that."

"Then hurry up and fuck me," I growled.

Jace made a guttural sound and finally let loose, rutting into me, so deep that it made me cry out. I forgot about my first-time nerves, hell, I forgot my own damn name. We fucked in a furious rhythm, our bodies straining, the bed shaking, every stroke making me beg and plead for more. No way I was going to last.

"Axel," Jace's voice hitched in a telltale sign I recognized. "I'm gonna…fuck, Axel, I'm coming."

His hands gripped my hips as he let loose, pounding my ass, nailing my prostate over and over, until I came hard, my vision blurring, pleasure stealing the breath from my lungs. I heard Jace shout my name as he came inside me, the heat in my ass intensifying. It was his cum. Holy shit, I thought coming inside Jace was hot, but this?

I collapsed on the bed, and he followed, blanketing my body. It was several minutes before we caught our breath, and another few before he finally slipped out of me. I winced at the pain but fuck, it had been worth it.

When he rolled to his side, I wrapped one arm around him, and we stayed locked together, not a breath between us.

"Are you okay?" Jace asked, licking his lips.

"More than," I confessed, leaning in to kiss him. "That was, Jesus, I can't even describe it."

He gave me a languid smile. "You're gonna be sore tomorrow."

"Thank God it's just a bus ride home."

He slid a hand over my hip, his fingers trailing down my ass cheek, then over my hole, massaging gently.

"Are we good at that or what?" he quipped.

I laughed. "Any better and we'll incinerate."

"I never would have thought—" Jace started.

"What?"

"That we'd end up here," he confessed, our gazes holding. "And that you're a secret cuddler."

His teasing comment had me nipping his shoulder in retaliation.

"I'm so *not* a cuddler," I grumbled.

"Are you going to let go of me?"

I grunted instead of responding. But I still didn't release him.

"See?"

"I'm just resting until I catch my breath."

"Whatever you say, baby." Jace rubbed my arm.

The one that was wrapped tight around him.

Before I could utter a response, there was a knock at the door.

"Just ignore it," I murmured and kissed Jace's neck.

There was another knock, louder this time. Then a voice called 'Jace.'

It was Finn. Jesus Christ.

"What's he doing here?" I whispered.

"Shit, his bag," Jace replied. "Get in the bathroom. Hurry."

"This better be the only interruption tonight," I grumbled and reluctantly let go of Jace.

He slid off the bed, grabbed his jeans off the carpet, and quickly stepped into them, zipping up. His hair was mussed, and I'd left hickeys all over his back and neck. There was no mistaking that he'd just been fucked.

Fucked by me. He was all mine.

"Stop ogling and get in the bathroom," Jace hissed as he motioned for me to move my butt.

While he grabbed his shirt, I padded off to the bathroom. The ache in my ass was really intense, but I loved it. Because it meant Jace and I were real.

Hiding behind the bathroom door, I left it ajar so I could hear what was going on. I counted Jace's footsteps as he walked to the door and then the click of the lock opening.

"Hey, Finn, what's up?" Jace asked, his voice hoarse.

"I need my overnight bag."

"Oh yeah, sorry," Jace returned. "Hold on, I'm just...ah... about to hop in the shower. Stay here and I'll get it for you."

The door slammed and Jace whizzed by. I heard what I assumed was Jace opening the closet door and then he was running by again. Another click, and another creak from the heavy hotel door.

"Here you go, Finn. Have a good night."

"You too, Jace. See you at breakfast."

I sagged in relief against the bathroom sink when I heard the door slam again.

Close call.

Dane being aware of what was going on was one thing, he was one of Jace's best friends. But Finn? I didn't know him that well or how he'd react to finding out me and Jace were fucking. Would he rat us out to Coach? Not that he, or anyone on the team, seemed to have an issue with Kayden and Maddox being a couple and playing together.

The irony wasn't lost on me given my first reaction to them and regret lingered like a nagging headache.

Trying to shake it off, I turned around and reached for the shower nozzle, turning it on full blast. Steam began to fill the room. Instead of waiting for Jace, I stepped into the shower and grabbed the tiny, white bar of soap, scrubbing myself vigorously, the water washing away the cum and sweat, and my good mood along with it.

Regret, however, still clung to me.

Not about Jace, not that. It was just me. One day I would get things right.

Jace entered the bathroom as I finished lathering up. He grabbed a towel, wet it, and headed back out. A few minutes later, he stalked back into the bathroom, threw the towel on the floor, and joined me in the shower.

"I got most of the cum off the window," he announced with a grin. "Hopefully."

"Good, because we don't want to explain *that* to house-keeping."

I leaned back against the tiled wall and watched the water sluice down Jace's body, memorizing every curve and ridge, hypnotized by him. He gave me a heated look in return.

"You alright?" he asked, running one hand through his wet hair, the other reaching for the soap. "You look like you know a secret."

"I'm more than alright," I insisted. "And there's no secret. Like I said earlier, I want to tell the team."

The bar squirted out of his grip and hit the shower floor with a resounding bang.

Lots of that going on tonight, and soap was the least of it.

CHAPTER 32

JACE

wasn't sure I'd ever walk steady again. And I wasn't sure I wanted to.

I thought I was experienced when it came to sex, but it turned out, I didn't know anything. All my smooth moves vanished around Axel. We were as real, insatiable, and messy as it could get. No holds barred. We fucked the way we played—all in.

And what made it even better? My heart was all in, too.

And because of that, I had to protect him. From me, as it turned out.

"Don't you want to think about this a bit more?" I replied when the shock of Axel's statement wore off. I reached down and picked up the soap. What was left of it. "You should only come out when you're ready. It's going to be a lot."

Axel pulled me into his arms, his wet, slick chest bumping mine.

"I told you, I can handle it," he replied and gave me a long kiss.

"I know," I whispered. "But you don't need to come out for us to be together. I'm not going to pressure you. And trust me when I say it's easier said than done. Everything is going to change. And not everyone is going to like the fact that you're queer. Are you ready for that? The stares and comments when you hold my hand in public? The trolls on social media?"

"I think I am," Axel replied. "Yes. If I can deal with the sharks back in Redgewick, I can deal with this."

"This is different, Ax. And there's hockey to consider, your future, going pro. You know how insular the hockey world is. And queer players still aren't well-represented."

"Things are changing. And it's your future too."

I nodded. "I know, but I've talked to my therapist about it, so I feel like I'm prepared. Or, as prepared as I can be. But this is all new for you. You need to consider how coming out will affect your entire life; not just hockey but most importantly, your mental health. You've gotta protect that."

"I'm dealing with my depression. And I know what I want." Axel let out a frustrated growl. "And I want us, you and me, more than I want to protect myself."

"I want us too," I offered, cupping his neck, needing to reassure him. "But I don't want you to have regrets."

"You're afraid I'm going to change my mind and deny everything," he stated, his body rigid. "That's what you're really worried about."

The thought made me feel sick, but yes, the fear was there. That Axel was going to wake up tomorrow and say fuck this, I don't need you.

"Going out with a woman would be a lot easier," I said quietly.

"Right back at you," he bit out as his grip on me tightened. "If I wanted easy, I wouldn't play hockey. Or sit through class or figure out a means to get away from my screwed-up family. Easy is bullshit. I'm not walking away from you."

Every word hit me deep in my chest and warmed me like his touch.

"Jace, I'm not walking away," he repeated, his dark blues imploring.

"I'm not either," I whispered and leaned in to seal our promise with a kiss.

I didn't know what tomorrow would bring. But, win or lose, I always played my heart out.

"Who I date is my business, mine, and I protect what's mine," Axel insisted.

"We're dating?" I quipped, hoping to lighten the mood.

He pinched my ass, and I squeaked.

"Fucking right we're dating," Axel grumbled, and I couldn't resist kissing his pout. "And don't try and distract me with your sexy kisses."

I smiled against his lips.

"So, as my official boyfriend, what kind of dates are you planning?" I asked.

His hands slid down my back to cup my ass. "Well, prior to the first date, I'm going to buy a jersey with my name and number on it so you can wear it every day. That way there's no question about who you belong to."

"Every day?"

Axel leaned forward, and playfully nipped my lips. "Every. Single. Day."

"And?"

"I'll pick you up next Friday evening and we'll walk across campus holding hands. There will be dinner and a movie, or maybe we'll go skating at the outdoor rink. After that, we'll go to Ethan's frat party and make out where everyone can see us."

"So, if the jersey doesn't tell everyone what's what, our lips will," I added.

"Exactly," he growled and kissed me, longer, deeper. "You're mine and that's final."

"And then?"

"Then we'll go back to my room and fuck until we break the bed."

I chuckled at his matter-of-fact tone. "That sounds like quite a date."

"It's romantic as hell," Axel insisted. "Or, as romantic as a hockey player can get."

"As long as I can touch your stick, I'll be happy."

"You and me both, Honey."

———

We woke up at six the next morning, an hour earlier than we had to, so we could have morning sex and then shower before meeting the rest of the team for breakfast. Axel snuck out of my room first, and I followed a good ten minutes after him just in case.

Thankfully, I'd packed a turtleneck sweater to hide my hickeys.

But, apparently, there was no hiding my sex-drunk expression from Dane. My friend took one look at me in the hotel dining room and said, "I hope you know what you're doing."

Axel and I had talked late into the night. He wanted to tell Coach and then the rest of the team now. I still thought he was rushing things. Until he showed me his phone and the jersey he was ordering for me with his name on it. Once Axel made his mind up about something, that was it. He was stubborn as hell and there was no changing.

Well, he'd changed his tune about me. And I couldn't really hold the past against him. Preston had lied to him too.

Speaking of my ex, I checked my phone. There was still no word about Preston, and it made me restless. I was dreading the idea of Axel being in touch with him again. Would Axel tell him that we were together? Would Preston convince Ax that I wasn't worth it?

We were finishing up breakfast and my urge to run to the bathroom reared up.

You can't control what other people say or do. You can only control your reaction.

Taking a slow sip of water, I repeated that mantra in my head until I talked myself out of making a run for it. I was feeling calmer.

Until the sharp ringtone of Axel's phone broke our team chatter.

"It's, uh, family stuff," Axel said to Coach, who nodded.

Axel excused himself from the table and I stared at him as he walked off, his posture stiff, and his voice low as he answered his phone.

"Everything okay?" Dane nudged me.

"I think so." I turned to my friend and whispered. "Sort of. We got word yesterday that Preston was arrested."

"Oh my God, for what?"

"Don't know yet. Axel's parents just said he'd been arrested, and nothing else. We tried searching in the news, but nada."

"What about—"

Dane's comment was interrupted by a sound I'd never heard before.

Coach was laughing.

Everyone at the table turned to stare at him, me included.

Banning never laughed. Like, ever. Occasionally, after a win, he'd smile but even that was rare. What had I missed?

"Dane." I leaned in and whispered. "I know I had a lot of sex last night and not enough sleep, so maybe it's my imagination, but did Banning just laugh?"

"He did."

Dane sounded as awed as I was at this turn of events.

"What?" Banning's smile turned to a glare as he looked around the table.

And just like that, things were back to normal.

"What's so funny, Coach?" Ethan outright asked, because, of course he did.

"Ask Silas," Banning returned and motioned for the server.

"Come on, Moss, spill," Ethan urged Silas.

"It was nothing," Silas insisted, ignoring our interested stares and reaching for his glass of juice.

"You can't make Coach laugh and not tell us the secret," Ethan replied.

Silas gave an enigmatic smirk and shook his head.

"It's no secret and it wasn't even a joke." Silas took a sip of his drink. "He told me that I was the oldest player he'd ever coached, and I told him he was the oldest coach I'd ever played for."

Everyone laughed and Ethan leaned forward. "You two geezers have to stick together, right?"

Oh shit.

Coach pointed at Ethan. "Since you're so young and full of energy, Walker, you can enjoy an extra hour of drills this week."

Everyone chuckled as Ethan smacked his forehead and groaned.

"I was kidding, Coach, I swear," Ethan insisted. "Unlike Moss, I *can* make a joke."

Silas gave Ethan his middle finger but pulled it back when he caught Coach's scowl.

"Save your shenanigans for the bus ride home," Coach warned as he paid the bill. "Speaking of which, we leave in ten."

We filed out of the dining room five minutes later and I headed for the bus. Axel was already seated, and I plunked down beside him.

"Hey." I tried to act casual but failed.

He reached for my hand and pulled it onto his thigh. That wasn't casual at all.

"That call was from Preston's father."

"And?"

"He was arrested for assault," Axel admitted. "There's also a restraining order against him."

"Oh my God."

I sounded surprised but I wasn't.

"Yeah," Axel whispered. "Apparently the charges were filed by a guy Preston was seeing. A fellow acting student."

My stomach churned hard, and I pulled my hand back, slapping it over my mouth. My breakfast was about to make its way back up.

"Shit, are you okay?" Axel asked as I sat there, trembling.

I thought I'd dealt with Preston and the past, but apparently, I still had some unresolved trauma.

"I don't...I don't know."

I bent forward and cupped my hands over my mouth, taking several deep breaths.

In and out, in and out.

Axel rubbed my back in soothing circles and suddenly, Dane appeared in the aisle next to us.

"Bud, are you okay?" Dane asked.

"We just found out that Preston was arrested for assault," Axel explained as he continued to hold onto me.

"Fuck," Dane muttered.

"Yeah."

Then it wasn't just Dane, but Coach who walked up to us.

"What's going on?" Banning asked. "Jace, are you alright?"

"Not really. Someone that both Jace and I know got arrested," Axel replied since I was still too numb to speak.

"I'm so sorry," Coach replied. "Is there anything I can do? Do you want to talk about it?"

"He's my ex, so I'd rather not," I quietly admitted.

I looked up to find Coach offering a sympathetic look.

"Well, we're leaving for home shortly. When we get back to Sutton, maybe reach out to one of the counselors?"

"I'll do that."

I'd message my therapist for sure.

"In the meantime, I'm around if you need to chat."

"Thanks, Coach."

Coach gave a brief nod and headed to the front of the bus. Dane took the seat across from us. I leaned back and closed my eyes, trying to stay calm. I heard footsteps and chatter as the rest of our teammates boarded, but I pretended I was sleeping.

A few minutes later, I felt the bus move as we rolled out of Albany.

Axel didn't push me to talk. He gripped my knee for a moment, squeezing, and then let go. But I could still feel the warmth of his body as he leaned up close against me, his right thigh and shoulder touching my left. Just knowing that he was there if I needed him gave me a comfort that I didn't expect. One that had me wanting to do the same for him.

With my eyes still closed, I tentatively reached out my hand, resting it on Axel's thigh.

Would anyone notice? Would anyone care?

When Axel interlocked his hand with mine, I had my answer.

The only one who mattered was him.

CHAPTER 33
AXEL

After Albany, everything changed.

When we got back to Sutton that afternoon, Jace and I parted ways to our respective rooms. I dumped my bag, did a load of laundry, and headed back to Jace's two hours later. He was still shaken up, and so was I, and the only thing either of us wanted was to hold each other. Between the game yesterday, dealing with my parents, and the news this morning, it was a lot.

We lay on his bed, on our sides, wrapped around each other, face to face, trading sleepy kisses and whispered confessions.

"Total cuddler," he teased me.

I ran my thumb over those wicked lips of his, and then, not able to resist, I leaned in and planted a resounding kiss on them.

"Maybe I'll get *you* a jersey with *my* number," he added when I let him come up for air. "But instead of my name, I'll have 'Hot Cuddler' printed on it."

I bit my lower lip, trying not to smile.

"I'd wear it."

"Really?"

"For you? Damn right."

"Now I know that you love me," he quipped, and suddenly, his eyes widened. "I mean—"

"Yes," I said to him, cupping his chin, staring into his eyes. "Ax."

"You don't have to say it," I whispered against his lips. "But it's true. You feel it too."

He nodded and kissed me harder.

I'd do just about anything for Jace, including wearing a jersey with that silly nickname.

Being with him, like this, meant more to me than anything.

We both crashed hard and woke up early Sunday morning with the urge to get back on the ice. Our normal routine helped ease some of the anxiety we were both feeling. Jace texted Silas and Finn and asked if they wanted to join us, but Silas was busy, and Finn didn't want to get out of bed.

So, an hour later, we made off, trudging through the winter slush that blanketed the campus.

Then we hit the ice, just the two of us.

Only this time, instead of fighting our anger, we fought to keep our hands off each other. It wasn't easy and the more I watched Jace skate, the more turned on I got.

"Come here," I said to him as I came to a stop at the blue line.

Jace skated by me instead, giving me a wink, and when he got near the net, took his shot, waving his stick in the air to celebrate.

"Jace." I removed my glove and motioned with my finger. "Come here."

I needed to get my hands on him, and I couldn't wait another second.

But my boyfriend loved nothing better than teasing me, skating slowly this time, coming towards me like he had all the time in the world. I pushed off and met him halfway, yanking on his jersey until there was no space between us, both of us panting and sweaty and with big fucking grins on our faces.

Right there, on the rink, under blinding fluorescent lights, and surrounded by air so cold you could see our breaths, I kissed Jace.

I forgot about where I was. Everything, except him.

I tasted his smile and there was nothing better.

"Rowland, Lund!" Coach's voice suddenly rang out. "My office, now!"

Fuck.

We pulled apart and when I glanced around, Coach was standing on the other side of the boards, staring at us, his permascowl in place. He stalked off before I could think of something to say.

My first thought was, *what the hell was Coach doing here on a Sunday morning?* And then, *shit, we're in trouble.* But, then again, we hadn't done anything wrong.

Instead of freaking out, Jace and I skated off the ice and trudged down the hallway to Banning's cramped, drafty office.

"Close the door," Banning said as we entered.

"Look, Coach, we—"

He shook his head, and I knew better than to say anything.

"I guess I don't need to ask how the extra practice is going. Or, the fundraising event."

Well, we did have work to do on the event. We'd been neglecting it, but we'd get to it.

Eventually. When we finally took our hands off each other.

I took a seat and rubbed my suddenly sweaty palms against my breezers. Oh man, this was more difficult than I thought. Coming out to myself was one thing, but saying it out loud?

"Jace and I are sleeping together."

Once again, I was the master of subtlety.

Coach was silent and still. I looked at Jace, who was fighting a smile and shaking his head.

"What?" I asked.

"Maybe use a little more finesse next time," Jace replied, the edge of his lips curled up.

"It is what it is. We're boyfriends," I stated bluntly. "We're together, as in having se—"

"Okay, Lund," Coach held his hand up. "I get it. Well, I don't, because I thought you two couldn't stand each other, but what do I know? Hockey's my specialty, not human relations."

"I'm going to come out to the team," I offered. "But given my past behavior when it came to Maddox and Kayden, I'd like to tell them first. Dane already knows."

Banning sighed and rubbed a hand over his head.

"This concerns me," Coach started. "Not just because of how you've acted around each other since September but the fact that you often play the same line. That's a lot of pressure for any player, and at this level, even more so. How are you going to cope with that? Axel, I know you were angry about my decision to name Jace center, and, Jace, sometimes your temper runs just as hot. Throw in a relationship, and we're talking about a lot of emotions."

"I know I wasn't ready for that role," I admitted, my face flushing hot. "I just didn't want to accept it. Maybe I will be, someday, but not yet. I've still got work to do when it comes to my confidence and my game."

That wasn't easy to admit, not about myself, and not about Jace. But it was the truth.

Coach glanced at Jace.

"We can do this. I can do this," Jace replied. "I can separate the personal from the game. It's why you trust me as the center. I swear, Axel and I are good. Well, better than good, obviously."

Jace and I shared a heated look and it had me swallowing hard.

Banning steepled his hands together and leaned forward on his desk.

"Personally, it's none of my business, but professionally, if your relationship affects the team, it is. Stick to your job when you step into this rink. That means no personal stuff while you're in uniform, got it?"

"Yes, Coach," we answered in unison.

"Even at practice," he emphasized. "Like today."

"Yes, Coach," we repeated.

He motioned to the door.

"Go on. Get. And send me an update on the fundraiser first thing Monday morning," he added. "And don't say 'yes, Coach', just go."

Relieved, I got up and headed for the door first, opening it for Jace.

"I think that went well," I whispered when we finally hit the hallway and were alone again.

"Are you sure?" Jace leaned in. "That's not exactly how I pictured Coach finding out about us. I mean, are you okay after that talk?"

I nodded. "I feel relieved. No more hiding."

"You heard what he said though. Are you sure you're going to be able to resist me in uniform?"

I returned Jace's smile.

"That, I don't know."

———

I made big decisions this week and felt like I was finally coming into my own.

I texted Kayden later that day and asked him and Maddox to meet up with me, Jace, and Dane in my room. After everyone settled down with a soda and a slice of pizza, I was ready to tell them about me and Jace. And to apologize to my teammates, yet again.

Maddox seemed shocked by the news, but Kayden, not so much.

"So, this is the one?" Kayden said to Jace with a knowing smile.

Jace nodded.

"You told him?" I asked as I took hold of his hand.

"Not the details, but yeah," Jace replied. "Just before the game Friday."

"He's crazy about you," Kayden added.

"Same goes," I confirmed and kissed Jace.

"Shit, you guys are hot together," Kayden announced. "Ouch. Mad. Not the sharp elbow."

"Really, Kay?" Maddox hissed.

"I'm just saying, you know." Kayden blushed. "Look at them. It's a fact."

Dane nodded. "He's right."

That didn't seem to help Maddox's mood at all.

"You know I only have eyes for my Bee," Kayden added as he pulled Maddox into his side, kissing his temple.

"Not in front of everyone," Maddox grumbled.

But he didn't pull away from Kayden and the look that passed between them had me reaching for my drink.

An awkward silence fell, and I put a protective arm around Jace.

"About what happened back in January with Coach—" I started.

Maddox's glare cut me off. "You've apologized ten times already. Enough. Let's move on."

"But—"

"You can clean my stinky equipment for the rest of the semester if it makes you feel better," Maddox snarked.

"Bee," Kayden warned.

"I said, *if* it makes him feel better."

"What my boyfriend is trying to say is, we accept your apology," Kayden replied. "And we're really looking forward to getting to know you as a friend, not just a teammate."

Dane held up his soda and we all did the same.

"I second that."

———

The next day, I transferred all but a few hundred dollars back to my parents as they requested.

Oddly enough, I was okay about it. I wouldn't have guilt about cutting off contact with them after this and if my brother called asking for more money, I'd have nothing to loan him. Or, give him. He'd never paid me back anyway.

Once that was done, I headed into town and visited Boots n' Burgers. Not to eat, but to ask for a job. Thankfully, Phoenix told me he was always looking for wait staff for the weekend shifts, so I managed to snag a spot, and with the promise of full-time hours when the summer hit. Which worked out great, since I had no intention of going back to Redgewick this summer. Or, as I told my parents, at all.

But I couldn't afford next year's tuition fees on minimum wage and tips. I was on the lookout for another gig, even though I wasn't sure yet what that would look like. Something, anything to get me through to my twenty-first birthday and my trust fund. In the meantime, I sold some of my stuff online; clothing, watches, and expensive shit that I was gifted for show but that I didn't need. I pocketed five grand in cash. It wasn't enough, but it would get me through the next few months, until this semester was done.

After that, well, I had to have faith in myself that I'd find a way.

Knowing how Jace struggled growing up, I figured a year of financial hardship was nothing. I was never big on material stuff anyway. Another reason I didn't fit in at home. Any money I had, I spent on hockey. But, except for the basics, I was putting myself on a strict no-buy policy.

The only exception was Jace.

I hadn't been kidding when I said I ordered him a jersey. It arrived the week after our trip to Albany, and just in time for our first official date.

But life, like hockey, is full of sudden shifts.

Just when I thought I had an advantage, I got hit.

CHAPTER 34

JACE

A week later

"Have you seen Axel?" I asked Dane as we slid onto the ice for Thursday practice.

"You're asking me? He's your boy—" Dane paused and looked around. "No, I haven't."

It was odd and I was worried.

Axel hadn't come out to the entire team yet. That was happening at Ethan's party tomorrow night. Our first date. I was so excited and yet, really fucking nervous. Which was ridiculous, we were already sleeping together. Still, a date was different than fucking. It was so much more. We were more.

Unless he's changed his mind.

That horrible doubt would pop into my head at odd moments this week. I put it down to everything being so new and intense, but Axel hadn't returned my texts all day, and now he was late for practice? I knew that something was off.

"Hey," Dane whispered as he nudged me with his glove. "It'll be okay. Maybe he's late from class or something. Stop angsting."

"Yeah, well, it's so new with us, you know? But I'm really happy and I…I hope I'm not the only one here."

"You're not. I see the way he looks at you."

"Oh yeah?"

Dane nodded. "I know that look. He's so far gone."

"I hope so."

Coach appeared and blew his whistle to get us started.

Ten minutes into practice, there was no sign of Axel. And that horrible feeling in the pit of my stomach just wouldn't stop rumbling.

Finally, thirty minutes in, Axel arrived. Coach wasn't happy to say the least.

"Lund, tack an extra thirty on to your time tonight."

Axel nodded but I could tell by his clenched jaw that something bad was going on and it wasn't about hockey.

Quietly, I skated over to him, and he reached for my arm.

"What's up?" I asked casually, even though my heart was pounding like mad.

"It's Preston," Axel replied, leaning in and whispering. "He's here."

My racing pulse froze in an instant.

"What do you mean, he's here?" I reared back. "He's in jail, in California."

"He made bail," Axel replied, then bit his lower lip. "His dad flew him back to New York yesterday, then he rented a car and drove up here to see me. He called me last night."

"Fuck."

"Yeah, it's messed up. And that's not all. The guy he assaulted? The student? He supposedly promised to help Preston get a movie audition and when he didn't deliver, they got into a fight. Preston's not denying he hit the guy, but he says he got struck first, and he was defending himself."

"Do you believe him?"

I couldn't breathe and suddenly my vision blurred as I

wobbled on my skates like a newbie. Axel gripped my arm to steady me.

"No," he insisted. "I don't. There's not a mark on him, not a scratch or a bruise, so he's full of shit. Anyway, he said he needed a break from LA and figured this was a quiet place to land. He's staying at the Sutton Inn. He called me today and I went to see him. I had to, Jace. I didn't want him coming here on campus to find you. Not that he seems interested in that. He only talks about himself."

"I can handle seeing him," I whispered. "I'm fine."

"You're not fine. Your face is paler than this ice."

"Why didn't you tell me this morning, or better yet, last night?"

"I didn't want to upset you."

"Too fucking late," I snapped. "Are you meeting up with him again?"

Axel nodded. "Only to convince him to go back to LA. That's all."

"Are you sure about that?" I threw out.

"Are you saying you don't trust me?" he lobbied back.

Dane skated up and gave us a warning look.

"What the hell's going on guys? Coach is ready to get back to it."

"Preston's in town. He arrived in Sutton this morning to see me," Axel replied.

"Are you shitting me?" Dane looked at me. "Do you need to leave practice?"

"No!" I exclaimed and suddenly other teammates turned to stare. "No, if anything I need to be here. I'm fine."

"It's okay if you're not," Dane replied calmly. "Coach will understand."

"I'm not going to let that asshole fuck with my head again," I bit out and yanked my arm away from Axel. "I'm here to play, let's play."

"Jace!" Axel called my name, but I was already off.

Just when I thought I was rid of the past, it had to come back and kick me in the ass. I needed time to deal with this news and to figure out what to do. I wasn't scared to see Preston in person, that wasn't it. I was stronger now and he didn't have any hold on me. No, the reason I was upset was because I was pissed at Axel. The fact that he'd talked to Preston, met up with him, without telling me first, set me off. Then I remembered they'd been best friends since high school. I'd only been with Axel for a month, and before that, the only contact we had was passing each other insults, along with pucks.

I'm a fighter. I fight for what I want. I'm fighting for you, too.

Was Axel fighting for me?

Axel

I couldn't concentrate and it showed.

Silas kicked my ass when we practiced danger zone drills, and then Finn did the same. Coach was even less impressed with me than when I first got here.

How could I focus when I was worried about Jace, my thoughts on him the whole time?

Coach's reminders about separating hockey and personal rebounded in my head.

I knew the second I'd taken Preston's call that I was fucked. But Jace was right. I should've told him right away. I should've known that Jace was strong enough to take the news. What was even worse was that Jace seemed to doubt the reason *why* I went to see Preston. Hadn't we already talked about this? How could I prove to Jace that he was the only thing that mattered?

When practice was done, I stayed behind to do my extra drills.

At first, I was too caught up in my head to notice that Jace stayed behind with me. Jace and Dane. When I turned around and found them leaning on their sticks, talking to each other, some of my earlier anxiety waned.

"I'll leave you guys to it," Dane announced.

Our captain slipped away and then it was just me and Jace.

"You heard Cap. Keep working," Jace announced as he skated by, swiping the puck as quick as lightning.

I chased after him, my competitive ego never far behind. He was faster, taking the shot, the sharp echo of his stick meeting ice and rubber. He'd been pushing hard all practice, and one slapshot was harder than the next.

"Battle drill?" I suggested.

It was entirely appropriate given how our relationship had started and where we were now. Only, I wanted to fight alongside Jace, not against him. I knew he was the same. I knew it. And I wasn't going to let this stupid thing with Preston ruin us.

Being so in tune with someone I was playing hockey with was both a blessing and a curse. I was aware of Jace in a way I wasn't with anyone else on the team, anticipating his every move, and yet, I was afraid to get too close, and afraid for him to get hurt. Did he feel the same?

It was yet another hurdle for us to climb.

He skated towards the net, plucked out the puck, and turned to me, his face devoid of expression. Laughing and smiling was his usual. A smart-ass comment, a teasing joke. But this coldness, it was so unlike him that my stomach twisted painfully.

Skating backwards, I took my spot and waited for Jace to make the first play.

I was so caught up in my feelings and my head that I didn't even realize he was already beside me.

"Ax."

"Yeah?" I replied, tapping my stick on the ice.

"Are you okay?"

I shook my head. "I'm worried about you."

"Don't be. I can handle it." Jace licked his lips. "I'm sorry I got upset."

"You have every right. I should've said something, but—"

"Hey, we're both new to this, it's okay. But we have to be honest, no hiding or delaying the truth. Have faith that I can handle bad news, and I'll do the same."

"I don't want to, you know," I paused, taking off one of my gloves and wiping the sweat from my face. "Trigger your disorder."

"I know, baby, but there's always going to be something," Jace replied. "It's what I deal with every day. Same with you and depression. All we can do is learn ways to cope and do our best, always moving forward."

"Jace," I skated closer, staring into his hazel eyes.

There. The fire was there. My Jace.

"What happened today is a blip," I insisted, tempted to lean in and taste his lips, but remembering Coach's warning. "He's going to leave, and that'll be that. I don't want to spend any more time thinking or talking about him. I want to focus on us."

Jace reached for my jersey, clutching it tight in his hand, and then I heard it.

Someone was clapping.

I turned around to find Preston standing on the other side of the boards staring at us. With his slick hair and California tan, he didn't look like a man who'd just been arrested. He looked like he was back from freaking vacation.

"Isn't this a fun little reunion?" he announced with a sneer. "My ex and my ex-BFF getting cozy in this dank, smelly rink."

"Go back to LA, Preston. Deal with your charges and get help."

"Help? For what?" Preston shrugged. "My father will make sure the charges are dropped. He's a lawyer, remember?

And I'm not staying in this shithole any longer than I need to. I just wanted to confirm the rumor for myself. Our friendship, such as it was Axel, served my purpose."

"What does that mean?"

"I'm sure you've taken hits on the ice, especially to that big head of yours, but even you're not *that* stupid," Preston replied. "But I'll make it simple for you anyway. Your parents owned that town and nearly everyone in it. Including my father."

That, I didn't know. And I didn't want to know any more.

"I have no idea what you're talking about."

"You grew up with so much influence, but you're so fucking dumb."

"Don't talk to him like that," Jace snapped. "Just stop with the mind games and get the fuck out of here."

"Jace, passionate as always. And I thought you liked games?" Preston cocked his head. "I guess the STD I gave you finally cleared up? It'd be a shame for you to lose the only thing you're good at."

"You piece of shit," I growled and started for the boards.

Jace held on to my jersey.

"I can't believe I ever trusted you," I bit out. "And, whatever you have to say, I don't care."

"But your parents will. And don't deny it. Jonas told me you were fucking a teammate. I wasn't sure I believed him at first. But now that I see you two together—" Preston paused. "I'm sure your parents will be very interested to find out you're fucking a guy. I wonder what they'd pay to keep that quiet?"

"Go for it," I snapped back. "Tell everyone. I'm never going back there, so I don't care. Just get the hell gone and leave us alone."

Preston's smirk faltered.

"You won't get anything from them," I added firmly,

aiming my final shot. "The money's gone. The Lunds are broke. Feel free to announce that too."

"I don't believe you," Preston replied, his voice low.

"Same goes."

Preston shrugged.

"Well, then, maybe it's best that I head back to LA. There's nothing here I can use."

"We finally agree on something."

"I'll make a stop at Redgewick on my way back," Preston called out over his shoulder. "Just to be sure."

"Tell my family I said hi."

CHAPTER 35

JACE

xel and I reached for each other, both of us shaking. We didn't speak, not until Preston walked out of sight.

"I hope like fuck he's really leaving town," I said as I finally let out the breath I'd been holding. "How did your brother find out about us?"

"I sent Jonas a text by accident the day we rolled into Albany. It was meant for you. He's the only one, outside of the guys, that knows."

"Why would he tell Preston?"

Axel bit his lower lip.

"Jonas threatened to out me. He asked me to send him more money, and I said no, that I didn't have any and I didn't care if he wanted to tell. Maybe he figured I was bluffing. Jonas probably thought telling Preston was payback. I don't know. I don't think I want to know."

"That's fucked up."

"I keep telling you that," Axel replied, his eyes darkening. "You sure you want to be with me? This might not be the last of him. Or, them."

I stared at him, at those midnight blues. It wasn't just frustration that Axel was dealing with, it was loneliness too. Loneliness and lies. And I hated that. He deserved so much more.

"Forget our Friday night date," I blurted out.

"What?" Axel's grip on my arms tightened.

"Let's not wait until tomorrow. Let's go tonight."

Instead of replying, Axel reached for me, cupping my face, slamming his lips over mine, all heat and hunger, and fuck my man knew how to kiss. We were both sweaty from practice and there was way too much padding between our bodies, but that didn't stop us. Until our helmets knocked against each other, and we laughed, breaking apart, finally coming up for air.

"Let's get changed and go on that date."

I glanced at the clock at the far end of the rink.

"You've still got seven minutes of ice time left," I pointed out.

Axel groaned and I nudged him with my elbow.

"Come on, we're headed into the finals, you've gotta keep in top shape."

"Sex doesn't count?" he quipped but relented when I gave him a knowing look.

"Fine," he grumbled and reached for his stick.

I chuckled at his put-out tone, feeling lighter than I had in a long time.

Despite Preston's unwelcome interruption, I was okay. Unsettled for sure, but not panicked. I guess years of therapy, the support of my aunt, my friends, and now Axel, meant that I was ready to face whatever opponent came at me. Even if it was an old one.

Axel and I finished up our practice as promised, then headed for the locker room to quickly change. We went our separate ways when we got to the dorm, with Axel insisting that he'd knock on my door when he was ready.

I showered, shaved, and slathered styling crème through my messy dark waves. After slipping into my favorite pair of jeans, I reached for a white t-shirt and layered on the jersey that Axel bought me. It was an exact replica of our team jersey, forest green, complete with our cougar logo in gold, and with 'Axel Lund' written across the back and his number thirteen. It should've been odd to see someone else's name and number on my shirt, but I didn't feel anything but happiness. Not just that, it was like he was right here, holding on to me, wrapped tight. A feeling of safety and love that I didn't take for granted.

I picked up my phone and turned my back to face the mirror, taking a snap and sending it to Axel.

> Axel: My phone's melting. Honey, you're the one who's Hot.

> Jace: It fits perfectly. It was meant to be.

> Axel: I'm on my way. I can't wait.

> Jace: Good, because I'm more than ready for this date.

Two and a half minutes later, there was a knock on my door. With eager hands, I reached for my jacket and gloves, and opened the door to find Axel standing there looking gorgeous.

And nervous? He wasn't the only one.

Dressed in black jeans, a matching button-down, and his parka, he leaned against the doorjamb and gave me the same once-over. He'd trimmed his reddish-blond scruff, and his shaggy hair was tamed (most of it). But it was his face that did me in, graced with that rare, wicked smile that had the power to knock my knees out.

He reached for me just in time, but then I remembered.

"Hold on," I urged him as I placed my jacket on the floor. "I have something for you."

I turned back and headed for my dresser, opening the top drawer and pulling out a white paper bag. When I passed it to him, he stared down at it in confusion.

"You didn't have to do that."

"Open it."

He opened the bag and pulled out a box.

"Red laces?" he stared at me. "You noticed?"

"Your first team, right?"

Axel nodded.

"I got a pair for you, and one for me. For game day. That way you know, no matter what, I'm thinking of you."

"Thank you."

He blinked quickly, then looked away, staring down at the box in his hand. Suddenly I wondered if I'd done something wrong.

"Or, I can take them back? I just thought—"

Axel placed the box back in the bag and put it in his coat pocket.

"It's the best gift I've ever received," he said quietly, taking my hands.

"I doubt that."

It was probably the cheapest gift he'd ever been given.

He leaned in, brushing his lips against my ear.

"It's true, Jace. It means everything."

I turned my head, teasing his jaw with my lips.

"Baby."

"And you already gave me a gift," he added, letting go of my hands and reaching for my hips. "Turn around so I can see it."

I turned in his arms, showing him the back of the jersey.

"It's way hotter in person," he confessed and then pulled me tight to his body until his hips collided with my ass, his face nuzzling my neck. "But it's going to look even better when you're wearing my jersey and nothing else."

I pictured Axel bending me over my desk, him fully dressed and me naked, except for that jersey, as he railed me hard. Oh God, that was hot.

"We're never going to leave my room," I groaned.

"Save that for later," Axel replied and teased my neck with kisses. "Dinner first, then a walk around town, and maybe a movie. I want everyone to know that you're mine."

"Are you sure?"

Instead of replying, Axel stepped back.

"Ax?"

I turned around to face him and he was picking up my jacket, holding it open for me.

I slipped it on, and he squeezed my shoulders, then let go. We stepped out of my room, and I locked the door, pausing against it for a moment as we stood in the hallway and stared at each other.

Axel offered me his hand, and I looked at it, then up at his deep blues.

I heard a nearby door open, didn't know whose, didn't care. The dorm was busy tonight, students getting ready to go out. Familiar faces walked by me, by us, but I didn't see them.

Just him. This tough, gruff hockey player with a sheltered heart. One he shared only with me.

Standing there, while interested passersby looked on, I reached out and took hold of his hand, interlocking our fingers.

And I didn't let go.

Axel

I walked—no, strutted—down the hallway with Jace's hand in mine, feeling like the luckiest damn guy in the world.

There were stares, of course, a few raunchy comments, and a whistle or two as we headed for the elevator.

"It's gonna get intense," Jace admitted.

"I play my best under pressure," I reassured him. "We'll be fine."

Maybe it was naïve, but I'd been dealing with haters all my life. And having to defend myself wasn't anything new.

While I was in the shower getting ready for tonight, I received a nasty voicemail from my mother. Preston worked fast. Still, I didn't care if she was upset with the fact that I was dating a teammate. I didn't care about the fallout for my father's business deal, either. If having a queer son was a problem, it was all theirs.

I was only a trophy to them; one they liked to pull out at key moments for appearance's sake.

But not anymore. Trophies were for sports, not people.

"This is surreal," Jace whispered as we stepped out of the dorm and started across campus.

Winter snow was melting, and fresh spring was in the air. And all the promises that came with it.

"In a good way?" I teased.

"The best."

We wandered down the pathway, and through the main gates, and then headed for the town proper. Sutton was all decked out at night, with tiny white lights strung up on every lamppost on every street corner. This wasn't just a holiday thing, but a year-round tradition.

We had dinner at Romano's Italian Eatery, but instead of the usual pizza, Jace and I shared three enormous plates of pasta. Their carbonara was my personal fave, not to mention the basket of homemade bread and honey butter. After our meal, we took a long stroll around town until we hit Boots n' Burgers. The outdoor patio in the back was bustling thanks to the heat lamps and stone firepit that offered a cozy place to sit and linger.

"There's a couple of seats over there," Jace pointed to the middle, where a couple was getting up to leave.

We snagged the two seats near the firepit just in time.

"You still hungry?" I asked Jace.

"I'm good. But maybe a drink?"

Phoenix appeared, making the rounds of the patio, taking orders, and when he spotted us, sauntered over to say hi. The instant he spotted our joined hands, he smiled.

"Is this what I think it is? Not that I'm surprised."

"You're not?" Jace asked.

Phoenix shook his head. "Last time you were here your convo looked pretty intense. Reminded me of when I met my husband."

"It's our first official date," I said proudly.

"That's sweet," Phoenix replied. "How about some hot chocolate to make it even sweeter?"

"That'd be great, thanks."

"On the house," Phoenix added over his shoulder as he headed back inside.

Sitting back, I put my arm around my boyfriend's shoulder and glanced up at the night sky, so clear, the stars bold and bright. It felt like I could reach out and touch their glittery perfection. Jace nuzzled his face into my neck and something much warmer than fire settled deep inside me.

"Hold on."

I grabbed my phone with my free hand and raised it up.

"Smile, Honey."

Jace leaned in and kissed my cheek as I tapped the screen, capturing the moment.

"Let's see," he said excitedly.

I showed him the picture, his beautiful face next to mine, and God, my heart expanded, like it was about to burst wide open.

Look at us. This is what love is.

"I think it's time we told everyone on the team that our

rivalry has a new chapter," I proclaimed and kissed him soundly.

"I love the sound of that," Jace whispered. "And how does that chapter end?"

I leaned in and took his lips, tasting his smile.

"It doesn't."

EPILOGUE

AXEL

APRIL

Everyone in the city of Sutton was here tonight at the Hot Shots fire hall fundraiser, including all the Cougars, and we had a lot to celebrate.

There was a roster of students from Sutton's other sports programs too, including the football team and the rowing crew. The mayor was front and center, along with Nora Renner, Sutton University's President, and Coach Banning, who made the rounds of the room, and of course, local business owners, and state media. But it was the appearance of Chicago's star defenseman Selwin Kirkland that had the room buzzing with excitement. He was accompanied by his assistant and his agent, and he couldn't move without someone wanting an autograph or a selfie.

The Cougars had three tables, room enough for all the players and their dates—those who chose to bring one—everyone dressed up in their best outfits. And every teammate wore a forest green beaded bracelet—made with love by Kayden—with their nickname and number on it. I agreed to wear it on one condition; Jace wore mine and I wore his. It wasn't the same as him wearing my jersey, but it would do.

Jace and I put in a lot of work these past two months to help the organizers of this event. It was stressful between school and hockey finals, but somehow, we managed. And it was a huge success, thanks mostly to Jace's charisma; he convinced more teammates to volunteer and had people opening their wallets to donate to the cause. And me? I kept it all in motion, so to speak. Kind of like how it was when we were playing hockey.

And my game? That had taken off along with our relationship, and my confidence. I wasn't just talking about playing the best hockey of my life, I was doing it. No, I didn't match Jace's scoring stats, but I was close. He teased me about catching up to him, but the truth was, I didn't need to.

I was exactly where I was meant to be; by Jace's side, both on and off the ice.

Not that this semester was without its struggles. It was still a long road for me to open up to my teammates, and to forge new friendships. But every day, I worked a little harder, and I was getting there. Jace and I often hung out with Dane and Jackson in particular, both of whom became two of my closest friends.

And after coming out to the team, I'd texted my parents one last time and told them the news. I didn't get a response, and I was okay with that. The only one in my family who reached out to me was Jonas. A month after that game in Albany, Jonas texted me to tell me that our parents were filing for bankruptcy and he needed a loan. I told Jonas that like me, he'd have to wait for his trust fund. Patience, however, wasn't my brother's strong suit. He sent me a long, vicious text, so I blocked him and got on with my life.

And my former BFF? Neither Jace or I ever heard from Preston again. I found out from Jonas (before I blocked him) that Preston was back in LA, acting, but not in college, because he got kicked out after the assault incident. No surprise there.

Not having any contact with my family or Preston meant I was finally finding peace. I'd be turning twenty-one in the fall and with that, I'd be financially independent. Even without my trust fund, I'd manage. Jace had shown me that with hard work and the right mindset, I could achieve anything I wanted.

I was still a Lund in name, but I was starting a new legacy. Instead of playing my family's game, I'd stick to hockey...

Halfway through the evening, with the speeches over and the dancing underway, the real party began. Some of Jackson's team joined our table, including Archie, and his crewmates, Jett and Hudson. They were cool guys who were all different in looks and personality, friendly but competitive to an extreme. Even more than our team, and that was saying a lot. And, of course, they wanted to know all about the championship game.

We'd clinched it, but that was a story for another day.

"I want to hear about the game-winning goal from the man himself," Archie insisted as he stared at me. "Come on, Ax, spill."

Silas shook his head. "Please, not again. Axel's going to get an ego bigger than his boyfriend's."

Jace bundled up his napkin and threw it at Silas, who laughed and threw it back.

Unfortunately, Coach Banning sat down at our table at that exact moment, and it landed on him instead of Jace. The look Coach gave Silas told me there was a lot of extra ice time involved in our defenseman's future.

"Silas," Coach bit out.

"Nice fit," Silas muttered.

Everyone looked surprised at his comment, but Silas was right. Coach looked sharp in a classic black tux and matching shirt and tie.

"But where's your whistle?" Silas continued, and everyone at the table laughed.

"I don't think you want me to tell you where you can find it," Coach retorted, making us laugh harder. "Are you done now?"

Silas raised his tattooed hands in mock surrender.

"Good," Banning stated and cleared his throat. "I wanted to take a moment to congratulate Axel and Jace and thank them for their hard work on this event. You've done the Cougars, and Sutton U, proud."

There was a round of applause from our teammates, and I squeezed my boyfriend's hand.

"I also have news to share," Banning paused and looked around the table. "With the approval of the university board and the dean of athletics, I'm pleased to announce that I'm offering a hockey training camp this summer, three days a week, June and July. I've sent you the official email with the details. This is an add-on for players who need dedicated coaching and mentoring. And there will be a professional player, or two, dropping by as well."

"Kirkland?" Silas asked.

"He's been asked, yes. Keep in mind, the camp isn't a right fit for everyone and there will be limited spots."

"When's the deadline to apply?" Finn asked.

"May 15th."

Silas leaned forward. "And the fee?"

"It's in the email." Banning stood up again. "Six spots are available, first come, first served. Any follow-up questions, drop by my office or email me."

"Thanks, Coach," Dane replied.

"Enjoy the rest of your night."

Coach nodded at us, then walked off into the crowd.

"Any takers?" Ethan asked the table.

"I'm interested," Finn announced. "I don't have a job lined up at home yet, so I think I'll stay on here. It sounds cool."

"What the fuck, Finn? Summer's about having fun," Ethan teased.

"Training camp's not fun?"

Ethan groaned at Finn's statement, and I knew the razzing was just getting started.

And summer for me and Jace? It was going to be as busy as our school year, with both of us staying on in Sutton. Jace had a part-time gig waiting tables at Boots, then he'd travel to Burlington three days a week for his kinesiology internship with a farm team. I'd managed to snag an internship too, fifteen hours a week, remote, for a sports agent based in NYC. Between that and working full time at Boots, my weeks would be packed. The money I'd earn might not be enough, and I'd probably have to take out a loan until my trust fund kicked in, but I'd be okay.

Jace's aunt Josie was coming for a weekend in July, and we'd already started planning out activities, including a hiking trip. I'd met her virtually and to say that my nerves were tested was an understatement. Jace had told her the whole story—edited of course—about me and him, but I worried that she wouldn't be supportive. She was protective of him, which I understood all too well. Once I made it clear that I was the same, that Jace was my everything, she gave her blessing.

"Hey, Axel, you never answered my question," Archie called out. "Tell us about the goal. Come on, spill."

"I don't know—"

"Come on, baby, tell them," Jace urged. "Shout it loud and proud."

Number eight was my number one fan and I laughed at Jace's comment. I was doing that all the time now. I saved my resting asshole face for hockey opponents. And for times when Jace and I got into heated arguments. Hey, we'd always fight passionately, it was just us. And he more than liked my grumpy face. The hot-as-hell make-up sex proved it.

"Not much to tell," I insisted as I glanced at Archie. "It was all teamwork. Jace made one of his lightning quick moves, a beauty of a pass, and I slid it home."

"That's it?" Jace exclaimed. "That's all you have to say? Where's the cocky dude from last semester?"

"I'm still here," I replied as I turned to him and put an arm around his shoulders. "I'm just cocky in other ways."

"Yeah, the dirty ones," Ethan chuckled.

Everyone threw their napkins at Ethan.

"Come on, Ax," Jace encouraged. "Tell them."

I shrugged and leaned forward.

"It all started on a frozen pond when I was six years old," I started.

This time, it was my turn to get a napkin in the face.

I chuckled and glanced at Archie. "Third period, less than two minutes remaining. I nearly get a stick in the face, but no penalty's called. The clock's running down. Jace gets the puck but then he gets boxed in, and since I'm on his ass—"

"Stick to the game!" Jett shouted and everyone laughed.

"Jace saw an opportunity," I continued. "Before I knew it, the puck was on my stick, and I was slamming it harder than any slapshot in my life."

"And that's how it's done," Jace added, squeezing my shoulder.

"Eh, just doing my job."

"You're way too modest, Axel," Archie replied. "But speaking of high-stakes games, when are we going to have that competition? Crew vs. Cougars. Let's see how fast and strong you guys are off the ice."

"It's on," Dane leaned in. "But it has to be a sport that offers a level playing field."

"Volleyball?" Jett suggested.

"Soccer," Ethan countered.

Dane considered and offered his hand to Jett.

"Soccer. Done."

"Losers have to shave their heads," Jett added. "And beards."

Silas looked horrified. I placed a protective hand over my head and glanced at Jace, but he just shrugged.

"We can do that," Jace replied. "It's offseason so no worries."

Ethan pointed at Jett. "What does the winner get?"

"Bragging rights." Jett offered a smirk. "What else do you need?"

"More than that," Ethan replied and rolled his eyes.

"You think of something," Jett countered.

"You're on."

This was going to be very interesting. I wasn't sure how quick any of us on the hockey team would be able to move on grass. But hey, both sports involved footwork, so that had to be to our advantage. Then again, the rowing crew was known for their stamina and soccer fields were a lot bigger than a rink.

"I can't wait to see you in a pair of tight shorts and nothing else," Jace whispered in my ear.

"Oh, Honey, same."

All night long, I stayed by Jace's side. Everyone knew that he was mine. And the way he held on to me? There was no mistaking that I was his too.

"I love you," I whispered in his ear.

"I love you, too."

"Even when I go caveman?" I quipped.

"Especially then."

I paused and drew back, looking into his eyes.

"You know something," I started, grinning at him. "It's not that goal that I'm most proud of."

"No?"

I shook my head.

"It's us."

The smile Jace gave me lit up the entire room.

"I couldn't have said it better myself."

Thank you for reading Play Maker! Click here if you want to read about Jace & Axel's summertime adventure.

Defenseman Silas Moss and Coach Damien Banning have something to prove and everything to lose in Heart Taker, Bar Down Book 3.

Want more of my MM romances? Check out all my books here.

BONUS STORY
CAMPING CAPER

JACE

I stood beside the rental car at the base of the hiking trail, hands on my hips, like I was readying for battle, not a weekend in the woods. Woods that had bears, and coyotes, and other creatures that outnumbered us. I loved Vermont, but I usually stuck to hiking and ski trails.

Camping overnight?

It wasn't really my thing. I preferred a proper mattress and cool A/C at night.

"Remind me again why we're doing this?"

My question went unanswered. Until I turned around and found Axel giving me a crooked smile. The one that wrecked me, every fucking time.

"Because it's something neither of us has ever done before. Aren't you excited?" Axel replied and pulled me into his arms.

"I'd be more excited if we were going someplace with an actual bed."

My boyfriend silenced my sarcasm with a resounding kiss.

"Come on, Honey, it's going to be great. You, me, a sturdy air mattress, and most important of all, no interruptions."

That sounded amazing. While sex with my boyfriend was always hot, fucking in a college dorm had its drawbacks. Namely, other students who loved nothing better than to interrupt our good times. Out here, however, there was no one and nothing to disturb us. Except, maybe, a wild animal. Or several.

"I love the idea of no interruptions, but do you think we're prepared?"

"Us? Please. We've got every necessity we'll need. And I've done my research."

That was true. Axel went on a buying binge in preparation for our weekend trip, and the proof was in our gear. Swear to God, we were carrying the entire Patagonia catalogue on our backs. We'd probably survive the apocalypse at this point. He'd taken to this trip like he was an outdoor pro, and it still surprised me. Axel grew up in in a wealthy household, so he was used to luxury; that is, glamping, not camping. But the idea came to him when we took my aunt, who visited two weeks ago, on a nature hike in these very same woods. Axel had such a good time that he insisted we make it a whole weekend, just the two of us.

I was up to try anything once, but part of me still anxious.

"I checked the forecast again and we're going to have warm, sunny weather, and no rain, so it's perfect," he announced. "We're gonna hike towards Amika Falls near the ridge and set up camp nearby. We'll swim, then build a fire, and make dinner."

That sounded perfect. In theory.

He kissed me again, dispelling some, but not all, of my worries.

"And then," he continued. "Sex under the stars."

"I like the sound of that."

It sounded romantic as fuck, but I've seen the Great Outdoors too many times to believe that this weekend won't end in unmitigated disaster. Worse, what if Axel can't stand the sight of me after two days alone together? We've been inseparable for months, and I know that he loves me, but still. There's nothing like a trip to test a relationship.

"Trust me," Axel whispered.

"I do," I insisted and held him tighter. "I'm just all up in my head."

Truthfully, it wasn't just the camping trip. There was a lot going on in our lives; summer jobs, getting ready to start a new school year, the upcoming hockey season. Plus, uncertainty about when we're going to get drafted. That last one worried me most of all. If we ended up on different teams, in different cities, which was probably going to happen, what would become of us? I thought about it every day and the knot in my gut wouldn't let up. I haven't said anything to him because giving my fears a voice was scary as fuck…

"I know," Axel continued and cupped my face.

He does. My boyfriend knows exactly where my mind's gone. I can't hide anything from him.

"That's why we need this break. To forget about all that stuff; school, our jobs, and yes, even hockey. Just for a few days. No outside noise. Nothing but you and me."

"You're right," I whispered, trying to focus on the present. "Let's do this."

"It should take about thirty minutes to reach the campsite," Axel reminded me. "You got your sunscreen on?"

"Yep."

"Bug spray?"

"Check."

"Bear spray?"

"Double check."

"Alright."

With a final nod, Axel stepped back, but he didn't let go of me. Instead, he took my hand and led me over to the entrance at the base of the trail.

The walk was easy, at first. We met a few fellow hikers along the way but other than that, it was quiet and peaceful.

The last ten minutes of the hike was way harder, but worth it when we reach our destination. I take a moment to glance around at the stunning view of the rolling green hills all around us. Then I glance at my boyfriend. Axel looks like he's made for the wilderness. He's got a sexy mountain man vibe going with the hockey beard, his messy blond hair, tight t-shirt, and camo cargo pants. All kinds of dirty scenarios pass through my mind, one fantasy hotter than the next.

Maybe this outdoor adventure was a great idea after all.

"Okay, time to get to work," Axel called out. "We've gotta get the tent set up."

"Right now? You interrupted my mountain man fantasy."

Axel raised one eyebrow.

"You're the man," I insisted.

Axel's returning gaze was so hot that I was ready to get rid of these clothes and get naked, now.

"Strip down and race to the falls?"

Axel shook his head. "Not until we set up the tent."

"Seriously?"

"Yep, it's an order."

"I thought I was the bossy one."

"I've learned from the best."

"Well, then, tell me where you want me, boss."

He stalked towards me and offered a swat on my ass. "That's Camp Sargeant to you, Honey."

Ooh, I liked that roleplay idea. Teasing him, I removed my t-shirt and ran my hands over my chest. Axel lets out a loud groan and I know I've got him. He loves tracing my cougar tattoo with his tongue.

"Not playing fair," he grumbled.

Chuckling, I bent over to reach for the tent.

"I'm giving you incentive to get this thing done quickly so we can get to the fun stuff."

Unfortunately, setting up the tent is not as easy as it looks. It doesn't help that Axel refused to read the directions. A half an hour later and we're only halfway done.

"We should've brought someone from the engineering department with us," I quipped.

"Hilarious." Axel rolled his eyes and pointed to the ground. "Grab the pole."

"Sounds dirty."

"Focus, Honey."

After struggling for another ten minutes, I finally convinced Axel to use the damn directions, and we got the tent setup finished. It looks solid, but only a night in this forest will tell.

After that, my bossy boyfriend conceded that it was time for a soak and a sunbathe. We gathered our towels and walked the short distance to the falls. With no one else around, we stripped down and waded into the water. It was crystal clear, cool, and refreshing. With the sun shining down, we float together, my legs wrapped around his waist, his arms holding me tight. The moment was pure, undisturbed bliss.

I ran a wet hand through Axel's thick hair, pushing it back so I can see his gorgeous eyes. Last summer, we barely knew each other, except for hockey games, and now look at us. Some days I can hardly believe at how much our lives have changed. I fall more in love with him with every passing day and sometimes the feeling overwhelmed me, but in the very best way.

We kissed for ages, and like any time I touch Axel, I want to merge with him in every possible way. All those fears that were bubbling below the surface begin to float away.

"Happy four-month anniversary," Axel whispered.

"Aw, baby," I kissed him back. "Happy anniversary to you too."

"By the way, I only brought one sleeping bag," he admitted. "We're going to have to share."

He pulled me in closer, and I smiled against his lips.

"I can't think of anything better."

Axel

Jace finally relaxed in my arms, and it was about damn time.

He's been his usual sweet bundle of energy lately, but I notice that every time there's even the mention of the future, he gets stressed out. Jace tried to play off like it doesn't bother him, but I know exactly where his mind is at. Which is why I insisted on this camping retreat. Just the two of us. No phones, no distractions, no interruptions.

I don't like the worry in his eyes and I'm going to make sure that by the end of this weekend, that uncertainty is gone. I know that what Jace and I have is special. This man has my whole heart, and no matter where we end up, we will find a way to be together. I've never been surer of anything in my life, not even hockey.

After paddling around the pond for a while, we made our way back to the tent and christened the sleeping bag. Like always, I was so caught up in Jace, and our sex, that at first, I didn't hear the bellowing.

"What was that noise?" he asked me.

We both stilled.

"That wasn't you?"

"Ax, seriously?"

The blood is now circulating back to my brain when I hear another bellow, louder this time, and deeper. Oh shit.

"I think we have company."

Jace slapped a hand over his eyes. "Oh my God."

"Whatever it is, it's probably miles away. The sounds echo up here."

"What do we do?" he hissed.

"I'm going to take a quick peek."

I reluctantly pulled myself away from my boyfriend and reached into my backpack for my binoculars. As quietly as I could, I slowly unzipped the tent and looked around. There was nothing visible in the immediate vicinity, so that's good. But then I heard what sounded like a grunt. There's definitely an animal of some kind out there, but what exactly, I have no idea. My view from here is limited.

I popped my head back inside. "I'm heading out to get a better look around. Pass me my pants."

"Are you crazy?"

"No. I can't get a 360 from this viewpoint."

"I'm going with you," Jace insisted.

All my protective instincts are now fully engaged. "No. If there is something, you stay in here."

"No way, Ax. Where you go, I go."

"Always?"

"Fuck yes."

I put aside the binoculars and reached for him, kissing him senseless.

When I finally let him up for air, I stared into his beautiful eyes. "Are you going to stop worrying about the future now?"

"Baby, if we survive this weekend, I'm sure we can handle anything that comes our way."

My smile couldn't be contained.

"That's what I want to hear. I love you."

"I love you too," Jace replied. "Now let's see who we've got as neighbors."

I reached for my pants and plaid shirt and slid them on, while Jace did the same. Then I grabbed the binoculars again, the can of bear spray, and a flashlight. Jace is right there beside me as we slowly stepped outside. I don't see anything.

Until I hear a cracking sound behind me, like a branch snapping.

Lifting the binoculars, I swiveled to look towards the southern slope of the mountain.

"Holy shit," I whispered.

"Is it a bear? Where is it?"

"Not a bear. A moose. Look."

Handing the binoculars over, Jace pulled them up to his face.

"Wow, he's huge. And he's eating some kind of plant."

"She. No antlers."

Jace lowered the binoculars and stared at me.

"What? I told you I did a bit of googling this week. Do you know that female moose are called cows? And yeah, they're vegetarian, so don't worry, they won't try to eat us."

"But they will charge if they feel threatened?"

"Um, yeah, they will," I admitted. "Especially if they have a calf. But don't worry, I didn't see one."

Jace looked over again.

"Hold on," he whispered. "I think we're okay. She's starting to walk off towards the east."

"That's good. Let's stay in the tent and be as quiet as we can for now. I'll have another look in a few minutes. Or, if you're worried, there's a cave near the falls that will offer us protection."

Jace paused and stared at me. "Who *are* you right now?"

"Me? I'm your mountain man, Honey."

Jace crooked his finger and offered me a sinful grin, the one that made my knees weak.

"Come here."

"Jace, I'm serious, we have to be quiet," I reminded him as I ushered him back inside the tent.

We quickly stripped down and reached for each other.

"I'll do my best."

It turned out, we weren't quiet at all and the wildest thing in the forest that weekend was us.

———

I hope you enjoyed Jace and Axel's bonus story. I've got more coming soon!

ABOUT THE AUTHOR

Ava Olsen writes steamy and dreamy MM romance with heartwarming characters, sexy banter, and ALL the romantic feels.

Sign up for my newsletter for the latest updates, cover reveals, and bonus scenes: http://avaolsenauthor.com

FOLLOW ME

ALSO BY AVA OLSEN

Bar Down: MM College Hockey Romance

Rule Breaker

Play Maker

Heart Taker

Stand Alone (enemies to lovers)

Happily Never After

Wayward Lane MM Rockstar Romance

PUNK-IN

B-MINE

4-EVER

Wayward Lane Backstage

Don't Fall For A Rockstar

Don't Fall For A Bodyguard

Don't Fall For A Dreamer

Voyagers Series

Oh Buoy

Starboard

The Cockpit

Endeavor

Nauti or Nice

Stand Alone (Voyagers spin off)

Co-Star

NY Nights

Novel Affair

Troublemaker

Unforgettable You

NY Nights Bodyguard Edition

Hate to Love You

Love Like Yours

Never Knew Love

Stand Alone (novella)

Long Time Coming